M000158516

WE ARRIVE UNINVITED

JEN KNOX

A NOVEL

STEEL TOE BOOKS
est. 2003

WE ARRIVE UNINVITED

"The psychotic drowns in the same waters in which the mystic swims with delight."

—Joseph Campbell

PART ONE: CELINE

Chapter One: Emerson, 2004

On the summer solstice, shortly after my twelfth birthday, Amelia predicted my mother's death. It was the last time I visited her small brick apartment on Dock Street in Columbus, Ohio. My younger sister, Lori, and I sat straight-backed at the kitchen table and waited as Amelia rushed past us on tough bare feet to answer the door. Dozens of small bells sewn into her floral skirt chimed as she moved.

We jumped at the second, more forceful knock. As we craned our necks to see what was going on, she whipped around, pointed her finger at my forehead, then my sister's, and said, "Stay in the kitchen. Stay put." When Amelia—our grandmother, *but don't you dare call her Grandma*—told you to stay put, you did. My sister and I leaned in to listen as she exchanged words with a pair of low voices before sighing. "Fine! Whatever. Tell him to give me some notice next time. My rent is good till the end of the month." We heard the loud bang of something heavy hitting the door.

"What do you think it is?" Lori whispered.

I imagined something magical, a large statue of a goddess or an armoire that would take us to Narnia. But before I had a chance to answer, two large men wheeled a refrigerator into the narrow kitchen. They seemed confused by Amelia's request to leave the hulking ivory appliance in the middle of the room and insisted on removing the old one. "This is my property. You need to go," she said.

"Yeah, you need to go," I said under my breath, thinking my sister would laugh, but she just put her head down as the men looked to me with eyebrows raised and, after asking Amelia to sign a paper, politely excused themselves.

A soft June breeze wafted into the kitchen as Amelia secured each of the six locks on the front door before calling my parents and lighting a bundle of herbs. She hung up and dialed again, angling the phone on her shoulder as she waved the smoke in each corner of the room. We stood as she created an outline of our bodies, back then front. The pine and mint tickled my nose.

"Where's your father?" she asked.

"Probably still at the doctor. Can you tell our fortunes?" I used my most persuasive voice.

"Not today. What's the doctor's name?"

I shrugged. At least once a month my mother saw what she referred to as a menacing rainbow. It would blur and steal her ability to think, drive and tolerate light. She'd cradle the back of her neck and forehead as she took awkward steps to her bedroom or collapsed on the couch. Dad would come home from work and turn off all the lights, imploring us to be quiet. Lori and I were good at being silent and still. It was our practice. But today Mom's pain had been extreme. Her doctor agreed to see her on short notice, which meant Dad had to leave us somewhere. Amelia's was the only option. "I hope I don't regret this," he'd said before dropping us off.

There was something exhilarating about spending time in Amelia's dorm-sized apartment. It was filled with oddities. Tapestries hung on dark blue walls and candles covered every surface. Herbal scents and unexpected adventures waited around every corner. The last time we were allowed over, back when Amelia was trusted to take us for the night, we rode a bus to the zoo and swiftly got kicked out after she tried to "liberate" a black and white colobus monkey. Adrenaline surged up my spine as I watched her climb over a partition in her pale summer dress, only for a guard to grab her heels. As we were escorted out, Amelia explained that the monkey had asked her to free him with his hands. "Always look to hands to see the truth. People are no different. Understand, Emerson?"

I didn't understand, but the idea of communicating with animals in this way intrigued me. I didn't understand the extra fridge or Amelia's urgency that day either, but I knew there was a reason she hurried those men away. Dad said Amelia's paranoia explained her sudden mood shifts. He was always yelling at her to take her pills, which she'd throw down the garbage disposal after he left.

Amelia began to unhinge and load three small infusers with dried rose petals and dark tea leaves. "Rose will relax us as we wait for your father," she said, handing me a small, ornately designed porcelain mug. Amelia would add so much honey and lemon that the tea would become thick and sweet like dessert. Sometimes Lori and I burnt our tongues trying to gulp the hot liquid like soda. Ordinarily, we would play Euchre. Amelia would tell wild stories until our eyelids began to get heavy. Most visits, after tea and our games, she pulled out a small blue fortune-telling book held together with masking tape, and she'd tell the future based on the shapes the tea leaves made at the bottom of our mugs.

I liked the feel of thick playing cards in my hands. I always got to deal first since I was oldest, so I reached for the yellow deck decorated with exotic birds. The other cards, gold-edged and adorned with goddesses, were kept in a silver bowl on the table, but we weren't allowed to play with them because *a card deck should be played for a minimum of thirteen lunar cycles before a new deck can be opened.*

I eyed the goddess deck. Marzanna, a Polish goddess, was the top card. She was dressed in straw with long, thick hair bursting into flames. Amelia's hair had the same thickness and wave, only hers was the color of settled ash. Lori hung over my shoulder and pointed out missed moves as I played a game of Solitaire. I nudged my sister away with my elbow. She nudged me back. With two refrigerators in the small kitchen, our chairs had to stay close to the round table, so when I almost toppled over the tea mugs rattled.

"Not now," Amelia said without looking up. The energy in the room was thick. Amelia's face tightened as she waited for the water to boil. She began pacing the small stretch of exposed linoleum, holding her jaw. She paused in front of the new fridge and ran her hand along its edge. It was clean and shiny, and it towered over her older, pea-green fridge. There were magnets on the older one: images of the moon, a willow tree and robed women in a circle with clasped hands and faces toward the sky. The women held a pink slip that said "30 days' notice" across the top. Wanting to change the mood, I asked Amelia if she'd like me to move the magnets to the new fridge.

"No point," she said, twisting her long gray hair one way, then the other.

"Why didn't you get rid of the old fridge?" Lori asked.

Amelia turned; her lips pursed so that I could see where lipstick had collected in the lines around her mouth. It looked like blood, like she'd been fighting. Enunciating each syllable, she said, "The landlord is remodeling so he can raise rent. He's pushing me out, but that's not important right now. I have work to do." She hit the fridge with the palm of her hand.

My sister, who was ten at the time, nodded and, in her pragmatic way, decided to make the most of the confusion. She reached for the plastic bear filled with honey and squeezed a dollop of golden liquid into her palm. She licked and repeated, keeping a wary eye on Amelia, waiting.

"I think the new fridge looks nice," I said.

"If you ever own an apartment complex, don't refer to yourself as a land*lord*." Amelia waved her hands as though playing a part, over-acting like the teenagers who starred in the free plays put on at the recreation center near our house. Bending down, getting half an inch from my face, she added, "If we have to be apart for a while, Emerson, it's going to be up to you. Now go watch cartoons or something while I work. Don't interrupt me no matter what you hear."

Lori ran to the living room, honey bear still in hand, and began turning the dial of Amelia's old-fashioned and rarely used television, trying to find cartoons but settling on the news. Two men with identical, gelled hair styles droned on while I remained in the doorway.

"I want to help. Maybe we can find Mom's doctor together? I think her name starts with B," I said.

She added salt to a pot of water and kicked up the gas flame. "There's no time now. I need to take her place. Celine..." She trailed off.

"What about Mom?" I said as forcefully as I could. Amelia didn't seem to hear the question. When she continued to pace, chanting my mother's name, I grabbed the phone, which had been left on the kitchen table, and stomped out to join my sister. Clips of Saddam Hussein and George W. Bush cycled alongside pictures of tortured-looking soldiers, while Lori stared on. I turned the dial and stopped on the nature channel.

As we passed the honey bear back and forth, allowing drops of thick liquid to settle on our tongues, Amelia remained in the kitchen. She yelled for me to call my father again and, if he didn't answer, to call a cab. I fumbled with the phone and tried to lower the volume of the loud dial tone. "At least we'll get out of here soon," I told Lori, who nodded somberly. I pressed the buttons slowly, willing him to answer, summoning all the magic I could.

He picked up on the first ring. "How many times have you called? Geez, my mailbox is full."

"Dad, Amelia's upset. She's scaring Lori."

"Hey! I'm not scared," my sister yelled.

She was right. *I* was getting scared. "She's been in the kitchen doing weird shit. She's pacing and upset. She wants you to pick us up. How's Mom?"

"Language! Your mother's better. She's resting." I noticed the room was getting smokier.

"Dad, you might want to come now." I hung up for dramatic effect.

Amelia's phone rang nonstop after that. She lit match after match to ignite a circle of candles and dripped wax on the muted yellow linoleum around a pile of flower petals. The water was boiling, and the steam was beginning to hiss. The smoke tickled my nose. "Don't answer that phone. He needs to hurry," she told us, placing a large knife, blade down, in the boiling water, then setting it aside.

I kept my arm tight around Lori. We tiptoed to the kitchen as a man with a British accent spoke eloquently about dolphins in the background. Amelia stared down into a cast iron pot of still water surrounded by lit candles and dried flowers. The doorbell rang, then came my father's sharp knock before the doorbell again.

I stood on my toes to reach the locks, and when the door finally opened, Dad studied me. He placed his hand on my head before rushing to the kitchen. "Sorry we left you here. I didn't think it'd be this long."

I shrugged as Dad began to yell. "You could've burned this apartment down with your grandchildren inside." His hair was pulled back in a small ponytail and his face was visibly hot. I wished Mom had come—she was the calm one around her mother. She knew what to do and say. She'd nod, listening carefully, responding with a series of questions that calmed everything down. Unlike the rest of us, she understood Amelia's way of thinking. She once told me that Amelia knew important things but didn't know how to invite us to understand.

Just when I thought my father was done yelling, he grabbed the pink slip from the old fridge. "Eviction notice?"

Amelia said it didn't matter. Her tone lowered, silencing the room, as she uttered four words I'd never forget. She said it plainly: "Celine's going to die."

"Don't say things like that," Dad raged.

"I'm trying to help her, but it might be too late. Take the girls and let me do my work."

We watched as Dad tried to grab the matches from Amelia's hands. She pushed my father away sharply, and when he came at her again, she threw the boiling water, scalding his arm, and reached for the knife. My father grabbed her by her forearms and pinned her to the linoleum, yelling for me to call 911 as I stood there watching my grandmother writhe like a wild animal. My sister dialed the numbers with sticky fingers and held the receiver away from her face. We both tried to explain that we were in trouble. I don't know what we said, but it worked.

As Dad and Amelia continued to struggle, their voices oscillated from yells to murmurs, I noticed a small notebook with a piece of torn paper on the floor near the flowers. My mother's name, Celine, was written on the pink paper alongside a series of numbers. I quickly stuffed it in my jeans skirt pocket, double-checking that it was hidden from view just in time for Dad to tell us to get our things.

Amelia insisted she had to continue her work to save my mother, and something in her sound current overtook me. I yelled, "Stop saying that!" They didn't acknowledge me. I yelled again, until my voice became shrill, then scratchy. "Stop! Stop!" I insisted. After a few blurry minutes, sirens drowned out our voices. My sister and I watched as an officer entered the smoke-filled kitchen and almost ran into the extra fridge. The chaos and shouting gave way to ghostly silence.

Our house was dark when the officer dropped us off that evening. I retrieved the extra key from underneath our porch and ran to Mom's bedroom, terrified that Amelia had been right. But there Mom was, slight and soft. Completely alive. She waved at the officer from the window, and he flashed his lights.

"Hey, girls."

"Mom. Dad needed to stay with Amelia," I said. I blathered on, the way I did then, recounting everything at manic speed as Mom blinked sleepily. I stopped before the struggle, confidently omitting what Amelia had said. What mattered was that Mom was here, just a little sick with her migraines and maybe woozy from the medication. Sitting next to her, I stroked her forehead the way she often did mine. "I can make you dinner."

"No food. I just need to rest, sweetie." She was holding her jaw the way Amelia had been.

"Do you still see the rainbow? Is it your worst one?"

"I have a little fever on top of the migraine, that's all."

I'd seen Mom in pain too often. I felt her head, expecting a fever, but she was icy and sweating at the same time, so I pulled an extra comforter down from her closet and tucked her in the same way she used to tuck me in, nudging the blankets underneath her sides and feet so that no cold air could reach her. I caught a brief smile on her face before her eyes closed again. My sister, who'd been hovering in the doorway, turned and rushed downstairs.

As Mom shifted in the bed, apparently trying to get comfortable, I told her I would stay with her till Dad came home. "Do you want me to call anyone?" I asked. When she said no, I reached in my pocket. As Mom eased in and out of sleep, I rolled the paper between my fingers.

I wanted to know what magic Amelia had been attempting. Closing my eyes, I could still see her steady gaze down at the water as she sat, lighting matches, surrounded by flowers. I imagined a different version of myself, unafraid, sitting next to her, and I felt the paper between my fingers grow warm.

I fell asleep at Mom's feet with the paper in my loose fist as the world silently inverted. I slept as my father went to "handle" Amelia. He'd later say she was threatening self-harm. The police drove her to a hospital that recommended a mental health institution a two-hour drive away. I dreamed as he steered the roads to Canton and Amelia sat silently. They arrived at The Lavender House with its narrow, ominous hallways in the deep of night, he'd later tell me.

When I woke, Mom was staring at me. I cuddled up to her, twirled her dark hair around my thin arm and accidentally yanked too hard. She flinched in a delayed, dull way. She seemed to be fading in and out of consciousness, rather than just sleep, and I noticed an orange pill bottle on the dresser.

"I'm fine, sweetie," she said. "Want to tell me what else happened at your grandmother's?" she spoke in her softest voice. Her eyes were the color of the ocean, with a speck of amber near the pupil. Today they seemed distant and cloudy.

"She was upset. She started saying your name, and she sounded worried about you. She lit a bunch of matches and began to chant. When Dad came, they screamed at each other, and she hurt his arm." For an ordinary family, this would seem a disjointed and unlikely tale, but Mom nodded.

"Your father is fine. What else happened?"

I wanted to tell her everything, to explain how she'd hurt my father and made a horrible prediction, but I couldn't. "Nothing else."

She took a long breath, and just like that, she was asleep. A chill rushed to my lower belly. I didn't realize it at the time, but I was experiencing what was happening in my mother's body—the weak pulse and lack of oxygen. My energy dipped, and I felt disoriented. I told myself everything was fine because it always was. I fell asleep curled into my mother's warm body.

Later, the doctors would say it was an overdose of a pain reliever she'd been prescribed a year ago for dental work. In combination with her new migraine medication, the quest for relief had stalled her heart. The swelling and slowing of breath, the deflation of her lungs. My mother didn't clutch her chest and fall to the ground. She didn't get sick and flounder on the bed; she didn't beg for help or scream out in pain. There was a rumble, beneath the surface, a softening.

I was next to her, sound asleep on a mercifully cool June evening at the beginning of summer when she died. The longest day of the year. The last night of my childhood. When I woke, my mother's heart was still.

Dad's arm was angry and red, already peeling at the edge of his burn. He blamed Amelia for everything. If he hadn't been away and taking care of her, he said, this wouldn't have happened. I didn't want to believe him. I wanted to believe that Amelia was trying to help, and if she was, who was to say it wasn't too late.

"Why?" he kept asking between angry sobs. I watched him go from shock to tears to a sort of heated rage that filled the room. He reached for the empty orange pill bottle and uttered something I'd never forget. He said it quietly, to himself. "Why are all the women in this family insane?"

Chapter Two: Amelia, 2009

The dead are tricksters. They enjoy whispering inconvenient truths. For this reason, or maybe to mess with me, they visit when I'm brushing my teeth or mid-conversation. Even when I was younger, when I didn't yet understand, they'd interrupt me mid-chore. Now, they speak loudest when I'm somewhere between consciousness and sleep—when my guard is down.

My daughter, Celine, arrived the same way. It was the anniversary of her corporeal death, and she appeared with a whisp of light. She told me to expect a visitor, and I immediately knew who it was. I wanted her to stay, to discuss, but she was still angry with me for trying to intervene the day she died.

"Have you been visiting them? The girls?" I asked. The question earned a sheepish smile, so I began my plea. "As a mother, you know you would have done the same." And just like that, just as quickly as she arrived, my daughter was gone. That night I dreamed of pressing my palms into a willow oak's bark until I became the tree, rooting into the earth. When I woke, it took time to orient to my room.

The Lavender House, a "mental health facility for the elderly," provided us single-serve coffee pots after we exhibited good behavior for six months. I had one of the smallest rooms, and I kept my journals on the nightstand, so I had to keep the coffee pot on a mat on the floor. I sat next to it and examined my appearance in a handheld mirror, trying to ignore the peeling wallpaper in the background. As my single-serve coffee brewed on the linoleum, I pulled three goddess cards and wrote an affirmation on the mirror in erasable marker. I wasn't allowed to light candles, so I imagined the full ritual, the welcoming.

I was still in my nightclothes on a pile of pillows on the floor when a nurse I'd never seen arrived and glanced at my affirmation, which was illegible to anyone but me. She kindly insisted on shoving pills down my throat, like the rest of them. I slid the small, pink ovals to the top right quadrant of my gums as I drank the full paper cup of water. This nurse wore all white with polka-dot socks, but her energy was red. Her blood pressure was high. I stared at a mole on her forearm as she took my vitals.

"I don't like you," I said.

"What did I do … Amelia?" she stammered, double-checking her chart.

I sized her up, answering with a shrug. This woman was a maker. She would be happier if she started selling crocheted purses or monogrammed mugs. She wasn't a caretaker; she was destined to create things that people could use with mild entertainment or pick up while on vacation to give to family and friends. Designing monogramed mugs would make her joyful. This work, on the other hand, would kill her.

"You really don't like me?" she asked.

I took a breath and spoke from my diaphragm so my voice wouldn't shake. "I don't like the pills. I don't like the walls in here. I don't like much about this place, and you're a part of it." When she nodded as though she understood, I pedaled back. "I think you should find new work. Old crazies like myself know things."

"I don't understand," she said, circling AGGRESSIVE on my daily summary sheet. I saw a scale for paranoia and hygiene as well. My diagnosis was schizophrenia, which is what the doctors labeled anyone they didn't understand. Years earlier, the word had been mania. Before that, hysteria.

Softening my tone, I said, "You know, my granddaughter will be visiting me soon. She's a special girl."

"That's … good. How old is she?" she asked with a half-smile as she glanced at my fingernails, then my hair. She circled ACCEPTABLE under hygiene.

"Almost an adult," I told her. She didn't register my answer at all. Many people ask questions without intending to listen to the answers.

Her finger traced the checklist as she looked in my closet and under my bed, then stuck out her hand.

"My name is Sophia. Have a lovely day, Amelia."

I smiled, waiting for the quietest moment before I unleashed a guttural scream from the top of my lungs. The shaking that came from avoiding pills for four days made it more intense, so I pushed the sound hard from my chest. I filled the room, the halls. It was a bit much, I know, but I was bored. And I wanted what was best for Sophia. She had to quit before she became complacent. The look on her face told me I'd done my work.

I got along with few residents at The Lavender House, but most were not long for this world. The residents who would hang on for as long as I would were mean because they knew, on a cellular level, that they had a longer sentence.

When 8 a.m. arrived, after a brief visit from the doctor, I journeyed to the cafeteria for a bagel. I rarely ate in there. It was sterile and full of bustling workers, spongy eggs and sad residents. Sometimes excitement came in the form of thrown condiments or hair pulling, but it was mostly depressing.

The library and fireplace were pleasant areas to sit alone or with the soft-spoken residents. The pond could be serene, and few people were there when the geese weren't patrolling it for scraps. After wrapping a bagel in a paper towel, I searched for my friends.

There were two residents I most enjoyed spending time with. I wanted to help them tap into their magic. It wasn't too late for anyone. Named Gloria and Glory—a similarity they'd bonded over as soon as they met—they were mild cases from a diagnostic perspective. Glory was senile. Gloria was obsessive-compulsive with trauma-induced paranoia. I liked to think of them as the quiet ones, and I was their entertainment.

Gloria had been a flight attendant. Glory had been a career waitress and mom eight times over. They said next to nothing when we played cards because they were both so wildly competitive in a Midwestern, passive-aggressive manner. They knew to defer to me when selecting movies on Sundays because I had a knack for picking the perfect one for the mood. I just chose films with handsome men.

Ours was a transactional relationship. I knew they'd sneak me their cookies or Danish to appease my sweet tooth, and they knew I'd keep them entertained. One day, they even asked me to pull cards for them, and I enjoyed their nervous delight as I shielded the bad news with mystery and exaggerated the good news. It was only a matter of time before they asked me to teach them.

I took a seat by the fireplace with my warm bagel and tore off a piece as I opened my notebook, recounting scattershot scenes from my life. When I wasn't consumed by other realms, writing was the best way to pass time here—to delve into correspondence with the ordinary future or past. I sometimes studied old times; well-worn memories that always revealed something new, but mostly I wrote to Jake. That morning, I was so immersed in the story of a young girl, a version of myself, falling in love. I didn't hear my friends shuffle toward me.

"Are you writing a short story? Can I read it?" Gloria asked, and when I nodded, she settled down next to me and read my notes with that tinny voice of hers. When she said his name, a surge of electricity shot through me. *Jake.* I would see him again soon, but I didn't share this information. After a few paragraphs, she ran out of breath. She said it read like a novel. This was an exaggeration, but the sentiment made me smile.

"Amelia, you should have been a writer. Can you believe this, Glory?"

More prone to jealousy, a sad thing at our age, Glory nodded hesitantly, then asked if we'd like to play Hearts. I told them I had another idea. "I want to find a willow oak. If we can find one, I'll show you something you've never seen before," I said. In our wing, we were free to roam around the pond. But today, we walked farther without looking back. I led the quiet ones beyond the paths and welcome signs. I made this trek weekly for the last few years, but this was the first time I felt called to share. When we reached the trees, I could feel the shift in the electromagnetic field.

You'd think we were in elementary school the way the quiet ones giggled as we took a step past the property line. We journeyed into the woods and got lost in birdsong. Still in her slippers, Gloria was slowest, and I continuously had to shush her when she yelped at the mud on her creased slacks or the sensation of a stick brushing her ankle.

Two deer near the mouth of a narrow trail stood stoically, symbols of grace. Glory scared them away when her walker hit a rock. Surprised we hadn't been noticed, we went deeper, albeit slowly, until we found a patch of damp earth. I was bending over to unlace my shoes when the rush of Lavender House staff arrived. We turned to find five staff members there, so serious in their head-to-toe white, and I began to laugh as I shoved my heels into the earth. The moment was interrupted, but the intention was set. Mother Nature heard my call.

Sophia laced a thick arm beneath Gloria's, so she wouldn't have to be the one to walk me back. She solidified her decision to quit that moment: I could see it in the way her pupils contracted, and her hands curled. I glanced around for the tree I'd dreamed of and thought I saw one in the distance, beyond endless pines. As we were led back, I asked why there were no guided walks in these woods, but the staff was huffy.

Upon our return, they locked the doors for the evening and called my son-in-law. I was in trouble, like a small child, and I sat in the library, waiting, as the "incident" was recorded. Jenny, a plucky young woman who sat at the front desk and would no doubt be at The Lavender House until she too was a resident, told me that while I was off galivanting, my granddaughter had called multiple times.

"I told her that you were indisposed. Amelia, stop getting in trouble. Some of these workers think you're better suited for the east wing."

"What's the difference?"

"I wouldn't see you, and I'd miss you." She paused. "You look a little pale. Would you like some blush?"

I let her adorn my face with the overpriced makeup she sold to all the nurses. The angle of the brush conjured memories of my mother's severe cheekbones. I told Jenny a story about an old crone who found the secret to youth only to realize that being a crone was far more rewarding, and at the end she clapped. Checking her computer, where notes about "incidents" were reported each day, she told me I was now scheduled to eat lunch at 11:30 instead of 12:30, to give Gloria and Glory their space. "According to what Sophia wrote here in your file, the two Gs were innocent bystanders." Just like that, I'd lost my friends.

"Jenny, tell me, are there willow oak trees in that forest?"

"There are all kinds of trees back there."

"Helpful. Thanks," I said, catching sight of my wrinkled coral-colored cheeks.

The day had been satisfying. I wiped the message from my hand mirror. "I am grounded in truth. I am the teacher now. I welcome my student." And as I waited for my corporeal visitor, I wondered who would visit my dreams or where I might travel. I hoped my daughter would visit again, maybe a messenger I had yet to meet. But instead, I saw my childhood self at around my granddaughter's age. Kat stood next to me, her heavy hand on my shoulder, and I screamed.

Chapter Three: Emerson

The two men who delivered the refrigerator were grim reapers who wore flowers in their hair. Smoke surrounded them, and the fridge turned into a coffin. I tried to summon magic in my dream, to change the events leading up to my mother's death, but it all unfolded as it had—the struggle, the ride home, and me curled up next to my mother's dead body.

I sat up in bed wide-eyed, cold, unable to move. Exactly five years had passed since my mother's death, and I felt the same weakening I'd felt that night. My body was separate from me, hollow. My mind squirmed. "I, Emerson, have control of my own thinking, and I am safe. I, Emerson, have control of my own thinking, and I am safe." I repeated this dozens of times before the sound of the vents kicking on in our old Victorian home startled me back to reality.

I'd been in therapy for two years by this time, ever since my first "episode" arrived out of nowhere at a bookstore, where the chill of death shot through me just as I was removing a heavy illustrated edition of *The Hobbit* from the shelf. I rushed to the bathroom that day and locked myself in, hugging my body and waiting to die. When a bookseller asked me what was wrong, I tried to explain what I was feeling. "I'm not in my body. I can't get back."

After she told my father what I'd said, it wasn't long before I was face-to-face with a mildly disinterested therapist who wore fall colors year-round and liked to quote famous people or offer "tools" that she read directly from her iPad. If nothing else, I appreciated that she worked with me to write simple mantras that would remind me I was safe. When I felt my body go cold, they helped to hide my fear long enough to wait the episodes out, but the taste of death always returned.

I stared at the exposed brick near my window as the world solidified. The sensation returned to my limbs and heart. After shaking out my body, I crept downstairs. My father was often up in the middle of the night, sitting in the dark at the dining room table with only the glare from his laptop as he worked through his insomnia. But this night I heard something like hushed laughter as I reached the bottom of the stairs.

A woman I'd never seen before was leaning in to whisper something to my father, her honey-blonde hair obstructing his face. They sat on the couch in the living room in low light. My father was thoroughly distracted His long curly hair, usually back in a ponytail, was down, and his signature haphazard beard was gone. They hadn't heard me.

Had my father forgotten we placed flowers on Mom's grave hours earlier? I wanted to interrupt them, but I couldn't. An unease settled behind my ribs as I grabbed a jar of peanut butter and the worn copy of *Women Who Run with the Wolves* from the top of the bookshelf at the base of the stairs. Undetected, I ran back up to pace my room as I read highlighted passages about the Baba Yaga. My mother liked to repeat the stories Amelia used to tell her about the old Slavic witch who lived in a home perched atop chicken legs. When I was younger, I'd fantasize about going to visit her and finding myself on a grand journey.

I tried to read, but the hardcover became heavy in my hands. The chill was returning, and I steadied my gaze. "Tell me what you want me to do, Mom," I whispered, and I waited. And waited.

Eventually, the dullness of reality sunk in yet again. At my computer with the heavy book in my lap, I ate a spoonful of peanut butter to ground myself and wrote my mother a letter asking her where I was supposed to go, what the panic meant. And, at seventeen just as I used to when I was twelve, I saved my questions to her in a file with only the date. I still wanted to believe, but there was no evidence of magic in my world.

The next morning, my father insisted on a family meeting in the kitchen. I glanced through the texts I hadn't seen. Ian, a new boy from school who had been my partner in a science project earlier that year, was asking if I wanted to meet up at the rec center. It was the second-to-last thing I wanted to do. The first being a family meeting in the kitchen. My best friend, Courtney, had texted to say she was thinking about me. I didn't text either of them back.

Hungover from my panic attack the previous night, I stared at my father and felt the acids in my stomach as they came to a boil. He wore a fixed, nervous smile. "I want to introduce you to someone." *I know, damn it.* My hands tingled as though numb. "I invited her to breakfast."

"Good timing," I said, or thought, as I stood there remembering how it felt to hold my mother's hand.

The clearest memory of Mom, and the one I liked to return to, took place on my twelfth birthday at a day spa that Mom could barely afford. We'd filled our bellies with breath and blew out our cheeks as our lotioned feet descended into tubs of hot wax. It was the one time we got pedicures, and Mom ordered the deluxe package for two after my sister said she'd rather stay home with Dad and her pet lizard. I squirmed around the soft chair, wary of the other patrons who darted their eyes whenever Mom and I broke their deadening silence with laughter. Mom's laugh was loud enough to be either contagious or alarming, depending on the person hearing it. She once told me that she was able to find the humor in adulthood because she'd felt like she had to be such a serious kid.

My feet tingled in the wax as I thumbed through a glossy magazine the thickness of a paperback novel. It contained images of homes I couldn't imagine anyone lived in, recipes I'd never eat and people who looked like dolls—expressionless and perfect. I read aloud an article that suggested six ways to pluck eyebrows in my best Mom voice, and she cackled.

Mom read an article on growing herbs in her best Emerson voice, which sounded so much like me at the time that I almost peed in the expensive leather chair. As the stuffy people glared, our feet turned into slippers. There was a slight tug as we lifted our knees on the count of three and gasped. Mom's wide smile then was something I was used to seeing, but I couldn't get enough, so I played up my reaction by clutching my heart.

"You'll never forget the day I turned your feet into wax," she told me, rubbing her hands together conspiratorially. She didn't realize how well this memory would imprint on my mind. Nor could she have known how much greater the impact when, later that year, she began to see doctors about her migraines and depression. Not long after our celebratory day, I began covering my head with a pillow and trying to ignore muffled sobs from the other side of her bedroom wall as I willed her smile back into existence.

Dad comforted her those days. He made pasta, her favorite. Buttered noodles for me, alfredo for Mom and Lori. He'd put on gentle music and take Mom's hand, twirling her around in our nest-like kitchen on good days. Or he'd grab one of the mementos she kept from her travels as a child and ask her to tell a story. She was often feverish and hesitant to launch into anecdotes upon request, so my father would place a warm washcloth on her forehead and show her an ornament from Honduras, reminding her about the little boy who taught her how to fly a kite or the keychain from Tate Britain where Amelia had got in trouble for holding her palms too close to a painting. It seemed he loved to hear her as much as I did.

I loved the story about how she and Amelia got lost in Geneva, Switzerland and had to stay at a bed and breakfast run by a woman who yelled at them in French when they wouldn't make eye contact or tried to sneak a piece of bread before dinner. It had been Amelia, not my mother, who would test the woman by reaching for the bread each time she turned around, but they never got kicked out because my mother would plead. Many of Mom's stories had been about negotiating with adults or trying to explain Amelia's behaviors.

"I'm too tired, honey," she started saying at the end when I would beg to hear another tale. When Mom wasn't feeling well enough to even listen, the stories faded from my life. I stopped asking, and my father began to read hefty science fiction novels late into the night, never allowing himself to go to sleep while she was in pain.

Dad should've remembered that. Instead, he introduced me to the interloper. His new girlfriend, Rita, wore a disarming smile. She had all the prepared graces of a middle-aged influencer and all the warmth of a sitcom stepmom. She was a woman inside a magazine, glossy and perfect, an inside joke for me and Mom. I took time to consider her outstretched arm and tried to ignore the deep knowing that she was here for good. We were standing by a counter of breakfast food.

"It's good to meet you," Lori said, sliding her slender body between us and offering her hand with the maturity I lacked. My younger sister wasn't bothered by Rita's presence so much as indifferent to it. Indifference was her superpower. The two of them spoke about my sister's sleek sweatsuit and how unfair it was that every pair of women's pants didn't automatically have pockets as we all began to set the table.

My father's phone rang, and he began to pace, keeping an eye on us. He spoke to someone in hushed tones, but I heard my grandmother's name and saw his face crumple like a paper bag.

"What happened?" I asked.

"Amelia. She went past property lines again. Not far, but they won't let her stay if she keeps this up. She brought other residents with her." He shook his head. Watching his girlfriend and Lori sit across from each other at the long mahogany table I thought we'd never again use, his forehead relaxed, and a whimsical smile crossed his face. "Sorry, kiddo. It'll be fine."

"I can't imagine being in a place like that. Sounds like she was just trying to go outside," Rita said.

"It's not just going for a walk." He looked to me, pausing, before turning back to Rita. "Amelia is a case study for someone who takes things too far. She can't distinguish fantasy from reality. When she leads people to the woods, it's not good."

"Maybe it was exactly what those residents needed," I said through gritted teeth as I looked down at my plate.

"She's acting like a cult leader in that place. It's not good, Em," Dad said plainly.

After an uncomfortable amount of silence, Rita said, "So, um, Emerson. You're still in high school, right? What's your favorite class?" I told her I liked them all.

"Do you run like your sister?" she asked.

"I have an issue with running if something's not trying to chase me."

Throughout the meal, Rita asked me more questions about my interests and offered generous laughter when I made sarcastic comments about my lack of interests. I tried to engage. For my father's sake, I tried, but it didn't matter how nice she was. Her warm hands and deep listening weren't enough. I couldn't care that she was a Pisces from Wisconsin who did aerial yoga. I counted the seconds until it was time to clear the table.

"When I look at her, I know she's not going anywhere. Why now?" I asked Lori as we rinsed the dishes.

"He can't wait forever. What was he saying about Amelia though?" my sister asked.

"She went to the woods. With other residents this time, I guess. But he seems more concerned about his new girlfriend." I sliced a gluten-free, sugar-free coffee cake Rita had made.

"Rita seems to make him happier than any of those skanks he dated after Mom. Remember Gabi with an i?" Lori said.

"Yeah, and the woman with the MLM business who was always trying to sell us floral-print headbands." I couldn't help but laugh. Those women hadn't worried me at all.

My sister shuddered at the memory. "Well, I like Rita. And Amelia's insane, but she'll be okay. Not sure about her *followers*. Want cinnamon toast instead?"

"I don't like that word. We barely get to see her because of that word. And yes, with peanut butter."

She sighed. "All the women in our family are insane, remember? Insane like wanting peanut butter on their cinnamon bread." She looked around the kitchen.

I felt my chest harden as I forced a smile. "Yeah. Listen, you were younger, you didn't know Amelia the same way. Going to visit her with Dad two times a year doesn't count."

"I know enough to know she's kooky."

As Dad led Rita to the backroom for an official tour, my sister and I went to war with our eyes. It wasn't a new argument. "Sorry, Em. But you seem stuck. Like stuck in time. Maybe get a boyfriend or something. Date that theater kid that keeps texting you." I kicked her in the shin hard enough to watch Lori stumble and hiss back, "Watch the legs."

At fifteen, my sister had a sort-of boyfriend and a small tightknit group of friends she ran cross country with each fall and track with each spring. She called them her crew. Our social lives didn't overlap, though one could argue that I didn't have a social life to overlap with. Schoolwork and my best friend Courtney were about it, and I told myself I was happier that way. I wanted to feel settled like the rest of my family, able to move on, but Lori was right. I was stuck. I would have done anything to reverse time, to not feel the way I felt.

I watched my sister's rehearsed movements as she went to work. Lori's version of cinnamon toast meant smothering a piece of wheat bread with butter and cinnamon-sugar, then microwaving it till it became the texture of wood. She handed me a slice on a brown paper towel and threw up her hands. "We must be out of peanut butter."

I took a few bites before the unease I'd felt spread, and I remembered the jar was in my room. "Do you ever wonder what Amelia was going to do that day?"

"Something bad."

"I was thinking about visiting her on my own. Would you come?"

"No way," she said, licking the sugar off her fingers and grabbing a small baggie of broccoli. She sprinkled amino acids in the baggie and shook it before rushing out of the room to feed her pet iguana.

"Don't forget to introduce Rita to Rocco before she leaves," I yelled, imagining the iguana's green tail whipping around defensively.

I rushed upstairs, feeling the intrigue of my idea to visit Amelia on my own. Now was the perfect time—it might help me to move on to know what Amelia was really trying to do that day, how she knew. It was an impossible conversation to have with my father around. I dialed The Lavender House in the solitude of my room.

No one answered, so I tried again. The third time, a reception-ist named Jenny offered a singsong, "Hay-lo. How may I help you?" I almost hung up, but instead told her who I was. "We just spoke with your father. Emerson, so sorry. Your grandmother is not allowed to talk ... she painted a wonderful bird this week though." Staring at the phone, turning it over in my hand, I hit the speaker button.

"You're saying I should call back then?"

"Sounds good. Have a blessed day."

As the dial tone sounded, I sat motionless, unsure what I was going to say to Amelia, or why I felt the urge to call, other than to defy my father. I'd spent years wondering if she was responsible for my mother's death as Dad seemed to think, or if she truly could have saved her. I wanted so desperately to believe, but I could never quite tease out what she was trying to do that day. I recalled the wildness of her hands as she ushered us out that day. Amelia had always gestured as though she could control the energy of the room. As I began to mimic, pointing my finger sharply at the phone as though I could will it to ring, I heard my sister rush downstairs and waited.

Rita's scream arrived right on time, earning a moment of levity. My father's laughter boomed and rolled. He was loud enough that the neighbors probably heard. A part of me wanted to smile, too, to head down and engage in whatever conversation they were having or see how Rita and Rocco were getting along, but I was stuck in the past.

I woke up late on Monday and barely had time to throw on a striped shirt and distressed overalls, grab my almond-colored lip gloss, keys, and notebook, before rushing out the door. I met Courtney at our regular spot by an oak tree near the gym. I hadn't slept more than a few hours all weekend, and the world was hazy.

"Look at you! Cute but … disheveled." She gave my arm a squeeze and laughed, offering me her sunglasses. Her nails were painted an intense teal, and her black cargo pants clung to her wide hips and sagged around her legs, weighed down by full pockets. She kissed me on each cheek, which made me stand straighter.

She pointed at the toothpaste on my shirt and smiled.

"I'm losing my mind," I said, and I tried to wipe the white globule away, but it left a smear.

"That ship has sailed." She leaned in close, examining me. "I don't think your eyes are opening all the way. Did you sleep?"

"Nope. But I'm good."

"Sure?"

"Absolutely, completely sure." I put on the sunglasses and looked around. Ordinarily, we'd discuss what test we had and go over homework or bemoan our fellow students who seemed incapable of doing anything more cerebral than recounting celebrity gossip and talking about themselves as though *they* were the celebrities. School seemed to be wrapping up from the first day of senior year. We were the studious duo, both set on college. But this day, none of that mattered. At least not to me. The sun was shining, and the world felt too small. "I think I need an adventure," I said.

"A woman after my own heart. You know how all good adventures begin?"

"With coffee." We ducked out during the bell for homeroom, walking against the swarm of teenagers with our backpacks heavy and eyes alert. Sometimes administration checked the perimeter of the school, even though we could make up assignments online, but we jogged beyond the track unnoticed. We walked alongside two tennis courts with cracked blacktop. The courts hadn't been used while I'd been in school. There were dandelions growing from the cracks. Just when I was about to confide in my friend, tell her I had another panic attack last night, someone called out. Maybe to us, maybe not. Either way, Courtney began to run away from the voice and gestured for me to follow.

When I looked back, Ian was waving at me. He stood tall in his

checkered pants and overenthusiastic smile. Instead of letting Courtney
know it was him, I picked up my pace. The ground was uneven in
the alley, and I tripped forward, catching myself on my hand before
scrambling after Courtney.

Panting and laughing in equal measure, we ended up at a tiny
brown house with a sign out front that read "Annie's Roadhouse Diner"
in orange lettering next to a hand-painted football. A bell dinged as
the door closed behind us, and a mature voice yelled from the back
that we could find our own seats. We sat at a small table and stored our
backpacks by the wall, as a woman with a curly mullet greeted us without
smiling.

"I'm Joan. Coffee?" She upturned our mugs and waited for us
to nod before pouring. When I asked for menus, she pursed her lips and
sauntered off to retrieve two laminated sheets of paper from the front,
where I assumed we were supposed to have grabbed them.

"It's your turn to treat me, right?" Courtney asked, tapping her
wrist as though there was a watch there.

"Sure." She stared, waiting for me to tell her what was bothering
me. I didn't want to talk about it anymore. What's one to say? *Hey, girl,
so um ... I've been trying to talk to my dead mother and having nightmares about
my grandmother's premonition.* I ran through better ways to say it in my head
before giving up and smoothing out two napkins on the table.

"My mother used to say that if we draw our future like a map,
it'll happen. We can manifest whatever we want." I snapped my fingers.
"Simple as that."

"On it," Courtney said, grabbing two pens. We sketched our
futures on napkins over coffee with flavored creamers and obscene
amounts of sugar, while picking at over-easy eggs and over-salted
potatoes. We created vague realities with thick outlines like coloring
books we planned to fill in as we went.

"Your future looks like homeroom," I said.

Courtney straightened her shoulders. "That's a microphone. I'm
interviewing someone important. It's a press room, and I have the best
seat. What the hell is that?"

I looked down at my drawing—the outline of a room with a fireplace. I'd agonized over the equation, trying to get the measurements right. I was going to draw a bookcase next, some art. I was going to create a nice home with a desk that looked out onto a forest.

"My future house. I'll own it outright and decorate it like a museum."

"Mine will look like an IKEA showroom." She paused. "Or maybe we'll be roomies, and we can meet somewhere in the middle."

"Can you imagine? Finally living on our own. Graduation can't come fast enough. I feel ... I don't know. Trapped. Silenced. I want to run away to another world."

Courtney nodded with a steady, knowing gaze. "A little dramatic, but I get it. What else? What will the office look like? Can we make the basement into a nightclub?"

"Of course." Chatting over breakfast food and imagining our future, Courtney and I willfully denied the fact that we had to get back to class, even as we talked about applications to Ohio State University and Denison that were due by January.

After a while, Courtney asked if I wanted to go walk around the outdoor mall before heading back to school. The outdoor mall comprised movie theater, a Starbucks, and a clothing store alongside a dog park. "Emerson, if you want to talk about your mom ... I know it's that time of year."

"I have an idea," I said.

"I'm all in for ideas. What?"

"Let's visit Amelia."

"Your witchy g-ma? Fuck yeah," Courtney said.

Joan offered a third refill on our coffee, and I asked for the check. I wondered why I was dragging my friend into this. If I really was going crazy *like all the women in my family*, maybe it was selfish to want her there on my quest to find out why. "Maybe I should go by myself," I mused as I counted out crumpled singles.

"Come on. I love your Amelia stories. No take-backs," Courtney said with a clap, asking for a to-go cup.

"I've never visited The Lavender House without Dad. I wonder if they'll let us see her."

"Sounds like prison. Let's break her out."

As I watched my friend pour five sugar packets into the paper cup before adding her coffee, I recalled Amelia's eyes as she paced the kitchen that day. The messages she was receiving were clear, and she didn't know how to tell us so that we'd listen. It was the look she had just before what my father called her "break" that day at her apartment... "Actually, Courtney..."

Courtney grabbed my backpack by the strap. "You really want to go back to listen to Mr. Smith drone on about thermodynamics for two hours? We'll catch up with him. Today is special. I can feel it. I know you like options, so here are options. We visit Amelia and watch a YouTube video about what we missed, or we go to the mall and pick out things to order on Amazon later?" She paused. "Come on. We'll be back for Mrs. Holden's class. Worst case, lost bus fare and a scenic ride." She counted out quarters for our bus fare.

"We live in suburban Ohio. Scenic is corn and cows. An adventure is banana ice cream," I reminded her, pushing her quarters away.

"Banana ice cream sounds pretty wild to me," the waitress said, clearing the table as we stood.

As if it had been summoned, the open-eyed lights of a COTA bus headed our way. "Is that our bus?" Courtney asked.

"I think we can take the 4S, yeah. It's an hour away, though. Are you sure you're up for this?" She grabbed my arm and tugged.

It was almost two hours when the driver announced our stop. Courtney slept while I played trivia games on her iPhone to numb my thoughts. After obliterating my friend's record high scores as her heavy head rested on my shoulder and she snored into my hair, I decided I wanted to turn around. I tried to move Courtney off at first, but the heat and weight of her body felt comforting against the cold air creeping in through an open window. She smelled of coconut and olive oil.

She was steady, while my right leg wouldn't stop shaking. The city gave way to the barn-dotted Ohio flatlands and then to a small, wooded area. It was here in the woods, miles in beyond old homes and barns, that we arrived at a long building with small windows.

In the last five years, I was always with my father when I saw Amelia in person. For the first time, this wouldn't be another hurried dinner or our regular stilted conversation over the phone. This time my father wouldn't be standing guard nearby, monitoring and worrying his hands, censoring everything she said. She might freak out, try to set fire to something or worse, and I'd be to blame.

The stop was near the turnaround for the route, which meant we'd have to wait for a bus headed home when we wanted to leave. It also meant we were in the middle of nowhere. I pushed my friend, but she didn't move. I kicked her feet sideways so that she fell off balance and woke with a start.

Her eyes struggled against the light, and I pointed out the window toward The Lavender House, which sat at the top of a hill. "She lives in that haunted elementary school?"

"You have any gum?"

"I have some gums," an old man, standing at the back door, said. He loosened his dentures to prove it before releasing a throaty laugh.

"Thanks, sir. Thanks," I said, holding my hand like a stop sign.

"Any day, any time." His laugh sounded like a gurgle.

"Yeah, I have gum." She dug around in her backpack, handed me a piece, and just before popping a small piece into her mouth, laughed nervously, keeping an eye on the older man as we headed deeper into the woods.

I had developed an image of Amelia staring out a window longingly, orchestrating events from her window and brawling with nurses when they tried to medicate her. I wondered if the old man who'd removed his teeth was her new neighbor. We followed the man, keeping a safe distance behind him as we shuffled toward The Lavender House. When we got closer, I noticed dark purple curtains that might fade to lavender one day.

Courtney was uncharacteristically quiet as we approached. After signing in, we waited in chairs that looked like recliners but didn't adjust. There was a row of wheelchairs extending down a long hallway with walls painted a shade of purple that matched the curtains, made worse by a maroon border with gold flowers. The décor's only redeeming quality was the few paintings offering the walls relief. One was an image of two yellow triangles, one facing up and the other down, meeting where the shadow of a torso extended; the shadow's arms reached outward toward the corners. It was so precise and out of place I fought the urge to touch it. It was the kind of art I wanted in my room.

The receptionist, Jenny, beamed at me. "I remember you! It's been a while. Where's your father?" She called back to Amelia's room without waiting for an answer. "Is she ready for company?"

I wondered who was with Amelia. Who monitored her so closely? Did each resident have a personal nurse? That didn't seem like something my family could afford. Jenny motioned to me.

"You're her oldest granddaughter, right?"

"Yes. And yes, I was here for Thanksgiving. I called the other day. You gave me eyeshadow a few visits ago," I reminded her.

She nodded. Jenny wore two braided buns that seemed to be falling out. When I got close enough, I could see that the buns were a different color than her hair, darker. Bobby pins stuck out haphazardly.

"You realize there are invitation days. And hours. Ten to twelve during the week and by appointment on the weekends," she said in a rehearsed, sing-song voice.

I nodded again.

"Amelia had a rough day yesterday. Can you come back another day?"

"No," Courtney said.

"Hm." She bit her cheek, as though trying to decide whether to kick us out or humor us. "How about outside, by the gazebo?"

I nodded. "We traveled a long way."

"Go on then, camp out. I'll get her, make sure she's dressed for the day. The two of you can chat or feed the ducks. We have a bag of stale bread out there. Or, you could find a clear spot in the back of the dining hall, though it's loud there and I can't guarantee that you won't be interrupted."

Jenny walked us to a small gazebo with a white-painted metal bench and two matching chairs. We sat in those chairs and waited for what felt like hours before a nurse led Amelia toward us. There was a chill, but the sun and the heater made the temperature bearable. Just when I felt hot, there'd be a breeze. When I'd begin to shiver, a wave of heat would encircle me. All sensation dropped to my feet by the time Amelia, with her long silver hair to one side, arrived like tired royalty.

She sat on the bench, examining me with flat eyes. "You look a lot like her now," she told me.

"Mom?"

She clapped her hands, looking suddenly alert. "You're here, Emerson! Finally, finally on your own. I've been waiting." I nodded, confused. I'd forgotten how quickly Amelia's mood could shift.

"Do people here treat you well?" Courtney asked in a calm, journalistic tone. She was leaning in with her elbows on her knees, fascinated.

"They're mad at me right now, but I don't care. This place is a freak show. Luckily, I will be getting out soon. Girls, my life ends with a love story." Amelia looked at me, eyes cloudy but intent. "I knew all of it would happen before it did. And I know what's coming. I knew the day he left me that everything would come out. I didn't know exactly what would come out, but I knew it was coming. Like a storm. The doctors are bringing it all back, but I won't tell my stories to them." She stopped and turned to Courtney. "Who are you, young lady?" she asked.

"My name's Courtney Marshall. I'm your granddaughter's best friend."

"Be sure to call me *Amelia*, hear?" She pulled at her long ponytail, twisting it so that it bent softly like rope and wrapped it around her hand with a sort of reverence.

"Yes, ma'am. You can talk to me," Courtney said.

Amelia lifted her index finger, examining my unease with surgeon-like calm. She looked to Courtney, then looked over her shoulder.

"You were supposed to come visit me earlier, so we have a lot to cover. This is your education." She pointed in my direction and gave me a severe look.

"What do you mean? I wanted to talk about ...."

"Your mother brought you here, Emerson. But slow down. You need context."

I sank into the metal chair as though I were a small child again. "I was born in 1921." She smiled slowly, mechanically, settling her gaze on the clouds. Amelia was beginning at the very beginning. I expected Courtney to roll her eyes, but my friend was enthralled.

Chapter Four: Amelia, 1921

The day began with smoke, lemon, bleach, decay. Hospitals were different then. Remembering the chill, my hands like ice, I tightened my jaw.

"Some of us arrive uninvited," I told the girls.

When a nurse tried to hand me to Mother for the first time, explaining how important it was for babies to feel touch, she refused. She said I looked sickly, that it would be more merciful to put me to rest.

The nurse, a new mother herself, argued vehemently. The argument would become infamous in our town. Both she and my grandmother, Grandma Grodzki, said I was perfectly healthy. At first, they thought Mother's request must have been due to her exhaustion and pain, but it soon became clear she was intentionally trying to get rid of me. There was no knowledge of postpartum depression then, though this wasn't quite that. I owed her for the inconvenience of being born, and she was never going to let me forget it.

Greta Grodzki, who would ultimately raise and mentor me, was a grandmother twice over and happy for it. A warm, salt-of-the-earth woman. She cupped my head and held me close. I settled into her generous chest, which buoyed me. If there was one place that felt like home, it was in my grandmother's arms. When she held me, I was connected to generations of women before her, women who knew more.

The girls' voices chimed in, jarring me from the trance. Courtney asked, "How could you possibly remember that early in life? Almost a century ago."

This question tickled me. I didn't often think of my age. A few years shy of ninety somewhere around the solstice. Emerson, being the conscientious girl she was, nudged her friend sharply, but she was thinking the same thing. She looked at me with a mixture of curiosity and disdain.

"We have more than five senses and more capacity to recreate the past than you can imagine," I told them. "I didn't learn this for years, but once we know how to recognize patterns, we hear and see everything. Time disappears."

Emerson scooted back, shifting uncomfortably while a badling of ducks, flying overhead, began to quack. She stammered, "I remember you telling me something like that when I was a kid. But what do you mean *we*?"

I smiled, noticing the quiet ones were at the pond feeding the ducks. I waved them over, but Gloria pretended not to see, so I refocused. "Life isn't linear, girls. Events and emotions come back like surges of energy, patterns, old riddles. You just have to know how to retrieve them."

"What I want to know is why your mother was such a bitch when she should have been mad at herself?" Courtney said, then covered her mouth with a guilty smile as if I'd never heard the word. I laughed hard enough to rattle my chest a little. Telling these girls my story would be even more fun than I'd anticipated.

"Shame," I said at last.

"But it was *her* fault."

"I was the walking manifestation of Mother's shame and suppression, a constant reminder," I said—giving in to a brief pause from the wayward memory before resuming.

In our small Midwestern town, Grandma Grodzki had always caused a stir with her refusal to attend church and odd requests for salt and herbs at the local grocery. People called her a Polish witch due to her slight accent, but Mother had been well-ingrained and was hardly controversial. She ran interference, saying the old woman was just a little batty and tired out after working in a potato chip factory hauling lard most of her adult life. "She's just a little confused," she'd say.

Given Mother's political prowess and her husband's honorable job as an officer, it worked. People left Grandma Grodzki alone and

looked to her as a socialite. That is, until I was born. Mother tried
everything to renegotiate my birth. She sucked hard on the smoke of
a thin cigarette in that hospital, but I was the one who felt the burning
sensation in my throat.

Meanwhile, I felt immediately loved by Grandma Grodzki and my
brother, who found me fascinating. He sat on the hospital bed and waved
at me incessantly, as though expecting me to wave back. He begged to
hold me, but Grandma Grodzki told him to wait.

"I just want to touch her feet to see if she's real. Look at those feet!"

"Gene, come be with your mother. I need you to hug me now."

"You'll be in charge of protecting her, Gene," Grandma Grodzki
told him. When Mother signed her release papers the next morning,
she insisted that she'd been given the wrong child. It was a last-ditch
effort. A nurse who'd offered Mother the cigarette to calm her down
also offered Grandma Grodzki one, while another nurse went over the
hospital's procedures and assured Mother that such a mistake of identity
simply could not have occurred. I was wrapped in a soft blanket, staring
at the ceiling as Grandma Grodzki held me up with plump, pink hands.

By the time I was school-aged, Mother had earned a reputation
around the neighborhood as not only indecorous but also a "refrigerator mother" because she was never around. No one at church or at my
school ever saw her near me. The other mothers, those with husbands
and no need to work, would sometimes ask me where she was. I'd hear
them whispering about my family, how Grandma Grodzki was witchy, a
lost cause, and Mother needed Jesus.

She was occasionally with Gene outside of home. The two of them
sometimes snuck downtown to buy new school clothes or have the
occasional chili dog at Phil's on 6th Avenue.

"Constant, constant shame. But your mother paid, too, Emerson.
This is what you need to know. You need to know everything to make
informed decisions. Multigenerational guilt is real, especially for women."
I pointed my finger at my granddaughter, envisioning her at the end of
this line of women, at the beginning of something else completely.

Taking note of the hesitancy in Emerson's face, I lowered my hand.

Pointing was such a bad habit. The night receptionist once told me how uncomfortable it made people feel, but I couldn't help it. Courtney ate another piece of gum and positioned her chin on her fist. "Tell us everything! My life is boring and I *need* you to keep going. Please?" she asked, and I wanted to hug her.

But I examined Emerson's stiff face again, and I knew she needed a little time. I'd need to ease her in. "Listen, girls, can you get me out of here? There's someone I need to see. I can tell you the whole story on the way. Do you have a car?" I asked.

"What kind of road trip are you thinking?" Courtney asked.

"One you wouldn't forget," I teased, loving the looks they gave each other.

"Amelia, we took the bus!" Emerson stood up, a tense little bundle of energy in jeans.

"Well, all right. I'm tired. Can you get Jenny? Maybe you can come back another day? Preferably with a car." I winked at Courtney who had an endearing audacity. This girl would make a good conspirator.

Emerson reached for my arm and helped me up. I didn't need the help, but I allowed her to think I did. I leaned in and whispered, "Thank you, Emerson. Old people *are* like windup toys, you know. We can only go for so long before we need to recharge."

"Amelia, I have questions about Mom. That night."

"Patience, sunshine." I kissed her cheek. "It begins with intuition. You have to learn to trust yourself and not be afraid."

She blurted out as if shouting over herself, "What were you trying to do that night?"

I couldn't tell her it was a failed self-sacrifice, but I could see her hunger for it. My magic wasn't strong enough. I knew it even that day. I knew it the day my daughter was born. Each generation's power is stronger than the one that came before. I examined my granddaughter, seeing the puzzle of women alive in her eyes, wondering what she was capable of. The path was open in front of her, but she was afraid. "Come see me again soon. I have a lot to teach you," I said. Her eyes lit up.

"I heard Mom. Or thought I did," she whispered, careful that her friend didn't hear.

There was desperation in her eyes, loneliness. "Look to still water. Watch your reflection till it changes," I told her.

Chapter Five: Emerson

"We're going back, right?" Courtney asked me, and I shrugged. "We have to, Emerson. Do you think we can get a car to break her out?"

I imagined my grandmother as the Baba Yaga. If only I had been right when I was a kid to believe Amelia was magical and not just crazy ... if only I didn't have to go home. We could steal off into the world and create a new life full of mystery. Courtney was right. We had to know more, come back when we had more time. "I wonder where Amelia wants to go," I said.

"Beats me, but I need an adventure! My family is so boring and predictable. But I guess we'd be arrested or something if we took your g-ma. Unless she taught us how to disappear or ... just being around her, it's ... enchanting."

"Do you feel that way around me?" I asked, feeling my face go red as we exited the complex and made our way to the bus stop.

She ignored me, tilting her head and looking sideways like I was joking. "I like her philosophy. Life is just a bunch of patterns, right? A way to describe life or to recognize the rhythm of it."

"Or stay stuck in the past," I said.

Courtney stopped walking a moment and stared at me. "I guess." Her voice dropped. "Let's visit next week. Way more educational than school, or we can go after or on the weekend. Say we're signed up for the chess club or some organization now if our parents give us shit. Also, if you want to talk about anything, come over whenever. I mean it." She punched me playfully, a little too hard. "You never reach out when you should."

I was about to tell her that I *was* reaching out. This whole escapade was about me reaching out, but with the whine of our bus rounding the corner I couldn't find the right words.

It wasn't long before Rita was hauling recycled boxes of perfectly folded pastel shorts into our living room and hanging pictures in corners.

"Help her out, Emerson," Dad said, his voice strained. I grabbed a clear container full of photo albums and rolled my eyes. Lori laughed at a box of ceramic cows, unpacking the bubble wrap with exaggerated slowness. "Um, Rita?"

"Be careful with those! They're family heirlooms. My grand-mother's."

I dropped the photo albums at the stairs and sat next to my sister at our faded dining table to help with the precise task of unwrapping ceramic cows. Rita sat with us, catching her breath after hauling in a decorative cabinet. "Moving is no joke, girls. Look, those cows. I know they're goofy, but my grandmother raised me. They're valuable. That blue and white one with the flowers was hand-painted and is worth a lot."

Lori turned him over. There was a small flower by his foot, and a small crack.

"They're kind of cute," I said.

"Thanks, Emerson. Where do you think they should live? Maybe we could move that old desk?" She pointed to Mom's writing desk, a desk she had haggled for at a thrift store. She would sit there and dream up worlds. Mom had been illustrating a collection of stories that she never finished. The writer, a friend of hers, delivered us a basket of pies and baked goods after Mom died. We never saw her again.

"I think I need a break," I said, looking to my sister and expecting her to join me.

"Come on, Emerson. Don't be like that," Dad said.

"No worries at all. Let her take a break," Rita said.

Unsure what else to do, I took a walk. I didn't want new

furniture. I didn't want new routines, and I really didn't want new people in my life that were supposed to replace Mom. The world was trying to erase her. Visual memories I had of her even, sitting in her oversized plaid chair as she sketched images of an old Honduran diner with a cracked checkered floor or the view of clouds from a plane window, were being erased. In place of the chair now was some white Ikea shelf.

As I passed the modest single-family homes on our street, I recalled Amelia's story, and clips of Mom arrived in my mind. Images so colorful it seemed she was with me, walking beside me. I no longer felt alone. I remembered her kindness, the opposite of Great Grandma Kat. I could hear her worried but supportive tone all those years ago as she asked me to reconsider, accident-prone as I was, enrolling in gymnastics when I was eight. I could still feel the smooth texture of her hair when she let me braid it as she told me stories. The way she'd crumple on the couch from pain but would spring to action as soon as her migraines let up, humming along to Paul Simon and looping Lori, who always needed to move, into her long arms as they danced in the living room.

Once I reached the end of my street, where there was a small city park with a single basketball hoop near two rows of gingko trees, I felt something nudge me from behind. Mom's melodic voice arrived, in a near-whisper. "It's time, Em," she said, and I jumped. Her voice was as embodied as the vivid images in my mind.

I looked around, wide-eyed, feeling the onset of an attack. My therapist had told me to notice three things in front of me and simply label them when I felt my heart slow, and body go tingly. I took a deep breath. *Grass. Basketball hoop. Bleachers.*

Mom used to watch from the bleachers at the community gym as I attempted to do a cartwheel and, inevitably, landed square on my butt; her voice soft, she laughed as my sister ran around with gymnastic ribbons she wasn't supposed to use and would put her finger to her lips as though we were all in on a secret. One time, she drew us on the bleachers in pencil in a sketchbook that now lived in our attic with her paintings and the rest of her things, including all the mementos, and she told me to look at the image and imagine myself walking down, doing the perfect flip. That day, I did it. I felt something take over me as I handsprung up and over with grace and landed softly on my feet.

"It's time, Em," she said again.

"For what?" I said aloud, looking around to see if anyone was within earshot.

Nothing. Mom's hints at alchemy had been subtle, channeled into her art. Our attic was full of paintings inspired by her travels with Amelia, alongside nature scenes she'd painted in the garage while watching Bob Ross reruns. "One of probably three people who attempted those paintings," Dad used to say. He also used to insist hers were better than his own renditions *most of the time*. They critiqued each other in honest and biting ways.

When I returned home, I couldn't bring myself to go inside. I was still waiting for an answer, or for the panic to set in. I wondered if I should tell my therapist about this. Would her iPad have an answer?

Phyllis, a neighbor around Amelia's age who baked cookies on every bank holiday, waved as she labored to pull stray weeds. I saw her holding her hands in fists. She moved with a lag on the right side, a pain that radiated from her hip since a surgery she often told us she wished she'd never had. I waved back, taking note of her roller set blue hair and kind, plump face. As I opened my hand wider, I called out to her that her garden looked beautiful as the same pain shot down the back of my leg. I absorbed it, taking a deep breath to metabolize it, and it melted away. In that moment, inexplicably, I could feel her body relax as mine did.

Peering at me with her hand up to shield the sun, Phyllis looked momentarily perplexed. I saw a glimpse of her as a girl then, on a boat in a powder-blue blouse and apple-red lipstick. I wanted to pursue the vision (or was it a borrowed memory?), to learn about her story and all she lived with and through, her dreams and defeats, but our front door opened.

As Lori sat next to me on the porch and patted my thigh,

Phyllis walked around to the side of her house without hesitation. Her hands now relaxed. Had I done that? I felt drained, as though I'd just run miles. A large piece of our stoop was crumbling, and I kicked away a chunk of the concrete. When I looked up, my sister lifted one corner of her mouth as she assessed me. I thought she was going to ask me what I was doing or why I was staring at Phyllis. Instead, with pure exasperation in her voice, she said, "Painted cows."

I nodded, snapping right back to the sad reality of our home makeover. "How many?"

"An army. I unpacked an army of cows."

"I want to go live with Phyllis," I said.

Rita and my father continued to unpack as two men dropped the last of the boxes at the side door. My father tied his long hair back in a bandana and motioned to us from the other side of the screen door.

We lived on the smaller half of a duplex, but we had a large front window that held a stained-glass panel one of my mother's artist friends had given her as a gift. As we stood, we could see Rita filling her bookshelves as she sang along to Prince. She began dancing her shoulders.

"You should go help her. Rip off the Band-Aid," Lori said. "She's a nice lady."

I rubbed the top of her head like a child, messing up her thick hair. "I'm the older sister. Remember that."

We both headed in and crouched down on the floor to help unwrap glassware. Without asking, Dad handed me a little bag of wood nails and told me to listen for his cue.

"Thank you, girls."

"Yep," I said.

As Rita went out to speak to the delivery men, my father leaned in. "Change is hard, I know. Rita's a beautiful person though. Inside. She's not here to replace your mother. I know you know that, but I want you to know I know it, too."

"Can we at least talk about Mom's things? They're all shoved up into the attic like trash," I said.

"Your mother had a lot of things. We'll go through what's left, but I think we should donate what we can to the church."

"Without her stuff, her stories are gone. My memories—my connection to her. Maybe if you talked about her every now and then, told me things I'm too young to remember, I wouldn't care. But her *things* are all I have."

My father didn't look up. "I don't know if the timing is right for this conversation, Emerson."

"It's never right. You're destroying memories. You're bringing this woman in, and . . . and I deserve a conversation." I began to feel heat throughout my body. "Fuck it. Never mind," I yelled and rushed to the kitchen.

"Watch yourself. Maybe it's time you started seeing the doctor again, about your grief. You don't have a connection. It's been five years, Emerson."

"Maybe I can still talk to her," I yelled.

Something shifted in his face then, and his jaw became stone. "Don't talk like that. Don't you dare talk like that," he said.

"Maybe you should let me say what I want to. Maybe you should let me process my grief." I heard the front door close.

I had been waiting for something more to happen for five years. After talking with Amelia once, I'd finally heard my mother's voice. I couldn't let the possibility of magic—of something more—go. I grabbed a large metal bowl and ran upstairs. In the bathroom, I filled the bowl with water before placing it on my desk, the only flat surface in my room. The water was rebellious. Every time I'd looked down there was another ripple, something subtle.

I thought of the Baba Yaga, all-knowing and selectively helpful. When she finally supplied the girl her firewood, it came with a spell that destroyed those who had abused the girl. Magic, it seemed, even the simplest magic, was unstable and unpredictable—especially in the hands of people like me.

I crept up on the water slowly. When I looked down, finding

some semblance of my reflection, I concentrated. I wanted to believe, but I couldn't help but worrying my father was right—it all felt so silly.

"What is it time for?" I asked. My eyes blurred as I focused. I was afraid to blink. Just as my reflection began to crystalize, I knew it was all pointless. I was crazy like Amelia. This went beyond a panic disorder. I was completely delusional, desperate to believe because I couldn't imagine the world being as limited as it was. Just as I looked away, a light flashed. The water was completely still as though solid. It became like wax, and I dipped my hand in to feel the heat and hug of paraffin. I heard my mother's laughter.

"You'll never forget the day I turned your hand into wax." I felt a feeling of peace like I hadn't felt in years.

"What is it time for?" I repeated, and as I lifted my hand, the warmth dissipated, and the peace evaporated as my door opened. Water dripped and soaked part of my sleeve.

I looked up to see a summer dress. Ultra-white smile. Rita beamed. "You forgot your phone," she said, placing it on the desk beside the bowl. "What are you doing?" A series of tiny waves commenced.

"Science project. Thanks."

I saw her out, but as she rushed back down the stairs, I gravitated to the hall closet where I reached for a thick rope. Heading up into the attic, I sat with old toys and Mom's paintings, waiting for the saturation of memory, but no more memories came. My taste of magic was over. Her voice refused to return. I put on one her old dresses over my clothes and began to cry. I begged for her to let me know she was there, still looking out for me.

The next day, Ian rushed me at school. He wore hexagon-shaped glasses. "Emerson. Do this with me. It's what I need for my college apps. I think it might even promise an internship." A part of me admired his relentless enthusiasm for life, but most of the time I was annoyed by it.

"Slow down, Ian. What are you asking me?"

He got a little too close as he handed me a flyer for a competitive honors program that was open to anyone with a 3.5 GPA. I noticed how flawless his skin was as I stepped back only to be startled as Courtney snuck up behind me and grabbed my waist. "Ass," I said, waiting for my heart to slow. "Does no one respect my personal space?" Ian rambled on as though he hadn't been included in that comment.

"Ms. Holden told me to make sure you knew. You both knew. Courtney, your mom will like it."

"Yeah, she'll like it. Who cares what I think," she said, placing an arm around my shoulder as she read. Courtney's Mom was a pious woman who was strict and had ambitious and highly specific expectations for her daughter. She always seemed to be analyzing my intentions when I went over to her house, as though calculating how much time Courtney was wasting with me when she could've been studying.

"You know what, this might be perfect," I said. Saying we're part of an honors class just to have an excuse not to come home till late. The "application" turned out to be enrollment due to low interest, so we could apply, and the classes were psychology-based, so they wouldn't be all bad.

We were to meet for our evening class every Tuesday and Thursday, but I planned to tell my father it was every day, so Courtney and I had the freedom to ride out to The Lavender House whenever we wanted. I hated that it had to be a secret, but I didn't want to have the "crazy women" conversations. If Dad knew I was seeing Amelia on my own, he'd do what he could to stop it.

Ian stared at me in a strange way, as though he wanted to ask me something. "Em, um."

"Thanks for telling us about this," I told him.

"Um...," he looked to Courtney, who offered a gentle, reluctant smile before stepping away. "Em, I'm not good at this, but do you want to get coffee or ... anything sometime?"

I looked around. "Um, maybe later. I'm not in a good place right now."

"You're one of the smartest people I know. I just want to pick your brain a little."

I was about to say no. A nice, confident, easy no. But instead I said, "Sure. Coffee. We could meet this weekend." I immediately wanted to retract what I said, but it felt like what I should do. What was expected of girl A when delivered a compliment, asked politely by Guy B. Just ... girl A was not me.

"Great! Saturday? I'll text you. Maybe I can meet at your house, and we can walk to that Happy Beans place?" The bell rang, and I looked around as my peers bustled to class.

My mother's voice arrived then, piercing through. "It's time, Em."

This time, instead of calm, the cold shot through me. I focused on Courtney, trying to ignore the panic rising from the soles of my feet, the lightening in my chest. "Things have been strange since we went to Amelia's," I managed to say.

"How so?"

"I'm getting ... shit, it's happening." I felt the numbness and chill moving up my arms, and I needed to get somewhere fast. Luckily, Courtney knew about my panic and was able to help. She walked me to the bathroom, where I sat in the stall and waited for my breath, my focus. "I, Emerson, am in control of my own thinking, and I..."

"I'm waiting until you're past this. I'm right here," Courtney said.

I could feel the death spreading up my legs and I hunched over, staring down at the stained tile. I had to get back to Amelia. I had to know why I was hearing my mother's voice but still feeling the panic—worse than ever.

"I'm good," I told Courtney. "Please, go to class. We'll meet up later. Wednesday, we'll go to Amelia's." I heard her approach the stall and listen. I tried not to breathe too heavily.

"Text if you need me," she said at last.

As I focused on the sound of her shoes squeaking against the linoleum, I worried this time it was truly the end. *Don't leave*, I wanted to say. Instead, when I heard her pause at the door, I steadied my voice and told her to go. I began my recitation, reminding myself that I was safe and all was well. They were just hollow words, but I kept repeating them, faster, and eventually they began to suppress the fear.

We followed one of the nurses, who wore all white, toward the entrance that Tuesday. "I'm here. I'm clocking in now, sorry I'm late," the nurse said, holding the door open for us without looking back. A resident with a walker and blue-silver hair took her time to wave at us. I nodded as the woman from the bus rushed to her and adjusted the tennis ball on the bottom of the walker.

"There you go, Glory," she cooed.

I couldn't help but wonder why Amelia's experience of this place seemed so draconian, when it seemed like such a nice staff. Jenny ushered us back to Amelia's temporary room, where there were more paintings and lacy curtains. It was a compact room, so we all sat a little too close for comfort. Just as I sat at the edge of the bed, I caught sight of a deck of cards in the corner of the room and realized they were *the* goddess cards.

Tracing my gaze to a cardboard box that held the silver bowl that held the cards, alongside a series of what looked like letters, Amelia suggested we go outside. "There will be fewer distractions." The small box of personal items was all I saw in the room, but I nodded in agreement.

Interlacing my arm beneath my grandmother's, we walked toward the pond. Courtney grabbed a fistful of old French bread out of a bag by the gazebo, and she handed Amelia a few chunks to throw.

"I have to ask you something," I said.

"I'll tell you about goddesses," she told me. "We'll start there. You remember your mother telling you these stories? The queen of hearts is Áine. She was abused by her husband, like so many. The Celtic goddess of summer, of sun: once she realized her power, she turned him into a goose." She threw the bread. "Then she killed the goose."

I remembered the name in script on one of Amelia's tapestries of a woman with a long braid who wore wheat and corn in her hair.

"That's one way to get rid of him," Courtney said, laughing.

"My grandmother used to tell stories about goddesses and spirits, all that we cannot see, and I told them to your mother. She told you, but not enough."

"I think she told me more than you think," I said, remembering the way Mom would abruptly stop storytelling when my father came in the room. Her stories of magic and myth were like our shared secret. She said good stories scared some people—my father included.

The image of my mother sitting at the edge of my bed painting worlds out of thin air arrived as Amelia launched into her personal narrative. It was like a quiet snap of the fingers. We were transported. It was early autumn, and the day warmed as I closed my eyes to listen with every atom.

PART TWO:
THE WORLD

Chapter Six: Amelia

The nosy people in town liked to ask about my mother in an investigative, accusatory way, and the church ladies were cheekiest. Although Mrs. Jamison's question had been vague, "How has Kat been? We never see her with the children," her tone was probing, and I was just old enough to want to hear the answer. I folded my hands and waited, standing tall. I didn't like the way she looked at Grandma Grodzki.

But my grandmother straightened her shoulders and gave the slender woman an unrelenting stare. She assumed her lowest voice, despite a fixed smile. "If you *must* know, she's just fine. Thriving even."

"Oh, wonderful." Mrs. Jamison took a step back, and I zeroed in on her pinstripe skirt and fish-belly pale legs, her shallow heels in the snow; she appeared to be floating, and one thing felt clear. She was not long for this world.

Lifespans are visible, I eventually learned. But in the moment, I just felt badly for the woman and wasn't sure why. I wanted to tell her to watch out. A strange, cold sensation took over. The way Mrs. Jamison tapped her thumb to her middle finger, the creases in her forehead, the color around her were all parts of a sort-of equation.

She was rambling on, saying, "I know it's been some years, but we all care about Kat, what with her being single, and she often seems so upset. She's never at church anymore, or at any of our gatherings. If I had lost a husband like that ... the way she lost Tom."

Grandma Grodzki began to resemble a cooked beet, and I could feel the heat emanating from her body as Mrs. Jamison blathered on. "Please do invite Kat to our book club. We meet at the church on Sunday evenings. And little Amelia, aren't you looking lovely today! Betty says you're her best friend in first grade, is that right?"

"Betty is swell," I said with a big smile.

"And how are your studies?"

"I enjoy Latin and art class." Latin was rarely offered anymore, and the Latin club, which I saw evidence of in hallway cases, had given way to classes on agriculture and sewing.

"Well, I suppose that's going to give you something to talk about anyway," she said. The woman was kind enough, but the lines in her face broke in too many places. I counted them.

"You should be careful today. Don't get into any accidents," I said with a smile.

My grandmother squeezed my arm hard then, as Mrs. Jamison narrowed her eyes before saying, "I'll tell Betty you said she was swell indeed. She'll appreciate the sentiment," Mrs. Jamison said. "And I'll be plenty careful." She seemed perplexed by my comment but unperturbed. "Good day to you both. God bless. God bless your entire family." She gave a little curtsy that I thought sweet.

"You have to be careful, child. We don't want a witch hunt," Grandma Grodzki said. I nodded, but I couldn't think of anything but my vision. Mrs. Jamison walked away on those pale legs, and I had to fight the urge to run after her. It was the first time I could remember seeing advanced news, time bending so to speak, and I wasn't sure whether to trust it.

A part of me wanted to protect Mrs. Jamison because I saw her pain. She was jealous of Mother's freedom in a way. Or that of my family's in general. After all, the mothers like this one—so plain and kind, wholly invested in everything their children did—were oddly competitive about it, almost as though whomever was most normal won at life. This normalcy, blanketed in sadness, was appealing to me in some ways though. Because normal or not, these mothers were actual parents. They were nothing like Kat.

That night, I begged Grandma Grodzki to tell me old stories, more about my father. She'd had a few women over, who paid her a few coins to read their fortunes "all in good fun," they'd often say. But I could tell they took it seriously. Grandma Grodzki flipped cards and interpreted what they said. She'd keep them well hidden during the day and only took these appointments when Mother was out late—when it was just the three of us.

Women in the neighborhood knew. They lined up at our door. After a long evening of such appointments, we sat around the living room, Gene practicing a card trick and Grandma staring stoically at an empty chair. Gene asked for a coin, which he stuffed into a small wallet his father had bought him. "I miss Father today," he said.

"Your father is with you," Grandma Grodzki said.

"Mom says he died because he was unlucky," Gene said. "Does luck live in a home? Does it pass on to children?"

Grandma Grodzki had become accustomed to his questions, but with this one she paused, staring at Gene with sympathetic eyes. "We all have bad luck sometimes. There's evil on this planet, but there's also a lot of good. We need both." She separated her thick hands and brought them back together as though molding invisible dough.

"And a lot of magic! I'll show you a trick soon." Gene held up the leather wallet, which contained the coin, then he shook it, opened it again, and it was empty. "Ta da! Mom doesn't like me having this wallet out, so hurry and look. It was Father's." He shoved it in my face, and I recoiled.

What hit me first was my mother's perfume. Beneath that sharpness, the leather was musty and rich with a vague hint of licorice. When I went to open the wallet, I heard a shriek. "What on earth is wrong with this city? It is downright frigid out there," Kat said, rubbing her hands together in the doorway. On cue, my heart sank.

"Welcome home, dear. There's a plate waiting for you," Grandma Grodzki said. She walked slowly to her rocking chair in the front room, causing it to creak as she settled in, trying to shield me. I could feel her warmth and pretended not to watch as she slid the money earned that day into her housecoat pocket.

Kat ignored her and made her way to Gene. "I told you to keep that wallet safe. The last thing I want is the girl here to destroy one of the last things we have to remember your father by." Kat grabbed and shook the wallet in the air. Gene took it back sheepishly then retreated.

"He's my father, too," I said, but the words tasted strange as they left my mouth.

"Of course, he was your father, too, but *you* didn't know him. You're too young to touch something so precious," she snapped. I scooted closer to Grandma.

I could see the entire story in my mother's face; it repeated throughout my life. I saw it when I looked in the mirror, but the illusion of being part of something normal, being more connected to my brother, was enough for me to feel obligated to try to make things work.

"Stop it, Kat," Grandma Grodzki called out without looking up. She uncoiled red yarn, allowing it to fall loose around her arm. I couldn't yet control the warm, wet tears from falling down my cheek. I wasn't supposed to cry, Mother had told me. That's what the world expected women to do.

"See what I mean?" she snapped. "Too young. Still a baby, a cry baby." She removed her white heels and rolled her neck a few times while watching me crouch on the floor as I leaned against my grandmother's leg. Mother, with an exhausted sigh, narrowed her eyes. "Alright now, stop the crying. Come here."

She enveloped me in her thin arms, and I offered a weak hug. She whispered, "Don't do it again. Promise?" I could feel her breath on my ear as I nodded, every underlying word pierced my eardrum. "Good. In that case, follow me."

I wasn't allowed near Mother's room. It was dangerous territory on any ordinary day, so to be invited was equal parts exciting and terrifying. She stood straight, tried to be present enough to absorb the moment. Her room, like Gene's, had peach walls. There was a vanity at the center of a wall framed by two windows that looked out on the neighborhood. All her things were meticulously arranged.

There wasn't a trace of dust or a stray sock. It was a far cry from the rest of our house. Even though it seemed Grandma Grodzki was forever cleaning, our house was messy with Gene's sports equipment and trains or knitting that I'd sometimes trip over, and the dust hidden from the duster only to reappear the second we were done cleaning. Mother never seemed to lift a fingernail, and everything about her and her space remained flawless.

"This is for you, Amelia. It's a handkerchief your father owned. I'm sure he'd want you to have it. He wore it in his pocket, like this." Her eyes were kind. "He owned a blue suit, and he always wore this particular handkerchief with his suit, see? This is how classy men dress—with a handkerchief that complements the suit, just a few shades lighter. I want you to remember that. You're starting to grow into your looks, and we might have more suitors than we know what to do with."

She pulled a small picture from the drawer in her vanity and held it up. I held the soft, pale blue fabric loosely. I looked at a picture of a man dressed precisely, smiling precisely, who looked so much like Gene it was eerie. I wanted to ask Mother why she was lying, pretending I mattered to her. Instead, I pressed the handkerchief to my heart, knowing it was more a gift than a connection to any myth of a father.

"You're pleased. Good. Now get out of here."

"Mother, do you think my father would've liked me?"

Considering this, she looked doubtful.

"I think he'd like you just fine," Grandma Grodzki said from the doorway, startling us both. "Come help me set the table, Amelia." She narrowed her eyes at Mother, who was reapplying waxy lipstick and didn't seem to notice. "I think it might be time for you to leave for a while," she grumbled, and the ground shook.

Mother *still* didn't look up. I heard my grandmother loud and clear, but Mother didn't seem to hear at all.

"I think I'll go back out tonight. The jazz club on 10th," Mother announced with a clap, reaching for her ivory gloves.

Beef and vegetable stew thickened the air; the rich, salty meat intermingled with the pungency of mustard seed and red pepper. Grandma Grodzki made this stew every weekend, often with my help to cut the vegetables. In fact, when Grandma nudged me out of the kitchen that day, I knew something was going on. I walked into the living room and saw Mother's thin fingers tapping the couch beside her. When I hesitated, confused, she continued to tap, faster, harder, as though she were assessing the cushion's thickness.

It was two days after my eighth birthday, and Mother announced that she and Gene would be visiting friends in California. "We'll take a few months to travel after, so we'll be gone quite a while," she explained, swirling her glass so the two ice cubes clashed in her vodka gimlet.

There was a dreamy urgency to Mother's usually distant and hurried demeanor. She wore the look she got when she told fictional stories of a single mother and her two children who traveled the world and had great adventures in jungles with lions and on ski slopes where they would see bears and have to rush away. When she would tell a story, she was usually drunk, but despite slurred words, it came to life in my mind. As I listened, I could sometimes see the walls turn to ice and their gray-white solidity would break apart into hard sleet and fluffy snow. I'd look down and imagine the skis on my feet and would begin to feel their weight—heavy but invited.

Mother was usually only tipsy enough to tell stories on weekends, when she played the numbers and drank vodka gimlets. She honestly believed she would win each week, so she was always energized by nights out. Her stories would come true one day, she said.

A regular loser at the game, she had a genuine belief that, each time, it was her time or, if not, it was nearer her time. "I'll win for sure next week. It's the law of averages," she'd say, her faith renewed by the thin paper full of numbers: possibility, hope. I memorized the numbers and rewrote them backwards and forwards in my notebooks, knowing if I got the right pattern, I could make Mother win. I willed it to happen until I knew with absolute certainty it would come to fruition.

Grandma Grodzki stood in the doorway, steadying herself near a chair, and I remembered what she'd said. "I think it might be time for you to leave for a while."

Mother had won what she called a small pot of cash, and she only had enough money for two train tickets. "I have to take the oldest. It's only right."

I wanted to run upstairs and destroy my notebooks, reverse what I saw, and make Mother give back the money. It seemed my own doing that I would be left, not only without a father, but without a mother or brother. I would be an orphan; it would lead to even more awkward conversations at school when parents were supposed to visit.

Now I felt the tears flowing in my veins. Gene, who had been sitting in the other room, worrying his pale, freckled hands, walked over and kissed me on the cheek, told me to buck up, and challenged me to a game of Rummy.

I avoided Mother over the next few days; I couldn't stomach being downstairs, where suitcases were collecting by the door, and I couldn't understand her high spirits, her unwillingness to consider that I should be with them. With my brother. When the time came, I waited silently with my arms crossed over my chest.

"You need to talk to your mother before she leaves," Grandma Grodzki said. "Say goodbye."

Why should I? I thought, but I nodded dutifully, earning Grandmother's curt nod.

There were three suitcases and two Macy's shopping bags lined up at the door. Gene and Mother were in coats and scarves. I walked from the dining room to the living room, still with arms crossed to protect my heart. I eyed Mother and felt my body recoil when those pale green eyes locked onto mine unapologetically. I glanced over to Gene's freckle-covered face. He was smiling tentatively; he had joked last night he would sneak me into the luggage. I rushed to him, fighting the urge to tell him I was breaking in half.

"Don't leave me, brother," I whispered. He ran a hand through his thick, red hair and watched the floor; the sun was so intense that summer that even his eyelids were spotted with light brown freckles. I looked down, too, at the dull yellow flowers that bordered the rug. It was as though they were marching laps around the room.

We waited like that, heads down, examining the carpet, as Mother rushed in and out of the room with such flourish that her movements seemed choreographed; she checked the luggage and twirled around, searching for a silver-backed brush and a favorite hat. "Gene, dear, do you have everything? Do you have your soap and extra shoelaces? Your books?" she asked.

Gene nodded. He looked up at my puffy face. Tears were going to erupt, and I didn't care to hold them in. By then, my entire body was made of tears.

Gene turned to Mother and said, "I don't want to go," matter-of-factly as he surveyed their home with a distant expression—his look seemed a retrospective appreciation that outweighed the prospect of leaving. She laughed it off, said she'd forgotten something, she knew it.

"How could I be so batty?" she asked herself and ran out of the room again.

Gene offered me a close-lipped smile and a shrug, as if to say, what's one to do? The moment was surreal, a million moments long, but also over too soon.

Mother ran back in, checked, and double-checked the bags. She announced that the taxi would soon be there. She threw her hand up dramatically. "It's time at last." It was as though she was the star of her own play, the way she projected her voice as though to an audience. She announced the time and said with a wide smile, "Amelia! Dear, come tell your mother goodbye."

I sat in my grandmother's chair and continued watching the flowers march around the carpet that warmed the creaky wood floor below it. I felt like that floor: forgotten, cold. A car horn sounded out front, and Mother's stockinged, high-heeled feet appeared.

"I don't want you to leave, Mother." I didn't move.

"Fine, don't hug your mother goodbye. Little girls who act the way you do deserve to be left behind, until they grow up. Here's a lesson for you: call me Kat from now on, got it?"

I looked up, absorbing this. Kat. It felt right. It felt like the name I should have called her my entire life.

Kat stood, arms akimbo. She wore long white gloves, far too

formal for daytime. When I revealed my face with tears rushing down cheeks, Kat sighed and bent over to hug me weakly, the lace of her blouse sticking to my wet face.

Gene approached me next, offering a kiss on the cheek and a whisper: "I'm not leaving you, kid. I'll come right back. I'll bring you a present. This is just one of those things. We'll push through."

A moment later, they were gone. Grandma Grodzki was on the front porch, waving goodbye. "Don't worry, child. It wasn't your fault. They had to leave. Truth is, they won't be gone long enough for me to teach you everything you need to know."

That evening, Grandma Grodzki told me to take a cold shower and stop crying, which I did, dutifully, and she took me to the back yard to harvest the chamomile tea she grew. She then directed me to take off my shoes and plant my feet in the earth. "You are not alone. You are connected to the earth. Close your eyes, feel its pulse," she said.

I stood there, uneasy at first, imagining what Mother … Kat … would say if she saw this. I imagined the church ladies recoiling. The kids I went to school with laughing. I felt embarrassed and small, but I kept my eyes closed. I listened to the pulse and dug my toes deeper.

The moon, the rustling, the wind, the ground. Everything slowed, and I felt alive.

Over the next few weeks, Grandma Grodzki would invite me to understand what Kat had willfully denied her entire life. She would teach me how to tap into my intuition in new ways, how to expand my world and connect in ways that were far too large for the life I thought I knew. She told me that I came from a long line of healers and intuitive women who had learned to hide their gifts.

She taught me the cleansing power of salt baths and salt sweeps. She shared with me copied texts by a woman named Margaret Murray, who wrote of folklore and witchcraft. She taught me how to anoint candles with homemade oils from plants, explaining that there were women who carried traditions from around the world. But she refused to let me write anything down.

"This is a verbal tradition. We just got the right to vote—we don't want to be tortured or "cured" by inept men for what is simply knowledge. The women in our family see a lot, and we need to ground. Amelia, you must pay homage to the earth while you're on it," she explained. "I have so much to teach you about your power. Everything your mother denies, but not fully. She is a woman who wants to be treated equally but doesn't accept who she is. She thinks status and money are the answer. I want you to at least understand. If you choose to deny, that's up to you, but I had to make sure you had an opportunity to hear."

The time was precious but bittersweet. She carried her stories in a regular deck of cards. Fifty-two cards for fifty-two weeks of the year, thirteen suits for thirteen moon cycles. The cards segueing to stories about goddesses and mythology that fed her practice. It was essentially illegal to use cards in this way or to share alternate stories, histories, perspectives even. Why would we expect to be able to share stories, when we couldn't keep our own currencies? Grandma Grodzki was able to be eccentric because she was old, she explained. I would have to keep quiet to keep safe.

"Imagine if Mrs. Jamison and her minions saw this," Grandma Grodzki said with a chuckle.

I learned how to make tinctures and read the lines on people's faces to see where they'd been, how to sit with candles and focus my mind. Grandma Grodzki explained that all I could see in the world, the patterns, were just a way of the world communicating with me. The patterns came when I wasn't consciously interacting, the communication was coming from somewhere deeper. The messages would always come, but my job was to listen. I began.

Then came the first letter from Kat. The tone of the letter was oddly maternal. Kat promised it would be all of them in the future tense; it seemed to me no adventure had yet been realized. She wrote about a new gentleman caller who was, of course, well-off, and mysterious, dark and handsome. Gene added his commentary at the end, explaining how boring it was and how he worked a lot, moving things or fixing things, and how Kat seemed to have already spent all her money. His blunt honesty suggested he did the mailing.

Grandma Grodzki and I would sit in the living room with tea, reading the letters ceremoniously in the evenings after dinner.

After fast-moving months, I was beginning to feel more myself. But I missed my brother terribly. I felt better prepared for the world as Grandma Grodzki explained how her mother had tried to deny her own magic too. "I think every other generation tries to rebel and fit in." I didn't want to tell her that a part of me understood that, understood Kat even. I wanted to fit in, to just get by and fall in love.

"The loneliness is the crucible, but you will learn to find balance if you don't deny your power. If you deny it, it will eat you alive or change you in ways that will make it so that you don't recognize yourself."

Grandma Grodzki had offered me tools. She told me how to connect to the earth and stars every night, offered stories of solidarity, stories of women who refused to let the world trample them, even if it often cost their lives. She taught me about apothecary and the power of fire to burn excess energy.

The tone of Mother's letters changed mid-summer; they became shorter and less formal. Over the next few years, Gene wrote less enthusiastically and less honestly, just recounting a detail or two, and Kat started bringing up new investments or schemes. She wrote of the fashions in California and the businesses in Chicago—her next stop "on the way back" to Ohio would become another next stop before she "visited us" in Ohio. I was beginning to think they'd never return.

After almost six months of no correspondence, Gene sent a postcard with a sunset on it, which arrived with tiny, sharp print and recounted little more than the weather and the dullness of his life on the road. He was looking forward to the end of summer, he wrote. He seemed miserable, which kept my heart halved.

One day he sent me a package with two books by Agatha Christie, and I read them to Grandma Grodzki as she knitted. Our life was peaceful and simple. I began to journal about all I was learning and became addicted to reading about mysteries and magic.

By the time I entered the firepit of high school, I felt new resolve. I had read each of the Christie books many times, trying to figure out how the author was able to keep everything straight. I wrote about the stories I'd heard, trying to capture the details in a similar way, but somehow, they became flat on the page, so I began painting them. I painted the goddesses, the witches, the wisdom into animals and trees. I sketched people with stories that lived behind them or in their pockets.

I returned to the inscriptions on my books when I felt alone. *You are my light, little sis. – Gene.* My books were kept on the top shelf of my bedroom closet, where I also kept my handkerchief and a picture of Grandma Grodzki at Kat and Tom's wedding. I read and reread them, until the pages began to fall out and the stories became puzzles that I had to reconnect in my mind. I kept them, with their broken spines and bent covers, safe above all the ordinary things.

Shortly after school began, Grandma Grodzki stopped telling stories, and I was desperate to capture them. Finding scraps and using notebooks from school, I began to record what I remembered and hid my notebooks in the crawl space behind the stairs.

"Just remember, you have the power to foretell, to heal, to decide who loves you, to sway events. This means you have the power to destroy. Learn from what you don't understand, learn from your mother. You have to learn from her so that you don't become her," she told me. She knew that when Kat came back, she'd bring a storm.

Chapter Seven: Emerson

Amelia rolled her neck, her long hair covering her face, as though just getting out of the boxing ring. Spits of rain swirled around us as we sat in the gazebo. The sky was not dark but for a small purple cloud. Courtney looked from me to her and back to me. I could tell she was ready to leave.

"Amelia, do you think my panic attacks will ever stop? Do you know what's causing them?" The desperation in my voice was palpable.

"No time soon. Could be a few things."

"You don't understand. It's like death is creeping into my body. I feel like I'm dying every time. Really dying. You *have* to tell me what you think it is. I'm in therapy. I'm doing everything right. Am I just doomed? Is that why I keep hearing…" I stopped as I looked over at Courtney, thinking twice about admitting that I'd heard Mom's voice.

"Just try to listen. Look to the water, doll. Every day. Pay attention to what you feel and hear. Find your magic slowly, and don't let it scare you."

"You're changing the subject. Are you saying my panic is magic? How does that work? I can barely get through the day," I said.

She pointed that bony finger at me and smiled, appearing the epitome of the all-knowing crone. Yet she asked, "You sure you don't want to break me out yet?"

Courtney leaned in. "I'm on it, Amelia. It'll take planning though."

A young woman dressed in a crisply ironed white uniform came our way and whispered something in my grandmother's ear. They began discussing meal preferences for the week, and the woman asked that we take a short walk as they discussed other things. I nudged Courtney, and we gave them their space to figure out the day ahead. As we walked, I felt my friend's heavy arm around my shoulders. She leaned in close enough that I could smell the mint on her breath. "Your grandma is a goddess herself. She's unreal."

"Or she's insane. Like me. I mean, look at that. These people here seem so nice, and she makes it seem excruciating here. And how would it be possible to remember those details? I can't remember what I had for breakfast." It didn't escape me that I was channeling my father's cynicism. The trees ahead of us danced with each other, swaying in ways that defied the wind.

Courtney snapped her fingers. "I saw it all, and I'm pumped! You're not crazy, you're just hard on yourself. I tell you that all the time. Shit tons of people have panic attacks. Besides, you had a cinnamon roll, girl, and you licked the carton clean. So ... your mom never told you about Kat or Grandma Grodzki?"

"She stopped talking about the past when she got sick, and I only remember a few stories about her traveling. I think she was careful about what she said. I felt like she was waiting for me to be old enough to tell me certain things." After a quiet minute, I decided to lighten the mood again. "But that cinnamon roll—sugary!"

Courtney smiled, presumably at my sweet outburst. Then her face changed and she nudged me. "Look, girl, maybe we can break your g-ma out of this place when we graduate. She can live with us. Do you know who she wants to visit?" Courtney's phone vibrated, and she looked briefly panicked herself, which meant it was her mother. "Shit. I have to answer. Excuse me," she said, turning away and pacing toward the trees.

Amelia walked toward me, body hunched and head down; she wore a devious smile. She watched Courtney in a surprisingly tender way, then assessed me. "They feed us too many potatoes. Fish and potatoes, meatloaf and potatoes, meatball hoagies and potatoes ... it's boring. Do you remember the goddess cards you were eyeing?" she asked me.

"Of course. I couldn't wait to open them when I was younger."

"A woman here said they were satanic and took them from me. I should have given them to you."

"Why would they do that? Is it the 1800s?"

Amelia assumed a trickier smile and held up her hands, spreading her fingers wide. Her gesture disarmed me, the way only she could, and I remembered the way she held her hands at the zoo the year before Mom died. I looked to my own hands that day and wondered what messages they contained. Today, as Amelia allowed me a moment to reminisce, I spread my own fingers wide and held them up to stare at the tops of my hands.

"Goddesses," she said, and I released my hand. "The goddesses lived tragic and beautiful lives. Like us. The Bona Dea was a goddess that only women worshiped. Only women could intake or believe her gifts. She was an oracle." she said. "I believe her story is a lot like ours."

"Like yours, you mean?"

"Ours. We know enough to be dangerous," she said, watching Courtney again.

"Amelia, I'm hearing her voice."

Amelia averted her gaze. She waved Courtney over, signaling it was time to hang up, and I could see my friend fumbling to close out her conversation. Her mother was not someone who was easy to get off the phone.

Amelia was quiet a moment, and I noticed her licking her lips. "All this talking. Dries you out. Talking is something that takes practice. You know they keep that place so stuffy in there, too, then we come outside, and our bodies don't know how to act."

"I'll get you water," Courtney offered as she approached, placing her phone in her pocket.

"Can you ask for some lemonade instead?" Amelia called out, then lowered her voice and locked my gaze. "Emerson, I'm glad you came. No one knows about my past. Only your mother, Jake, and now you two girls. I trust your friend, I like her. Start studying the stories your mother told you. She was preparing you. Look up the Bona Dea. Dive into as many stories as you can from all over the world. Not the popular ones; the ones that are buried or that are ridiculed or called outlandish—that's where the truths are."

I looked down at my hands, wanting to ask hundreds of questions.

"Your mother and Jake, the man who was supposed to be my husband, were both taken from me in different ways. They both understood more of this world—enough to keep their minds open. And Jake is still out there. We'll visit him when you break me out." Amelia examined me carefully. "You're going fix things—both of you are."

Courtney was running toward us awkwardly, trying to navigate the goose poop that covered the yard. I was confused and full of adrenaline. The way I used to be around Amelia when I was a child. I wanted to believe that there was some deeper story, some esoteric truth, but it all seemed so vague.

"It's vague because you're not ready," she said then, reading my thoughts. I refused to react. She used to do this when we were kids. Lori doesn't remember, but if I was thinking about how much I hated watching the painting show both she and my parents liked, she'd call me out on it. Back then, I thought she could not only predict the weather but control it. I believed everything until the day she made her prediction about Mom.

We watched the trees.

"Here you are, Amelia," Courtney said, catching her breath. "Those people in the cafeteria are nice, but that woman at the desk—I don't know about her. She asked me where I was going with a urine sample. I told her I wouldn't be caught dead with a urine sample, and there was this whole odd back and forth."

"Guess you'll never be a nurse," Amelia said. "That's a good thing. They're no-good, second-rate drug dealers here."

I shot Courtney a don't-get-her-off-track look, and she seemed to understand it, saying, "They seem nice to me. Amelia, can you tell us more?"

"Tell us about Jake," I added.

"I'm tired, girls. I'd like a nap before my coveted meatloaf sandwich." She scrunched up her face. "Think you can entertain yourself?"

I nodded. We had a half an hour, and part of me wished we'd taken the last bus, but I understood. *Wind-up toys.*

I told Amelia I'd walk her back. She made the same gesture with her hands, seemingly locked within herself before she let out, "Poor Kat. She didn't know what she was doing." It was something she seemed to be saying more to herself than us, but Courtney's eyebrows creased.

"It gets worse, doesn't it?" she asked.

Amelia's eyes lit up as she seemed to notice how Courtney and I were hanging on her forthcoming words. "If you'd get a car already, you can come and rescue me. Heck, buy me a bus ticket. We'll go see Jake."

"I'll work on it, Amelia," I said.

On the way out, I stopped at the desk and knocked on the counter because no one was there. There was new art on the walls, abstract flowers that were mesmerizing. "Hello?" I called.

Jenny popped her head out. "Hey, sweetie! Good visit? I'm sure it meant the world to Amelia." Her lips were Pepto Bismol pink now, and I was sure she'd changed her shirt. When I glanced at Courtney, it seemed she was making the same assessment.

"Yes, it was great, but ... she said someone took her cards. She had a deck of cards. Do you know about that?"

"No, but we'll look into it. Sometimes they misplace things and think we took them."

"She said someone called them satanic."

"That would be something else. What was on the cards? I play poker myself, and I'm a card-carrying Christian woman."

"Goddesses."

Jenny wrote that down, pursing her lips, and I took a long breath. "Goddesses aren't satanic. Not to my mind. Probably a misunderstanding, but I'll let you know if I find anything out," she said in her sing-song voice.

Courtney and I walked along the perimeter of the property, finding a wooded area. We traced the trunks of ash and oak trees, picking up awkward conversation.

"I am going to tell your grandmother's story somehow,"

Courtney said. "Do you think she'd let me audio record? Maybe I could author a book. Or make a docuseries."

I nodded, tracing the smooth bark of an Ash tree to the ground. The earth was dry. I pushed my palms down and felt the world lift to meet me. "Try it," I said, feeling exactly twelve years old again. Courtney and I tried to recreate the moments Amelia had painted with Grandma Grodzki, but we just felt silly. Then Courtney's phone rang.

"Shit. It's Mom again. She's been on me ever since we missed that one day at school. It was my mistake telling her, and now I'm a hoodlum. I have a 4.0. I mean, what can I do to please her? I can't take one day off?"

"You could tell her it was because of me. That I needed your help with my panic attack, and that you were indulging me."

"I do like to indulge you," she said, cupping my chin. It was only a moment, but as it swelled I wanted to lean in and kiss her.

Chapter Eight: Amelia and Gene

My brother was a hero long before he was a soldier. After only a few weeks, everyone at the school knew and loved Gene. Even people I didn't know somehow knew and adored him. He was funny and charismatic, the transient student who would soon be a pilot and hero, and he was cashing in on his fame.

Grandma Grodzki laughed off his nights out, saying he'd come back a bundle of hormones. Conversely, since they'd been back, Kat was uncharacteristically quiet and rarely left her room until evenings, when she would slip out to who-knows-where. She hadn't bothered to regale us with her great adventurous stories over dinners. In fact, most nights, I would deliver food to Mother's room, knocking twice, and get little more than a "Hope you remembered the salt."

Kat's absence was a relief. I felt guilty for thinking this way, but when Mother was in that room, tucked away, the floor felt stable beneath my feet. I was able to continue to learn from Grandma Grodzki and trade stories most evenings.

I was learning to trust myself that year. The visions seemed to arrive in a less threatening way, and though I didn't understand them fully, I was beginning to feel their power. I remembered the day, so long ago now, that Betty's mother had asked about Kat. I'd felt the warning, Mrs. Jamison's impending pain and when Betty didn't show up for school for a week after, I'd found out that Mrs. Jamison had gotten into a severe car accident that had shattered bones in one of her legs.

I began to record my intuitions in a small notebook I kept well hidden, and I read papers women had written on mythology and folklore. My little notebook contained all I knew, all I'd been told, so I knew I'd have to memorize and burn it once full. Grandma had warned me that our beliefs were not welcome, not by our community and not by my mother.

I tried to capture the voice exactly, the patterns that would emerge in sound and color, the whisper-like song that sometimes reverberated in my ears and sometimes turned cold, shocking my system like an icy bath. I wasn't sure it was a blessing. Mother had to be denying it for good reason. But I figured I better pay heed to it.

As I began to take note of the nuances, the energy I saw moving around people—even people I didn't know—became less of a burden and more of a pattern. I saw lifelines and places where it seemed there was a build-up, a festering. I could see quarrels and anger and accidents. Yet, I also began to see potential and good fortune.

Sometimes I just wanted to see what was in front of me like everyone else.

After school on a Friday, a game day, I offered to help Grandma Grodzki cut potatoes for dinner. Ever since our months together, I loved to help in the kitchen and felt ease as I chopped herbs, knowing the way they healed. I cut each potato into six pieces and threw them into a large maroon bowl. We never spoke of magic, or our connection to nature, not aloud, but we found deep company in each other's presence.

"Are Gene and Mom here, Grandma?" I asked.

"Kat's upstairs. I think the boy will be out for a while. News?"

"Yes. Big."

"Don't tell me you have a gentleman friend. I don't think my heart could take it right now. You're just beginning to understand how to be a woman. Once you start with those boys, I tell you—"

"It's so much better than any boy."

Grandma Grodzki laughed from the gut, deep, and patted me on my head. "How about you finish up here? I think I need to relax a moment." There was a glimpse of something then, the way she stood, but I willfully ignored it.

After dinner was prepared, there was coaxing from Grandma Grodzki to get Kat to come to the table. Mother was in full-on drama mode. She wore a leopard-print robe that hugged her curves and exposed enough of her cleavage to make me think of the women on magazine covers I'd seen in Gene's bag. Kat was overfull with tortured thoughts stuffed into high necks and gloves. Suddenly, the timing didn't seem right.

"Amelia has something big to say." Grandma Grodzki shoved a saucer of green beans in Kat's direction.

"Hm," Kat said, disinterestedly, and looked down at the beans as though they were diseased. She shoved them away and took a single roll, then glanced up at her daughter as she doused the roll with butter.

"Out with it, Amelia," Kat said.

"Maybe it's not that important. I didn't mean to make a big deal of it. I didn't mean to interrupt."

"What do you mean interrupt? There's no one here." Kat spoke sharply, as though she'd been accused of something.

Grandma Grodzki pretended not to notice and looked at me, nodding to my feet, which I ground down to stand taller. "You were flitting around the kitchen like you had wings earlier, little girl. Don't be so humble now. Let us in on the secret."

"Well, I won this thing. An art competition at school. I beat out all the other boys and girls. And my drawing, my draft at least, is here. The painting looks just like it, only in color." I ran into the front room to retrieve my bag. "See? The teacher told me that this picture is their favorite, and they're going to hang it in the school's main hallway. It will be displayed there all year!" It was one of the rare moments that time stopped, and I felt like a child.

The picture was of a woman leaning forward with her leg lifted behind her as though falling. Her head away, she saluted a man in a military uniform whose face was shadowed.

The art instructor had said it appeared as though the woman might be taking off, as though she were about to fly, and that it was this ethereal quality he admired most. I hadn't meant it that way consciously, but that was the thing about art. To my mind, the woman was saluting because that's what she was supposed to do, but there was a rebellious glimmer in her eyes. The woman didn't want the man to go, but she relished in the possibility of freedom. She contained the future as well as the present and was losing her footing as she began to ascend. She was a goddess, the embodiment of all women.

I might have been trying to put too much into the drawing. Even the background, the two trees and sky, had taken me hours to get exactly right, to render all the magic they contained—the way they held these characters up, despite the illogic of human action. Maybe I wasn't thinking all that when I drew it, but I was intending as such one way or the other.

The patriotism was just a reflection of my own pain, thinking about Gene leaving again, then thinking about how that transcended communities. I sketched it out. It was a pencil drawing, a simple thing, but people liked it, so I painted it for class. I stood there in front of Kat, holding the original delicately, proudly. "I need to get a frame."

Kat stared at the drawing for a long time. Grandma Grodzki clapped her hands. "Oh, that's just splendid." She stood to get a closer look. "Well, this is simply perfect. Our little artist." She gestured to Kat. "You know, your mother was quite the artist when she was young, too."

"Really, Mother? I didn't know that. Do you like it? I mean, is it okay?"

"It's lovely," Kat said, surprising me.

Her gaze returned to the honey-soaked roll that she'd been picking at. Her body curled forward slightly, and, within moments, my unveiling was forgotten. Kat was in tears, breathing furiously and gasping. She was mumbling something about California, how she shouldn't have come back so early, how she shouldn't have given up her dream for her children.

I put my arms around her. My mother's shaking body was like ice, and I closed my eyes, trying to absorb her pain. Kat pushed me away and lurched back up the stairs to her room. She stayed there for two days, only emerging to use the bathroom or steal a few bites of food from the refrigerator late at night.

I waited for her, pleased to feel in some way needed by Kat. After a while, I realized that my mother was not one person but many. She was to be admired, to be feared, to be avoided at all costs. This realization led me to the sketchbook. I drew nature and the family I knew with more insight. Birds represented those fleeting moments of compassion which appeared outside of day-to-day experience. A swallow flying over a peacock.

Chapter Nine: Emerson

The room felt too small. The house felt too small.

"You know I can't do that," Dad said. He furrowed his brow and rubbed his neck. He paced the kitchen as Rita and I worked on a crossword puzzle. I didn't love the woman, but her constant presence and growing familiarity worked in her favor. My sister read *Runner's World*, drumming her fingers on the glass table as she waited to be excused.

When my father was fully exasperated, he handed the phone to Rita, who said, "Hello, Amelia. It's good to talk with you. Yes, I look forward to meeting you soon! I'll bake you my famous vegan cinnamon rolls. Soon! Yes, I promise!" Rita tried so hard for Dad, for all of us. She seemed to genuinely like being here. I looked at her and tried to see beyond the loss she reminded me of.

When Rita handed me the phone, I thanked her. Before I even said hello, Amelia asked, "When are you coming back?"

I stared at Dad. I wasn't sure how he'd react, knowing I went to visit her on my own. "Oh, um. Hi, Amelia," I said. "I love you. My, um test? When is it? Oh, yeah, it's on Tuesday. Tuesday around 10 a.m."

"Good cover, kid. See if you can sneak me bourbon. These nurses are draconian. Just a little, those tiny bottles, like they give you on airplanes. Your father keeps a few."

I laughed. "I'll try, Amelia. Love you. Bye," I said, my heart pounding as I handed the phone to Lori. Dad tilted his head up and removed his glasses, examining me a moment before returning to his coffee.

Before I started visiting Amelia, I'd drag out these conversations for as long as I could, asking her about the weather, what she ate, what she was thinking.

My sister took a deep breath and said, "Hey, Amelia. Miss you. Love you. Okay then, see ya." She hung up and rushed to the front room in her tight neon pants with two water bottles in hand saying she had to stretch.

"Bye," I called after. Lori waved without turning her head. I stared at my father. "Dad, we need to visit Amelia more often. We're neglecting her. I read this article on the elderly, and so many people are neglected by family and friends. There's no other family on Mom's side, and I know it's strange for you, but she deserves to have family visiting her regularly. Everyone deserves that."

My father's face hardened.

"Of course. That's a fine idea, Emerson," Rita said, reaching out to touch my arm.

"And can we maybe stop doing the baton pass of the phone on Sundays? I think it must make her feel shitty," I added. "Maybe we could all chat with her at once. Or we could try to get someone there to set up a video conference. The two-second phone thing feels so impersonal."

"Where is all this coming from?" Dad asked. It was coming from my ability to imagine myself in this position, only worse. With no one to call me.

I shrugged. "I've just been thinking about it. What it would be like if it were me? Or Mom?"

Rita nodded, somewhat hesitantly, in agreement as she looked at my father. Dad sipped his coffee and said we could give it a shot, his face softening too quickly, almost as though he was just trying to get me to shut up. He stood and stretched, almost hitting the ceiling with his fingertips.

He reiterated, "Amelia doesn't think like you, Emerson. She has her own ... version of logic. But I appreciate the sentiment. Just remember we can't have any expectations. She can be manipulative." I was about to ask him what the hell that meant or explain how it might be because she's been stripped of her independence and had to manipulate to survive.

"When I graduate and get a job, I'm taking Amelia in the way a responsible adult would," I said. "I'm not abandoning or dismissing her like the rest of the world seems to."

"If it wasn't for that woman," he started, his voice low. I knew what he was going to say next, but Rita's hand on his arm held him back.

I felt my fists tightening. They were eating, and Rita smiled warily as I walked past them.

"You're not eating?" she asked, nodding to the veggie pasta she'd made.

"No thank you, Rita," I said and joined my sister in the front room.

My sister, wide-legged on the floor, was texting. She shook her head disapprovingly, and I wasn't sure if the gesture was directed at me or her phone conversation. I sat on the stiff new couch and waited for the enthusiastic knock I knew was coming. My stomach growled, and I looked back at the food but caught my father's gaze and looked away. When Ian angled his head so that he could wave from our front window, I glanced around at my family, registering their shock as I said, "I'm going on a date," and after I left, I slammed the front door.

I was thoroughly distracted, but Ian seemed oblivious. All shiny, white teeth, he elbowed me softly in the ribs and said, "Thanks for giving me a chance. You didn't just agree to spend time with me because you felt bad, right?"

"I'm trying to do normal teenage things, to be honest. If I wasn't with you, I'd probably be having a panic attack in my room and writing letters to my dead mother."

He started the car. "Sounds like a nice time. I'm even more flattered now."

This made me laugh. I noticed the felt-like appearance to his skin. Mine had looked like that the few times I bothered to wear makeup. "What kind of foundation do you use?" I asked.

"It's an all-natural brand."

"Why do you wear it?"

He turned to me and smiled. "Like it? ... There are multiple benefits. The built-in sunscreen and symmetry, the color balance." He looked at me. "You don't need any. Such lovely skin."

"Why the mascara?"

"The theater never leaves me, my dear. Besides, ordinary life is boring."

His words would prove true. The rest of the time he wanted to try out lines and ask me for critiques or recount his previous roles and the subsequent reviews he got from the school journalists, including Courtney. He wasn't a great actor by my standards, so I wasn't surprised when he quoted a line by my friend that said, "An admirable try by a devoted actor who is just shy of his potential."

He had the whole review memorized, had dissected it line by line, and I appreciated this because it made me feel as though Courtney was with us. I texted her. "Save me?" But she only replied with a laughing emoji. "I'll remember this," I wrote her.

The days were getting cooler, and when we left the café, I had a greasy peanut butter cookie and throbbing temples. "Hey, can you give me a ride to Canton tomorrow after school? It's kind of out of the way, but I'd really appreciate it," I said.

"You got it. But only if you go to the movies with me." Ian tried to kiss me before we got into his mother's Lincoln. I thought about pulling away. Part of me did, perhaps, but another part wanted to know what it was like. I let him lean in, unable to close my eyes, noticing the way the makeup sat atop his pores. His lips were dry, and the kiss felt exactly as I thought it would—like nothing at all.

"Well, that was interesting," I said when I arrived home.

Dad had his laptop set up in his usual spot. He looked at me from over his glasses. "I'm proud of you."

"For what?" I asked.

"For getting out there and having fun. He seems like a nice kid. Weird. But nice."

"He's narcissistic and wears makeup."

"I'll take it," Dad said. "Hey, Em." He pulled out the chair near him. I didn't feel like sitting, but I walked closer. "I've been thinking about our conversation. You know you can talk to me if you don't feel well. I won't judge you."

Laughable. I said, "I'm fine, Dad. Just normal teenage stuff. I'm going out with Ian again tomorrow after school." A part of me wanted to tell him—or anyone—that *no, I don't feel well. I feel fucking insane like you, Dad, predicted. I leave my body daily and am terrified I won't get back. I've started to hear my dead mother's voice, and when it comes to the earth plane, I feel inauthentic and pathetic.*

"Alright then," Dad said with a smile. "You going to eat that cookie?"

The next day, Ian drove twenty miles an hour the whole way to The Lavender House. Courtney sat in the back and drilled him about the upcoming performances and whether the rumors of school budget cuts to the theater program were true. This kept him talking as I sat with my head angled on the window trying to remain in my body as everything went icy in my chest.

It was raining hard enough that we could barely see the road, and I imagined we were riding on the seafloor. I closed my eyes and heard my mother whispering alongside the rain. The hard pelts on the windshield were hypnotizing. When we arrived, I had to roll my head a few times. I realized I had been gripping the seat and had to open and close my fist to allow circulation. I asked if Ian wanted to hang out to be safe. "I'd hate for you to get in an accident on our account. Besides, the receptionist has a nice spread of foundations." I said.

"I'm touched that you care, but that's a hard pass. Retirement communities freak me out," he said, staring at me. I looked back at Courtney, who was concealing a chuckle.

"Come on, lovebirds, get it over with."

I gave him a quick half-hug and pulled away. "Thanks again. Bye."

We ran at full speed the full four feet from the drop-off, but it was just enough to get drenched. When we fell into the door, a woman in a wheelchair gasped. "You two look like drowned rats," she told us. "Here, let me get you all some towels before you drip all over this nice carpet. Wait, are you Amelia's granddaughter?" she asked.

"Yes! I'm Emerson," I said, extending my arm.

"Figures." She eyeballed me before slowly turning her wheelchair. As I rung out my hair in the foyer and Courtney shook an umbrella out the door, the woman proceeded to move about an inch a minute.

We watched, dripping wet, cold, until she was out of sight, then we signed in at the unoccupied front desk and ran toward Amelia's room.

"Look at you girls," Amelia said, delighted. "Have a seat, have a seat. The cafeteria isn't available for a while. I cleaned for you." She wore light blues and baby pinks. Lacy curtains hung in her window overlooking the pond. She didn't seem to notice we were soaked through.

Because we were stuck in the room, having to pivot to find a place to settle, I realized it had the feel of a small child's room, right down to a few dolls on her dresser and an old music box with a tiny plastic ballerina standing in front of the mirror inside the lid. Aside from the dresser, there was a TV stand, a twin bed, a closet no one could walk in, and a windowsill. She even had a child-size coffee maker on the ground.

We tried to fit near the window, sitting on a towel, but couldn't comfortably, so I stretched out on the floor as Amelia motioned Courtney to the bed.

"She moved my chair. Same person who took my cards, probably." She gestured toward the silver bowl on the top shelf of her closet. "But never mind that for now. You know what, girls? You two made my day. Absolutely made my day. And I was already having a good day, comparatively, so what does that tell you?"

"That you're happy to see us?" Courtney guessed.

Amelia smiled and began to doodle on a piece of notebook paper. "Did you bring any booze? Are you going to break me out of this fascist place?"

I held up my hands, and after a disappointed nod she asked if we wanted more story. As she spoke, I noticed her eyes seemed brighter than before. She was looking forward to our visit, to telling her stories. Perhaps we were the first to ever hear them. I leaned in as she continued.

"Sorry," I said. "Can you still tell us about Kat?"

"I'll work up to that. I want to hear about you girls."

"I'm boring. Your granddaughter has a boyfriend though," Courtney said with a smirk. I nodded along, and Amelia gave me an extended glance.

"Hardly," I said.

"Tell me about him."

"I went to a coffee shop with a kid we know who talked about himself the whole time. It was kind of horrible," I said, more to Courtney than to Amelia.

"You did, huh?" Amelia said.

"We're going out again," I added, again looking to my friend, who didn't look back. "To a movie this time. More of a classic date, I guess.

Maybe dinner."

"Tell me more." She stared at me a while, and when I didn't respond because I didn't know how, she gave me a stern look as though letting me off the hook this once. "Fine! I'll do the work here. I'll tell you a *real* love story. Not sure you know this, but when I was younger, I was an artist."

Chapter Ten: Amelia

When Kat finally emerged from her room, it was as though nothing had been wrong. It was as though I never came to her side to support her. It was Friday, the day of assembly and the unveiling. I had been reading at the breakfast table, trying to ignore the tingling in my stomach.

I tried everything I could to find something to occupy my mind, but nothing was working. I'd turned and tossed the previous night, barely able to keep my eyes closed, and still my body was full of excess energy.

I imagined the other students admiring my picture, staring at it for a long time. I imagined the other students laughing at it, wondering how I'd won the award. When I looked up to find Mother humming, heating up water for tea, I pretended it was the norm.

"Morning, Amelia. Morning, my beautiful daughter," she said, pulling my chin up with her cold fingers. She was dressed in a neat, pinstripe business suit and sharp heels. Everything about her seemed new and refreshed, but I could only force a smile and offer to make her eggs. Mother lived for moments in the spotlight. I tried to imagine how she'd be if she were the one about to unveil her art.

When Grandma Grodzki appeared in her mint-colored housedress and slippers, she didn't look surprised to see Kat giddy. "You look well," she told Kat, giving me a warm smile. "Did your mother tell you? She's thinking of going downtown to look for a job for the holidays. Hallelujah." She clapped her hands.

"That's splendid news," I said, feigning a smile as Grandma Grodzki shoved me aside to make Kat's breakfast. I was grateful, eager to leave the house and feel the open air on my face, yet I wanted to pull Grandma Grodzki aside and ask her to share some way of making me less afraid. I wanted to care less, to be collected and calm.

To finally unveil my drawing at a ceremony seemed like a chapter from someone else's life. It would be a moment of inclusion and recognition. I hadn't told anyone at school yet because I wanted the day to be special; I wanted to have my moment of stardom, that mixture of pride and embarrassment, and the more I thought about it, I was ready. The announcement would be made before lunch at a school-wide assembly, and I hoped that the teachers might even call me up on stage like they sometimes did when recognizing a student's perfect attendance or athletic achievement. As a mediocre student, I had never been called on stage for anything.

I imagined my smile and insincere humility. Caught up in my own head, I didn't hear my brother slide into the kitchen in his socks.

"I won't work for long," Kat said, stirring her tea loudly. The clinking of the ceramic set my teeth on edge.

"It *is* splendid news. It's about time Mother comes off it," Gene said, grabbing the orange juice.

No one even knew he was there—he must have snuck in late at night. I beamed, trying to forget he shipped out in less than a week.

"Don't speak like that," Grandma Grodzki said sternly. She whacked Gene on the side of his head, and I chuckled.

"Ouch. Damn it." He rubbed the tender place she'd whacked. "I'm only being honest. So, she made a bad investment. Get over it, I say. Mother is smart. She'll find another way to make money."

"You're damn straight I will." Kat placed her pink mug on the counter and spun around. "So how do I look?" She looked stunning, and I said so. Her bangs were curled under so that they accentuated her narrow but piercing eyes. She looked as if she had walked out of the pages of a novel or was in a movie, playing opposite Clark Gable or James Stewart. As though in response to this thought, Kat gave me a wink and put two fingers under my chin, again lifting her head. "You're coming with me today."

"Where to, Mother?"

"Downtown. Take a brush to that hair, and let's go."

"I can't. It's a school day."

"Well, last time I checked I *am* your mother. That means I'm in charge, and I can give you permission to skip just this one day. I need you today, to be my sweet little lucky charm."

"I have my unveiling today. I might even get a ribbon."

"You said your little picture will be displayed for the entire year, right, doll? Right? So, you can celebrate and collect your little prize tomorrow. How about it? Come with me. I'll buy you a milkshake at Lazarus, and we'll lunch at the diner on Main Street, like some real working girls. Mother needs you."

I stared at Mother, then through her. In that instant, my nerves were gone, replaced with fire. Kat was trying to take my recognition away, minimize it and make the day all about herself instead. Gene rolled his eyes and, seeing my distress, rushed over to Kat's side and cleared his throat loudly. "I am your lucky charm, Mother, remember?"

"Oh, you are, but just look at this little girl here. What person would deny a job to a woman with such a precious little girl? Gene, you're a man now. No one will feel obligated to give me work if they see you; they'll just think, look at the strapping young boy. He can support his mother."

"Not if I wear my uniform. A uniform will get us respect. I can put on the old charm."

"Mom, please take Gene. I'll go with you any other day. Please," I said, even though I wanted to yell. It was the one thing I knew better than to do in front of Kat, so I wasn't surprised when I felt the sting of Mother's palm. My cheek grew warm as I backed away.

Kat told Gene to hurry and change, then get his coat. She didn't look back as she walked out of the room. She only said, "Don't bother coming another day, Amelia, my little artist. You won't be needed another day."

I realized I was late now and would have to run part-way to make it on time. "Bye, Grandma," I said, giving her a hug before running out the door and down the street. I ran so fast that my hair became windblown and the rubber on my shoes began to grow hot. I ran so fast that I felt I was running through time.

Just before I arrived at school, sneaking past a cluster of teachers, who were smoking and gossiping, I got down on the ground and pressed my hands into the dirt near a tree trunk. I didn't realize I was in front of a window, but when I looked up, I could see my reflection. My cheek was swollen, and my hair a mess. I looked like a crazy person in the dirt, but for an instant, I felt total acceptance. I tapped into something larger than myself.

Sneaking into the assembly, closing the heavy door behind me as everyone took their seats, I found an empty chair near the aisle, closer to the front than I'd intended or would have liked.

"Why is your cheek red?" the boy I sat next to asked loudly.

"My mother slapped me," I whispered, widening my eyes, then added, "Nosey." The adrenaline and lingering anger made me bold. I sat among both students and teachers in assembly, knowing my own name might be mentioned and that I had almost missed it. My cheek burned.

The principal was announcing plans for a new menu at lunch, a healthier menu, including carrot sticks, apples and peanut butter sandwiches made with Wonder Bread. I knew he would announce the art display, and I was consumed by thoughts of tripping on stage. Maybe teachers would assume my red cheek was just a blush of embarrassment. I tried to summon what my grandmother taught me, a detachment with petty worldly pursuits and instead trust myself, but everything about me in that moment felt like a normal kid. I was concerned with what people thought and, at the same time, completely full of myself. I recognized the loss that comes with adoration. Either way, it felt good … addictive.

"If my mother smacked me," the boy whispered as the room quieted down, "I'd smack her back. Then I'd run before she could catch me and take the first train to New York City." He smacked the back of his hand.

I couldn't help but laugh. It was so inappropriate for a boy to say, just as it was inappropriate for me to think. I began to fantasize about what it'd be like to stand up to Kat, though I imagined I'd cut my hand on her sharp cheekbones.

I'd never seen this boy. He sat smiling, as though the thought of sparring with his mother brought him amusement, too, which was sick. But he was handsome, slender with long legs outstretched in front of him as though he was sitting leisurely on a park bench, passing the time and feeding the pigeons. He had a thin nose and wide eyes.

"What's your name?" I asked.

"I don't think we have time to cover all that in whispers in assembly. Maybe you could meet me in the hall by the cafeteria before lunch and I'll tell you."

I rolled my eyes with the emphasis I'd seen Mother employ when speaking with men. "Always treat a man like you don't have the time for him," Kat once said to a woman who was briefly her friend. I had been listening as the friend sobbed over a fight with her husband, and Kat offered hard advice. She'd said, "Men like to think they have a challenge. They like to play games. And they like ladies who play games with them. They sure don't like the sort of lady who'll cry over nothing."

I looked at the boy, trying my best to continue to appear annoyed, but a surge of interest I couldn't deny flooded through me, and I added, "I don't care to hear about you. I just wanted to know your name."

Someone kicked the back of my seat. "Shhhhhhh. You'll get in trouble. Mr. Clark is watching." I turned to see Betty and smiled, which made my cheek throb more.

I could smell the cinnamon and feel the warm tingle of my friend's breath in my ear as she asked what happened to my cheek. I just shrugged. I was happy to have reinforcement so close by. The boy smiled wider as he watched us exchange a look of excitement. As I turned back around, I cut my eyes at the boy, then stared ahead, worrying my hands. The dirt underneath my fingernails dusted my dress.

As the assembly went on, I snuck glances at the boy. I noticed his smile seemed to take up half his face, like the Cheshire cat in *Alice's Adventures in Wonderland*, and this was probably the only reason I eventually smiled back.

"I'm Jake," he whispered.

And with that, nothing was ever the same. I felt strange; a twisting sensation that replaced the thumping in my belly and chest, and suddenly my entire body was as warm as my cheek. I tried to pay attention to the announcements being made. I had to remember to listen for my name.

There was static in the microphone. "In other news, we have new artwork by students. The art will be displayed in the red hallway, next to the trophy case. Our own student, Miss Amelia Grodzki, is the winner of our art competition, and Mr. John McCrellis is the runner-up. Everyone, please, let's take a moment to recognize these students."

A round of tepid applause echoed in the large assembly room, and I looked down at my feet until it was over. I was both disappointed and glad they hadn't called me up on stage. Mr. Damon continued, "Will these students please stand? Don't be shy."

I half-stood and smiled; my hand covered my cheek. I couldn't bring myself to look at Jake, whose response I so desperately wanted to see. Kat's voice chimed in my head, clear and loud. "Men like the spotlight, doll. They *do not* like sharing it."

"Congratulations," Betty whispered.

I glanced back at my friend and mouthed my thanks, dropping my hand. As I went to sit back down, I glanced at Jake again. His gaze, straight ahead, was one I'd often employed myself in class and recognized right away. He was lost in thought, completely uninterested in me or the assembly. This intrigued me.

Chapter Eleven: Emerson

The coolness wafted beneath my skin before turning icy. I shifted in my seat and tried to remember my breath. I kept thinking of Ian kissing me and how different Amelia's story was. I needed him to be a distraction, but even here, in the aftermath of what normal teenagers do, in the midst of hearing Amelia's tragic love story, the panic rose as though trying to conceal something. We were sitting in the gazebo now, and the air was still heavy from the rains. Mist emanated from the pond, but all else felt still outside. Inside, I was dying, and I repeated my mantra silently.

"Let go. It's time, Em," my mother's voice insisted. Her voice crystalized as calm arrived, as though her message lived beneath the panic.

"Time for what?" I asked.

Courtney gave me a perplexed look before Amelia signaled for me to stand and come toward her. She closed her eyes as I did, and gently reached out to feel my pulse. She pressed hard, almost hurting me, then released a long sigh that sounded exaggerated, as though she was purging something from her body.

"Do it with me," she said, sighing again. I looked to Courtney, who shrugged, before I followed suit. "Again."

"I feel silly," I said.

"One more. Deep breath. Sigh it out." She waited. "Good. You're feeling good?" she asked, and when I nodded she gestured. "Now sit!" she commanded before returning to her storytelling voice. "My life changed when I met Jake, but not because of him. I met him before I was strong enough to know what to do. You girls might not be ready to hear this whole story. You know, it might just be too much for you. What if you find out things that you can't deal with?"

Courtney nodded vigorously but was watching me, familiar with the way my body went rigid when I was panicking. "We're not perfect angels, and I've been mad at my mother, too," she said. "I know what it's like to be so annoyed by someone you want to beat them up." She gave me a sarcastic wink. "Do you recall the day we met, Em?"

I laughed, steadier now but wary. It was as though Amelia had done something medicinal. "Of course ... Amelia, that's a story we should tell *you* one day." I wanted to hug her, to thank her for erasing my panic, but the moment had passed.

Amelia lifted the palm of her hand to the sky, and we began to feel warm raindrops return, a brief moment of gentle awareness preceding another storm. Thunder rolled overhead, and Courtney took off her jacket to hold it over Amelia as we walked back to The Lavender House, meeting Jenny at the door. The rain picked up just as we stepped inside.

"Let's get her warmed up so she doesn't catch pneumonia," Jenny said, and a nurse showed up to walk Amelia to her room.

"I'll be back, girls," Amelia called. "Don't leave!"

After attempting to warm ourselves under the bathroom dryers, Courtney and I settled in the comfy waiting room chairs, shivering, as she recalled what it had been to be the bumbling new kid in high school, wandering around the cafeteria the day we met.

"Do you remember it as vividly as I do? I swear, it's like yesterday but different people," I said.

"We were angsty then."

"Yeah, not anything like now."

We laughed, recalling how I had bumped into the condiment aisle and a glass bottle of ketchup fell next to her. I remembered watching it happen in slow motion; the ketchup splattering all over her khakis, and her body barreling toward me. She was new to school and self-conscious, she later told me, but all I saw was rage. I was out of my league as she pushed me to the ground without pause.

I started flailing my arms, trying to fight like I used to with my sister, but she just pinned me there, and my exaggerated movements. I saw kids closing in around us, provoking, recording it on their iPhones and laughing. We were both given two days of suspension and weeks of detention, during which we learned about emotional intelligence via a loop of very sadly done videos.

It was two years after my mother died, and I hated Courtney vehemently. I channeled all my anger toward her, until the third day in detention, when I decided I hated the videos on emotional intelligence more and said as much. I remember hearing her laugh, mocking the video in a nasally voice. "Mutual trust means deep listening," she said before releasing a loud laugh like my mother's, and I couldn't help but add my own mocking rendition.

"Emotional calibration means recognizing extreme emotions and taking a moment to pause," I said. We forgot our mutual hatred long enough to cackle. "I think I could take you down now," I said, trying to catch my breath.

"Do you remember those videos?" I asked, nudging Courtney as the smell of baby powder arrived shortly before a resident walked by.

Courtney snorted, causing a resident who was walking by to pause and stare at us for an uncomfortable amount of time. It stopped our laughing. I thought she was going to say something. It seemed she did, too, but then she turned and moved on down the hall. Her thin hair made a curlicue on the back of her head. "Do you think they all have stories like Amelia's? All the residents?" Courtney asked.

"If they do, I don't know if they are able to tell them anymore." I closed my eyes and imagined what this woman's story must have been. Suddenly, I felt thirsty and dazed. I was thinking about a younger man or a different time, a loss and the long wide fields they used to drive past as they headed into town together. The woman turned a corner, and my shoulders released, the image was gone.

I shivered. I wondered if my mother's fear was to end up in a place like this, one of those residents with no visitors and no stories. Or no faith that anyone would listen or care. I wondered if this was my fate.

The stories of the women in my family were too tragic to ignore. I imagined the world quickly locking me away, a wisp of hair pasted to the back of my heard, stories swirling in my mind that no one would ever hear, and I began to feel the wave of panic. I glanced down at my watch, feeling my energy shift. "The next bus!"

"You're always in a hurry," Courtney said.

"We'll be here a few hours if we don't make it," I reasoned.

As we gathered ourselves to make a run to the bus, Amelia arrived in a new outfit, a pale blue blouse and dark blue pants that came up to her breasts. She was beaming. "Fresh and clean," she said. "How about ten more minutes, girls? Don't head out just yet."

"We have to," I said, hesitating a moment before adding, "but we'll be back."

Amelia turned to Courtney and played her best card, "I could tell your future if you come back to my room."

"Em, let's stay a little while. We'll figure it out." I looped my elbow around hers and tugged. If I had to drag my friend out of there, I would. "Next time, Amelia," Courtney said.

Once we were running for the bus, she heaved. "Bully."

"We'll come back soon." As I said this, the chill returned and tore me in half. I bent over, trying to breathe, and just as Courtney went to help me up and ask what was wrong, it subsided. It was the most intense and brief episode I'd had.

"Emerson, are you OK?" Her eyes traced to the exact point where the chill had come and gone so quickly. My hand was instinctively applying moderate pressure, squeezing my own pulse. When I released, I felt relief.

"I don't know. I don't know, but I don't want to feel this anymore." I began to break down. If Amelia was right, if this was some kind of magic or knowing opening up inside me, then I didn't want it. I didn't want any of it.

When Ian's Lincoln arrived the next night, my father introduced himself and tried to conceal his excitement that his teenaged girl was going on a teenaged date. I brushed past him, and went to a movie that Ian had picked out about an artist who accidentally killed someone and must find his way to redemption. No one else was in the theater, and it was darker than I remembered. The audio was overwhelming, and when I looked over at Ian trying to understand what it must feel like to be attracted to an awkward but sweet boy who was objectively handsome beneath an annoying persona, I couldn't. But I needed to. When he whispered that the bartender was someone—could I guess who?—that's right, the sister of the deceased girl, his breath was warm, and I leaned in to kiss him.

I had one goal that evening, and it was to feel something. To feel normal excitement. No magic. Just normal teenage shit. After the movie, we paused in the narrow theater hall, where local art was displayed. It was a community theater that supported local artists, and I wondered aloud if they'd consider hanging some of my mother's travel pieces here. Ian, likely feeling emboldened by my kiss, allowed his fingers to settle on my hip. "You'll have to show me some of her work sometime."

"She never got too serious, but she loved it. She had a few pieces hanging in a restaurant for a while. Maybe I'll ask." The workers upfront, both young men around my age, were busying themselves with popcorn and some kind of game on their phones.

"I'll ask for you," Ian said. "They're nice here. I'm sure they'll hang a few pieces." His encouragement was sweet. He gave my hip a gentle squeeze, and I almost felt something.

Staring at the depictions of mountains and oceans, the images of Ohio farmlands, old Columbus neighborhoods blurred, and I saw people looking beyond the frames for more. The stories told through art were ones I'd always felt I could hear, and I wondered how many people only told their true stories this way.

When Ian reappeared near me again, saying they'd love to consider her art and I just had to submit samples to their website, I shushed him, herded him toward the women's room near the back exit and into a stall. Shoving my body to his, I willed myself to feel something. He was confused but went with it. A full foot taller than me, he looked down, his breath warm. Long fingers settled on my lower back as we kissed. I moved his hand between my legs, and he hesitated, unsure what to do.

"Are you sure, Em?"

"No, I'm not sure. I don't know what I'm doing, but I want this." I took in long breath and unbuttoned my jeans. Our eyes met, and I saw his kindness. He lifted me up and tried to fumble through. When I closed my eyes, I saw love. Not him. Not this moment. But I saw the possibility.

PART THREE: PROFIT & LOSS

Chapter Twelve: Amelia

Everyone who stopped near my work on the way from assembly sent a nervous surge down my legs. Betty and I walked slowly; we were the last ones in line at the heavy double doors. I walked with my math book clutched tightly to my chest, pretending to look humble when I really wanted to strut.

Betty giggled when she saw my giant A in the lower righthand corner of my painting. "Yours? Amelia! That woman you drew has a big chest."

"She's a goddess. I drew her from a picture."

"She looks like a model. I wish I looked like that picture." Betty stopped to look closer. A couple of students were huddled around the painting as I examined my creation, trying to imagine what they were thinking. "My friend here made this masterpiece," Betty called out to the lot of them.

"I really like it," a red-haired girl said. "It reminds me of that woman in the Coca-Cola commercials. She looks sophisticated. And the soldier she's saluting would be proud."

"It's just a picture that she traced," JoAnne said. JoAnne entered the competition and hadn't placed. She was a scrawny girl with horn-rimmed glasses and a ruddy face. She was the type of girl who always questioned the teachers and thought she knew everything but didn't have a clue.

"It was not traced," I said. "I designed that dress myself. I just used a model, like artists are supposed to. You can't trace with paint anyhow."

"You don't know anything about art. Anyone could do this. Your fast mother probably did it for you, and you signed your name," JoAnne said, motioning to the piece as though it were something to be waved away and forgotten about.

"I suppose that's why I won, and you didn't."

"Wow, Amelia, I've never heard you raise your voice like that before. Don't listen to JoAnne. She's just jealous because she's not good at anything. No one picks her in gym, and she never gets courted." Betty turned toward JoAnne. "Don't talk about my friend! You don't have any friends because you're downright nasty. And you look the way you act!"

JoAnne stood tall and flared her nostrils like a bull, but Betty didn't stop. "Oh, and your father is lame."

JoAnne shrunk at this last comment, as though it hit her. She must have been shocked because she responded as a younger child might, "So is yours!"

"My daddy is a man of the cloth. Besides, I have an uncle in the war. He's still military. It's not like *your* father—your father was lame, couldn't serve, and he still is."

"At least my mother isn't easy like Amelia's." JoAnne's anger pinched her brow. She looked to me, then Betty. The girls at McKinley High School had great pride in their brothers and fathers who served. Kids were disappearing from class after a visit from the principal, only to come back with the life sucked from their bodies, their brothers, fathers, uncles and friends having been drafted.

"You're a waste of space," Betty said.

The American soldier was the hero of the time, and it was only those girls whose brothers or fathers had not served who did not discuss their fathers endlessly. Well, them and me. JoAnne was a lame girl from a lame family, and there could be no more cutting insult, except that a girl didn't have a father at all.

I was between the two of them, standing next to my artwork, so when JoAnne reached for a clump of Betty's long, blonde hair, she clipped me on the chin. I was pushed back into the glass that displayed my work, and a surge shot through me. It wavered but did not fall or crack. It could have destroyed the one thing I had to be proud of. It seemed no one wanted to allow me this moment of recognition, and this realization sank into my skin. I was lucky to have a friend who would defend me, and I wasn't about to let this girl hurt Betty. So, I ignored the warning I felt, the red I saw, and began to fight.

I didn't pull hair and kick, but pushed and swung, the way I'd seen my brother swing on the boy down the street when the boy had called him a fire head. I imagined Mother standing in a doorway, arms crossed, wide smile. I continued to swing until I felt a large hand on my neck. Two of the administrators dragged me away and into the nurse's office to sit on a cot and wait.

"Can I have some water?" I asked the nurse.

"You shouldn't have a thing. You should be ashamed of yourself, Miss Grodzki. This was a day of celebration for our boys in service, and you made that lovely piece of artwork, and here you are getting yourself into needless trouble." The woman sighed. "Girls like you shouldn't fight. You could get removed from school for such a thing, you know?"

"I know. I was trying to defend my friend."

"There's no good reason for a young lady to fight," the nurse said. She brushed a piece of lint from her pristine white uniform and tilted my face up toward the light. "It looks as though she got a good mark on that pretty face of yours. Such a shame. A pretty girl like you should never take such a thing for granted. You know, not all girls have that kind of beauty. You have more opportunities with that face, so don't go wasting it. Imagine how hard it will be for you to find a husband if you had a mangled face? You have to use your noggin."

The nurse smelled of pine and cinnamon, which made me think of Christmas and almost made up for her unremitting lecture. I could see she was unhappy in her own marriage, so I wondered why she sold it so much.

"I know. I'm sorry."

"I'll get you that water. Stay there, and don't get into anything," the nurse said, leaving me alone on the stiff bed. Kat and Grandma Grodzki would be called and notified of my behavior, and I knew the night would be hellish. I thought about crawling out of the window at the end of the room and running until I found a new life.

I relished in the idea of hopping trains and selling my drawings in the towns I would visit; maybe I could join a traveling show and learn to act like Ava Gardner. Everyone was always telling me I was beautiful, but what did that matter? A woman was still a human. And I knew I could find real happiness in a life of movement; not in the way Mother wanted to move, but in a freer way. I wanted to live for art, not for some husband I wouldn't be able to stomach.

When the door opened, it startled me. It was Betty, who looked unmarked, though her dress was ripped at the neckline. Her hair was disheveled.

"I'm sorry," Betty said. "But that girl deserved it all. She needs to crawl in a hole somewhere and die."

"Don't be sorry." I thought a moment as Betty took a seat on an adjoining cot. "It was mean to say that about her father though."

"Yeah, well, I don't like that girl." Betty hopped up and walked over to the phone. She smiled slyly and picked up the receiver, covering the mouthpiece so that no one could hear her breathe.

"Stop it. The nurse will be right back. We'll get kicked out if she catches you on the phone."

Betty glanced at the door and clicked something. She replaced the receiver. "I think they're notifying our parents. My mother is going to make me scrub the bathroom every day this week." The way Betty told it, Mrs. Jamison had become as unpredictable and moody as Kat since the accident. She seemed to have gotten strict for no reason, Betty had often remarked. But I figured Mrs. Jamison was just reacting to the fight. Betty was always getting into trouble. I didn't want to think about what Mother would do. "Is your mother alright?"

I shrugged. "She's going back to work soon. She went downtown today with my brother to shop for slacks and try to find a job. She wanted me to go with her, and I guess I should have gone now that all this has happened."

"I think your picture is lovely, Amelia," Betty said. "And I'm going to get us out of this trouble. You just watch." She smiled and sat back down just in time for the nurse to walk back in with a small mug of water.

"They're multiplying," the nurse said, looking from me to Betty.

"I won't lecture you, young lady, but you know better, right?" she asked Betty, who nodded affirmatively and from nowhere, it seemed, began to sob.

"My father will be so disappointed in me," Betty said between gasps. "But I just miss Uncle Ryan so much. I pray for him every day. I don't understand why he had to leave. He's halfway around the world. Can you imagine?"

The nurse, whose face scrunched up with the slight pain of sympathy, grabbed a box of tissues and began dabbing Betty's pale cheeks. When the assistant principal came in, I got a flash of the small, precious-looking daughter of a minister crying for her soldier uncle and her school's nurse moved to tears herself. Betty's plan worked. We were let off with a stern warning, and as Betty wiped tears, only to begin sobbing again, the assistant principal told us that JoAnne had been suspended. As my friend cried, I felt a strange mixture of worry and envy. I couldn't help but think about Gene, who had assured me he would be safe.

I sat watching Betty, who had suddenly stopped crying. I imagined what it must be like to have a father. I wondered if Betty had made up the bit about the uncle. I went to her side, as the women stood there a moment, in a huddle, before the administrator straightened and informed us that we were excused—but, oh yes, she had contacted Mrs. Jamison and Kat. We walked home in silence. Betty lived three blocks closer to the school than I did, and her mother was waiting on the porch with a cigarette and a glass of something golden. She looked severe, and when she caught sight of her daughter, she smashed her cigarette under her heel and took a long drink from the glass, nearly emptying it. Betty said goodbye and ran into the house. Mrs. Jamison shot me a look as though it were all my fault and limped in after her.

Gene answered the door. "My little sister, the boxer." He smiled, white teeth gleaming. "After a day of running around with Mom, that call I took for you sure cheered me up. It might be the most I've ever laughed."

I wondered if he told.

"Look at your face! C'mon. I wouldn't rat you out. I put on my best woman's voice and told them I'd discipline you good. Let's walk."

"I just walked the whole way home," I said.

"We don't have to go far," Gene said, still amused. He chuckled and shadowboxed with the air. "Did you mess her up?"

"I feel bad now. She's a poor girl, and I should've just let her call me a tracer. I should've laughed it off."

"You damn-well should defend yourself! You think we're rich, just because Mom gets people to buy her furs? We don't have anyone else to do it for us. No Dad around. We have to be out for ourselves." He examined my face and added, "And for each other."

I stared at him for a long time, trying not to say what I eventually said. "But you're leaving like all the rest of the boys. Everyone's leaving, Gene. I just want to go fight for you. I want to get out of here. I can't have anything here. I'll be like Joan of Arc."

"Who?" I remembered Grandma Grodzki telling me about her heroism during the Hundred Years war, how she was vilified even as a hero, which was one of a thousand examples of why women needed to be careful wielding their power. I imagined what it would be like then to carry a gun and step in front of my brother, ready to defend him or anyone else.

When I didn't answer immediately, he went on, promising that he'd be home in no time. He said he knew what to do, and if he had to, he'd find a way back.

I knew he was wrong. This was bigger than him, and I could feel it. "You're leaving me with Mother. She doesn't like me."

"The whole problem she has with you is that she thinks you're soft. She likes strong people. You should tell her you got in a fight."

"Gene, if she knew I was strong, she'd hate me more. Don't you ever get mad at Mother? Don't you ever want to smack her back when she swipes your cheek?"

He stepped back, examining me as though he no longer knew me. His caterpillar-like eyebrows lifted, which always made me laugh. "Well, I reckon I'd be a dead man if I ever tried. She gets under the skin sometimes, but it's just who she is. Shake it off." He didn't believe his own words, I could tell.

"Easy for *you* to say." He seemed to consider this. We'd never spoken about how different we looked from each other. But he had to know, too. He had to have heard the gossip. Then again, my brother seemed immune to all the pains I felt.

He stroked his chin, as though there were a beard there. "You should have seen her doing business with those men in California. I sometimes heard people whisper about her when she'd leave a room. They didn't think I heard, but I heard them call her all sorts of things. She has trouble getting along with people sometimes." Gene stretched. "Little Amelia Grodzki, I'm going to miss you." He laughed. "My scrappy little sister."

He sat on the curb near a mailbox, and I sat next to him, conscious of the fact that people were staring and a wholesome girl doesn't sit on the curb. But next to my brother, I was invincible. I just wished it would've lasted. My cheek throbbed, and I wasn't sure if it'd been from the fight or from Kat's slap. It didn't matter.

"You would have been proud of my artwork," I said. "They displayed it in the school hall."

"My sister, the fighting visionary."

And then he was gone. Just like that, like magic. His absence made my chest heavy and my shoulders sag, but after that fight, I found a voice at school. Time seemed to march on faster than before. Even Kat, emerging from her dark moods, seemed to be more hopeful.

"I was downtown ordering a cinnamon roll at the café in the basement of the Lazarus. I saw a sign posted on the steps, and I grabbed it. The address wasn't far, so when I found it, I went in, and no more than twenty minutes later, I had a job. Just like that," Kat reported over dinner.

I smiled and nodded encouragingly as I chewed on waxy green beans. I found it remarkable that something as simple as a job would change so much in Mother's demeanor so quickly, but I was relieved.

Maybe she just needed purpose; a modern woman, after all, like the essays I'd read. I couldn't help but want a job of my own, too. Independence, however, seemed a million years away.

A spark had reignited in Kat, and it almost seemed she had that same longing and hope she had before she'd left with Gene to make it big. My days were calm, and I kept my head down at school. Nights, Grandma Grodzki and I had twenty minutes to ourselves before Kat would come home and talk endlessly about her days; the way the keys had to be hit hard on the typewriters, and how it hurt her fingertips; how she was getting used to the office life and felt quite productive; how some of the other girls gossiped and got next to nothing done. She would always complain about the hard days with a smile. She adored working, said it gave her a sense of purpose and would lead to bigger and better things because when she made enough money, she would begin to buy land.

"The value of land only goes up. You remember that, especially when you meet your husband. He should be investing in the home you two live in," she told me.

It was only when other women in the neighborhood asked Kat if she had a gentleman friend or suggested she might be even happier if she was out looking for a husband ("…not that she'd ever find one," I heard Mrs. Jamison snarl at the market) she would grow quiet or snap.

If anyone were bold enough to ask outright if Kat was being courted, she'd point to me. "There's our little wife, right there. I'm too old to look for a husband, and I'm not keen on having one anyway." When she was in fanciful moods, she would sometimes say that Tom had been her only love, and she shouldn't be greedy; no, she was content with the short-lived gift of her time with him.

One night, I walked down the hall toward the bathroom, still half-asleep, and traced my fingertips along the smooth wall. Kat stood near the steps with her hair swept up and tight in a French twist, her makeup theatrical and perfect. She gestured to her back and turned to reveal buttons that she couldn't reach. I blinked a few times, then reached to secure each soft ivory button until I reached the top one at her neck, a decorative pearl that barely fit in its delicate loop. I was careful, moving slowly as not to break the loop. After fumbling, the pearl finally went through.

The country was suffering financial collapse, yet Kat appeared to be well off, more so than she was. This was her version of magic, a life of financial abundance despite reality. At the end of the hall was a full-length, adjustable mirror she loved. It was her favorite thing in the house; she'd said so more than once. I sat on the step, rubbing my eyes to wake up, then watched her remove two pins from the front of her hair so that the twist fell; she tilted her head and spun around in the mirror.

"I tell you, little one, this job is the best thing to happen to me. I feel free. I could get back on the road any day now. There's talk, you know, of all us women losing our jobs when the boys return from that little war, but I don't think so. I think women will continue to type. The men will have to find other jobs. Did I tell you that I'm the fastest in the whole office? There's twelve girls, and I'm tops."

"That doesn't surprise me, Mother."

"Oh, my beautiful little girl. How is school?"

"It's fine. We draw in art class every day. We do something called free drawing, and I even get to draw a little in geometry."

Ignoring everything I said, she responded, "You truly have become beautiful. Glad that eye straightened out. Well, I guess not entirely, but it sure isn't as noticeable as when you were younger." She sat next to me and lifted my chin, the way I hated, examining my skin. "You have to moisturize. It looks dry and a little pale." She examined me as though assigning value, determining whether I was worth the price. Maybe to Mother, only one woman in the family could have freedom.

Ordinarily, Grandma Grodzki would hum as she made her beige breakfasts of oatmeal and toast. This day, however, she was sitting on the couch with a washcloth over her forehead and her knitting tossed to the side. When I asked what was wrong, she said, "Just a headache. You'll have to fix yourself some dinner tonight."

"But it's morning," I reminded her. When she didn't answer,

I kissed her on the cheek, covered her with a blanket, and poured salt around the floor, sweeping it away to clear the space for healing. The way Grandma had shown me. I left the house without breakfast and ran all the way to Betty's house.

When my friend didn't come out, like usual, I made my way around to the back of the house and threw a small rock at the pane by Betty's bedroom window. It made a cringe-worthy pinging sound; I hoped Betty's mother wouldn't come out and yell like she sometimes did. Betty's face appeared in the window ghost-like. She held up a finger and widened her eyes, signaling annoyance.

I realized I hadn't checked the time before I left, and without breakfast, I was almost half an hour early. There was still an hour before school would start. I went back to the front step and sat down, pulled out an English book, and began to read.

"You silly, silly girl," Mrs. Jamison said.

"I'm sorry, ma'am. I didn't realize how early I was," I said, turning around to face Betty's red-cheeked mother.

"Well, you might as well come in and have a glass of orange juice. Betty is in the bath." Mrs. Jamison, wearing a long robe with a Hawaiian design, limped into the kitchen.

"Thank you." I was rarely invited inside Betty's home. We usually went downtown, to the park, or just stayed after school. Mrs. Jamison was strict and had Betty on a ridiculous curfew since she'd been getting into trouble so often. Also, Mrs. Jamison didn't believe in sleepovers, so Betty rarely got a chance to socialize at all, except right after school.

"Take off your shoes, dear," she called back, "then take a seat on the couch there and grab one of those coasters. That kitchen table needs repair, so it's out of order."

I did as I was told, looking around at all the crosses. The couch was adorned with flowers; it was in a style Mother would have called old-fashioned. There was a small coffee table in front of me and the largest ivory cross on the wall mesmerized me; it seemed to be staring at me as she stared at it, and for the first time in a long time, I saw patterns and got a cold feeling.

The home resembled a church, with wood crosses and scripture etched into wood scrolls all over the walls. Betty's father was a minister, and he had made each of these items in his garage. Betty said he cut off the tip of his finger making a wood frame last summer and he'd come into the house bleeding and screaming about how he'd never try his hand at carpentry again.

The next week, he was back at it, swearing this time never to make anything that isn't for the lord. He began taking drives after that, long drives to get wood from a special shop that sometimes took him two days to get to and from. If it were late enough, he couldn't drive at night due to his poor eyesight. But while he was away, Betty said she missed him dearly.

I accepted a short, flowered glass jar of orange juice and set it on the coaster. I asked Mrs. Jamison if it was okay if I looked at the family photograph in the corner.

"I suppose. Just be careful."

The photograph was in black and white, but light pink lipstick was painted on the women, and some of the dresses had a green tint. Betty looked miserable in the photograph, as though she had a stomach-ache. Her father was standing proudly at the center, with Mrs. Jamison at his side with a thin, forced smile. There were two elderly women in the picture as well. One had a small boy in a headlock, and the boy seemed pleased about it, grinning like a fool. It was an interesting picture.

Another picture, an older one, showed an entirely different Mrs. Jamison, smiling genuinely, still the pretty town gossip I remembered as a kid. She had changed after the accident. The way the minister leaned into her in this older photograph made it look like a scene out of a love story. In the newer family photo, the two stood erect, separate as rooks on a chessboard.

I wondered if I could talk Mother and Grandma Grodzki into taking such a photograph so I could remember our times and watch how things changed. I realized I didn't even have current pictures of Gene, so I was forgetting what he looked like again. I imagined him coming home and how my own family portrait would appear to an outsider. Gene could take the center stage as the man of the house, and three women could stand around him, immortalized, a strong family, despite the obvious missing link. I imagined such a photograph would cost a lot of money. Perhaps I could draw it and put myself in the center like a queen.

"Betty, are you out of the bathroom yet, dear?" Mrs. Jamison yelled. She wanted me out of the house; I could tell.

"Yes. I'll be down in a moment."

"Did you hear that, Amelia? Betty is on her way down. You better drink that orange juice. Don't waste it now. We can't afford to waste anything these days." Her eyes were bright, insistent, as she watched the glass. I lifted it to my lips and took a healthy gulp. I despised orange juice when it contained pulp. The little mushy pieces seemed to collect at the base of my throat and float around there before I could force them down.

"Good girl. What's your mother up to?"

"Mother's well. She has a job as a secretary."

Mrs. Jamison nodded. "She's an intriguing woman, your mother. She always has been. Your grandmother? Is she still against the church?"

"She's not against…"

"She's forgiven. My husband's doors—God's doors are always open."

Betty bounded down the stairs and, kissing her mother quickly on the cheek, rushed into the kitchen, took a piece of dry toast, and downed the same pulpy orange juice with a few seamless gulps.

"Come on, Amelia, let's go!" She seemed exceptionally happy today. "I'll be home right on time, Mother. Right on time, you can bet on that. Tell Daddy to wait on me."

Mrs. Jamison forced a smile and nodded. "He's not going anywhere tonight. He'll be here. You just focus on your studies for now. Don't get distracted."

As we walked, Betty maintained a goofy grin. "My father is supposed to come home tonight, and he's bringing me a present. He's been on some trip for a few days."

"Where does he go so often?" I said.

"He does these church trips and volunteer work. But whenever he's gone for more than a day, he brings me back a present. It's like I'm six years old again, the way I look forward to his presents, but the last time, he got me this." She turned around, holding her long coat open like a model to show off a scarf. It seemed more like something an adult would wear, hanging from her shoulders the way it would from a hanger in a store window.

"I remember you showing me the day he got it for you," I reminded her, in a sterner tone than I had intended. "Must be nice, having a father."

"Oh, Amelia, I'm sorry. I guess this is insensitive of me. I forget sometimes that you don't ... Hey, how's your brother? Is he going to be a captain or something?" When I didn't answer, she reached for my forearm and leaned in close.

"New topic. Who is that boy always staring at you in the cafeteria?"

"What boy?"

"You know what boy." She elbowed me a little too hard in the ribs. "I've seen you looking at him, too. You're keen on him—that tall boy with the dark hair. He looks rich. And I think he's on the wrestling team."

"Jake. He's just okay. I only talked to him once, before our fight."

"I think he's trying to court you."

"I don't know if I want to be courted," I said, my face hot. I couldn't help but smile a little as I looked at her friend and added, "But I guess if I was to be courted, I would want him to be the one to do it."

Betty giggled. "He's adorable. I think I like him, too, but don't you worry. I'll admire him from afar. I think he's smitten with you and only you. What do you think about this plan—okay, so we go to one of the wrestling meets and cheer him on. Afterwards, you can go up to him. If he loses, you can say that he'll get 'em next time. If he wins, you can swoon. It'll be a perfect opportunity for you to chat with him. It won't be all crowded like in the cafeteria."

"I don't want to just go for him. It'll make me too nervous." I paused. "Let's go to watch the match."

As we approached the school doors, Betty stopped me by grabbing my shoulder. "I'm sorry about the father thing. I forget how lucky I am sometimes. Also sorry about what Mom says about your grandmother. I don't believe she's a heathen."

"She didn't say that!"

"She says it all the time."

Immediately, I felt the chill spreading across my shoulders and down my back. For the first time, the chill was accompanied by a whisper; I couldn't make out any words but closed my eyes to try. I hugged my friend tightly, trying to ignore the sound, and said, "Don't worry about it. I understand."

Chapter Thirteen: Emerson

Pregnant. No way was I pregnant, but the word repeated in my mind. The chill returned again and again, the same as before Ian, and I wondered if it was truly panic, or worse, a premonition. I didn't want the burden of knowing too much.

Courtney and I sat at the dining room table playing trivia as I tried to figure out how to tell her what I'd done and how stupid I was. Instead, I said, "Cyndi Lauper." She threw her hair tie at me.

"You dominate in 80s trivia. I want history."

"When did women earn the right to have their own bank accounts in the United States?"

"Sixties." I dropped the card and scooted toward my friend. I was going to confide in her, ask her advice, but as soon as the thought arrived, the texts began. Again. Ian wanted to know how I felt and if we could get together again. He wanted to know if I was on the pill. He texted me so many things that I had to silence my phone.

Fine. No. Everything's fine. Maybe later. I wrote it all as one long text.

Courtney glanced down at my phone just as he texted back a series of question marks. "How'd your date with Ian go? I hope you're not breaking his heart."

"Boring. I—I'm stopping it. I'm not dating him anymore," I said. And it had been. What I wanted from him wasn't available.

She laughed at the card she selected, and before she read it stared at me. Through me. "Do you want to talk about something?"

"No." I worried she could see what I'd done, my fear. Instead, she let me off the hook.

"I've been thinking. We need to be doing what's right. Your grandmother's story, my grandmother's story ... women not having their own fucking bank accounts."

"What is right? What's right, to me, feels crazy," I said.

"What's right is not wasting space." She scooted in even closer to me. Courtney was wearing baggy jeans. Her neon bra peeked out beneath a thick-strapped black tank, and her hair was in a messy pony. She never wore makeup, never tried too hard, and I loved that about her. She was herself through and through. No optics, no fakery.

"You don't know the meaning of wasting space," I told her.

"Tell my family. Mom is still convinced I'll be a lawyer. I read her my best essay, the one about the environment I wrote for Dr. Macioci's class."

"That was award-winning work," I assured her, ignoring the loss of balance I felt.

"With as hard as my family worked to get where they are, I feel guilty wanting to write. The odds are against success, but writing is like a call. It's like it's in my blood."

Without thinking, I reached for her arm. "You have to do it then. And I have to figure out what the hell it is I am going to do."

"You'll figure it out," she said. In that moment it felt as though we were closer than we'd ever been. There was a magnetic pull, and I wanted to kiss her. I was feeling what I'd tried to force with Ian. But as soon as I got caught up in my analysis of what was going on, Courtney did what I could only think about—she leaned in all the way and pressed her warm lips to mine. In that moment, I was present. Then the texts continued, and I pushed her away hard. Harder than I meant to.

"I'm sorry," I said. "It's too much. I made a mistake." I looked down at my phone.

Want to get together and talk? I promise not to tell anyone, Ian wrote.

"Yeah. No worries." Sorry about that. Um. Is that Ian?" Courtney asked, her expression flat.

I nodded. "He's persistent, yeah. Look, I did something stupid."

"Yeah. Let's move on. The kiss wasn't that bad. We've been friends forever," she said.

"No, not this. I did something the other day. I don't know why—I guess I wanted to care about something like you do writing and

Amelia or my mother did art. I just feel so stuck in my family's story, and it's like I don't have my own, so I tried to find one."

"You don't make any sense, Em."

"It's like I need to figure out my family to know how crazy I am. It's like I need to decode their stories before I can do anything normal. Relationships. Anything. Have any kind of future."

Courtney placed her hand on mine and took a deep inhale as though breathing for me. "Maybe your future is in 80s trivia." She smiled, trying to lighten the mood, but there was tension now. I reached for another card. As I looked down, a wave washed through my body and the card I stared at became a Queen of Cups, a card that looked fifty years old. I could see that the hand holding the card was no longer mine. It was that of an older woman. Grandma Grodzki.

"Connect with the patterns," a voice said. Not my mother's.

"Did you hear that?" I stood, stopped the record player.

"Yeah, I think it's your father," Courtney said.

The jangling of keys sounded in the door, and Dad rushed in. His brown pleather coat was well-worn, and he tossed it on the chair as though mad at it. "That commute is not getting any better. Look at you two! Who's winning?"

"Me," we both said.

"Hope you didn't order too much pizza. Rita's at the gym, and I'm heading out. We're meeting some friends." He picked up the scrap paper we'd used to write down our order.

"No worries, Lori can eat for a dozen," I said.

"What's the longest river in the world?" Courtney asked my father.

"The Nile," he said.

"Tallest mountain? Em?"

I was almost too dizzy to stand up, but I did. "I'll be right back." Excusing myself to the half-bath, I sat as still as possible and allowed the panic to rise like waves. Watching my hand, now my own, I wondered what it'd be like in a mental hospital. Would I turn, becoming a horrible person, like Kat? Resentful? Would Courtney ever talk to me again? Sure, she was acting like everything was okay, but I knew better. And when she found out about Ian, she'd hate me.

Courtney's voice arrived with a knock. "Are you all good? Mom's calling me. She's upset about my B+ in pre-calculus. Can you believe she called the school to ask them? What in the holy hell! And she wants to have 'The Talk' about my future. I might need you to tutor me, girl." She knocked again. "You okay? You're not mad at me, are you?"

"No. I'm good. Coming," I said, breathing deeply and splashing water on my face before toweling dry and rejoining my friend in the living room, who had already picked up all the cards. As Courtney got ready to go, I reached for her, leaned in not even knowing what to do. Apologize? Kiss her? I wanted to do both. "I'm sorry. I fucked up," I said.

As Courtney stared, trying to decipher what I meant, she looked at my phone, which started to beep every few seconds. "We can talk later," she said, placing her hand on my forearm before heading out. As the texts came in, my father darted down the stairs in a whirlwind of cussing. "Shit. Fuck. Shit, shit."

"Shit what?" I asked him, placing my phone on the foyer table.

"Shit, The Lavender House again. This is getting old."

"I'll call them back. I've been talking with Amelia a lot," I said. My father examined me carefully.

"Be careful with that. Rita said she saw you doing odd things in your room. Is Amelia feeding you weird ideas?" he asked.

My face grew hot. "Does it matter?"

"It's not healthy. You're bright. Do you want to end up like her? In a place like that? That thinking is addictive. It's why your mother..." He stopped. "Look, I'm calling them, not you. I'll do it now. This is a conversation for later." As Dad dialed, I could see Courtney still at the door, and I felt like I might implode. She looked genuinely concerned.

"I'll fill you in later," I told her, then began whispering to myself. "I, Emerson, am in control of my own thinking..." I focused on my breath, and Courtney walked me outside, grabbing my phone.

We found my sister on the porch, holding the post and stretching her calves on our step as she panted. Her face was post-run red, and it looked more intense with her cobalt blue running outfit. Her outfit had a sheen that made her long legs look like stilts, and her look disarmed me. It brought me back.

"You look like a clown with heat stroke. What's up?" I asked.

"Love you, too, asshole. I ran home from school. I'm going to start doing those three nights a week."

"That's eight miles."

"I'm driven. *You* should try having a goal. How are things in Emerson's world? Or is it the Emerson and Courtney world?"

"Courtney's about to take her world home," Courtney said seriously. On her way out, she handed me my phone, which was unlocked. The texts were displayed on the screen. They told the story for me. I examined her face, trying to figure out whether she'd read them.

"You coming to my race on Saturday? It's just a 5K. I'm confident I'll get the gold in my age group. You can come, too, if you want," she told Courtney.

"I'll try. What does one do while you're running? Just sit there waiting?"

Lori considered this. "I guess, yeah, if you ever want to, though, it'd be cool. Maybe the half-marathon? That one's a big deal."

"I'll come," I said, realizing how much I missed my sister. I added, trying to keep the mood light, "You smell like rotten garlic and the basement after it rains—you should shower." She laughed and punched me in the bicep. I waited for Courtney to laugh too.

"At least I don't smell like the school bus after football practice mixed with old socks and blue cheese."

"I can't keep pace with sister insults. See ya. I'll try to come to support you, Lori." With that, Courtney walked off without looking back. Something felt wrong, and I fought the urge to call after her, almost doing so, when Dad slammed the door. "You've been skipping school senior year, Emerson?" He didn't wait for me to answer. "I'm going to be late, but we need to talk."

"Amelia should have company. You can't just leave a woman alone to rot in a place like that."

Glancing at his watch, Dad explained that Amelia was in a holding room after trying to leave the property yet again and threatening staff. "The nurse said that having company lately seems to be egging her on and feeding her delusions. She said she was teaching you girls magic. She's in full-blown fantasy land again, talking about going to visit people. I don't know what you've been talking about, but Emerson, you can't even joke about breaking someone out of a mental health institution or indulge the fantasy. You're playing with fire, and trust me that you're doing more damage than good."

"I never said that. Amelia was joking."

"She must be off her pills again. Look, we'll be home late. And for the record," He lowered his voice, "The Lavender House is expensive, and they provide good care. Other places don't. I have a meeting with the manager and her primary doctor for Saturday, but I'm worried they're going to ask her to leave. What will we do then?"

Lori sighed.

"I need to go with you," I told Dad, then looked to my sister. She sighed louder. "Why don't we go in the morning? It's better there in the morning, anyway. Can we go before the race?" I added.

Amelia needed an advocate. I was in this with her. He stared at me with pure exhaustion crossing his face, and I stared back. I tried to tune in, to feel what he felt, and when it hit me—his worry and pain. I realized he wasn't trying to be malicious. He was trying to regain control he didn't have. I felt what he felt so acutely, the loss of my mother and genuine belief that logic was the only way. I could hear his thoughts, his fear, and though something told me not to, I willed him to soften.

His face changed. "Fine. We'll take a road trip."

"Can Courtney come?" I added.

"I don't think that's appropriate or that she wants to, Emerson. I don't know what you did, but she looked mad when she left. We'll go Saturday," he told Lori, "We'll meet you at the race."

"You sure? I'm more than capable of celebrating my win by myself," Lori said, and my father ruffled her hair the way he used to when we were kids. He smiled at my sister, the sane one.

"I'm off. If we miss our reservation later, Rita will never forgive me," Dad said.

Lori rolled her eyes. "She'll forgive you. You do know Rita is already locked in, Dad. We have her curio cabinet."

He quickly put on his jacket and knotted his hair back in a ponytail holder—he always had one in his pocket or on his pinky finger—and smoothed his goatee before rushing off.

Later that night, I called out to my sister. I was sure my heart had stopped, and I couldn't feel my legs. Doubled over, I could barely move when she opened my door. A shooting pain radiated from my pelvis. My little sister, stoic and steady, rushed me to an urgent care, while I moaned like a wounded cat, sure that this was it. I was dying.

We sat in the waiting room for hours. There was no music, no color in the room. Only audible signals of pain and the shuffling from the reception area that was separated by a plastic half-wall. The waiting room chairs were full. Those who waited with me were pale or gray-faced and others looked fine. The sensation was like nothing I'd ever experienced, a twisting of my body and loss of control, and despite everything inside of me that wanted to be tough for my sister, I crumbled. I couldn't look at anyone without the fear compounding.

"What's wrong?" she kept asking.

"I don't know," I said. I couldn't remember my mantra. Couldn't focus on anything in the room. I doubted I was pregnant, but what if I was? I tried to imagine having a baby and couldn't. As we waited, I recalled Amelia's story. I hadn't spent so much time with my sister since we were little kids. Our conversations were frequent but stilted and rarely lasted longer than a few minutes unless we had a mutual complaint. "I've been going to visit Amelia, Lori. She's been telling me about her life," I confided.

"I bet it's wild," Lori said. "If she gets kicked out, she'll probably come live with us. Can you imagine?"

"I can," I said.

Chapter Fourteen: Amelia

The woman on the porch was an omen. She chain-smoked slender, hand-rolled cigarettes which gave off a sweet smoke unlike any I had ever smelled. Her delicate but plump features defined pretty—thick hair that was curly and bouncy, and her face was a perfect heart. She had the retro look of a flapper and all the moxie.

"Hi there," she called. She took a long drag on the cigarette, then offered it to me. I was tempted but shook my head. The woman shrugged and asked, "Are you little Amelia Grodzki?"

"Yes."

"Well, little Amelia Grodzki, my name is Helen, and I'm your mother's friend. We work together as typists. She's an industrious worker, your mother."

"Yes," I said, worried.

"Do you know where your mother is?"

"She should be home soon. Grandma should be here. Would you like to come inside and wait?"

"That would be swell. Such a nice girl." She patted me on the head and extinguished her strange cigarette on the wall, keeping the remainder of it, which struck me as strange for a woman who dressed in such a sophisticated manner.

When we entered, Grandma Grodzki was sprawled out on the couch, snoring as loud as any man. I put my finger up and gestured for Helen to head silently into the kitchen, where we could speak without disturbing the peace. I made sure Grandma Grodzki was fully covered by the thin blanket she had bunched around her legs. I kissed her on the cheek, then crept off to the kitchen. "Mother isn't here. If she were, the upstairs light would be on and her purse would be on the table. Would you like a cup of tea?"

"That would be lovely. So, little Amelia, while we wait on your mother, why don't you tell me about your pretty little self? Your mother speaks of you all the time. She says you're an artist and a good student. She told me you were beautiful, but she didn't tell me how beautiful."

"Thank you. I don't feel exceptionally beautiful."

"Oh, now that's crazy. You're as gorgeous as your mother, and don't you forget it. Don't tell your mother this, but I think you got her beat by a long shot. Your eyes are bigger, and those cheek bones. You could be a model and an actress, little Amelia. Come here."

I set the teapot on the burner and walked toward Helen. The woman's spicy scent seemed to invite and repel at the same time. Helen cupped my face and examined my skin with the attention of a doctor. "Flawless. A flawless little girl. You'll be a star." She gave me a quick pinch on each cheek and smiled. "Perfect, creamy skin. You'll never have to work like your mother, and I do. Never. I guarantee that. You'll be married as soon as you graduate high school." She smiled. "You better hope a good, wealthy man falls for you. If you find the wrong one, you can waste all that beauty."

"Maybe I don't want to be pretty then," I said.

"Believe me, life will be easier."

"No thank you. Marriage sounds like a prison sentence." An inventory of all the married women in our neighborhood, how zombie-like and sad they seemed, kept me from indulging this woman the way she wanted. I always knew, though it was never brought up, most women were miserable because of their husbands. For some reason, I felt comfortable around Helen.

"One of our neighbors took rough beatings from her fat, angry husband. Her face was destroyed, and she could have saved time by doing it before they married." As I said it, I realized how harsh I sounded. I also realized this could be a plan. I knew Jake would never be like this, but I also didn't think of him as a husband. He was too good for that.

"There are good stories, too. Don't you fancy anyone?"

"This woman, she bakes cookies at Christmas time and goes door-to-door, handing them out to all the neighbors, but I think she is secretly wanting us all to take her in. It's like she's a prisoner."

"One bad apple, precious Amelia."

"She disappears for days, and I sometimes catch a glimpse of her nursing her plants quietly when she thinks no one is watching. I can see the pain on her face, the way it settles in the lines around her eyes."

"You are quite the firecracker. This tea is amazing. Let me tell you a story..."

I thought of the bruises that would sometimes cover our neighbor's face and arms and wanted to go on, but instead I glanced over at Grandma Grodzki who was half-awake now, slowly getting up.

"Some men are absolute brutes," Helen agreed. "But I know a woman who thought she had it all. She was everything, and the world didn't have anything better to offer her. Then she met this man. Let's call him Bob. He wined and dined her and defended her against the brutalities of life. Women are put on this earth to balance men out, so you remember you have the upper hand with them. You remember that, and you'll find a good one." She stopped a moment and rotated her mug. "The nicer you are, the more likely you'll find a downright mean old husband."

This struck me as something Mother might say. I sat next to Helen and tried to think of something less intense to discuss. "Do you like working?"

"It's satisfying to earn my own money, but I could take it or leave it. What makes working fun is getting to chat with all the other girls. Your mother is my absolute favorite, even though she has a wicked little temper. She's always bossing the other girls around—everyone but me, of course. She's a real riot."

"Mother is strong. She likes to take control."

"Oh yes she does," Helen said, laughing loudly.

I wanted to shush the woman but didn't want to be rude. I glanced over at Grandma Grodzki again, who had repositioned to listen. She winked at me, then gave me the look to straighten my posture. "Sit like a goddess," she would whisper when my shoulders were hunched.

"You know what, little one? I might just leave. I know you went to all this trouble to make me tea, but I forgot there's somewhere I need to be. Will you pass a note to your mother for me?"

"Oh, of course," I said in a near-whisper, to offset Helen's loud tone. Helen fished around in her purse for a pen and wrote a few words in cursive. She folded the note four times so it was now a little square and placed it in my hand, curling my fingers around it. "Don't read this now. It's top secret. Just give it to your mother tonight."

"I will. And I won't. I promise. I mean—"

"I trust you, pretty little Amelia." The woman kissed me on the forehead softly and walked to the front door. Her skirt was tight and the way she walked, shifting her weight back and forth as she went, was so deliberate it was almost cartoonish.

Helen hadn't even closed the door behind her when I unfolded the note. *Meet me at 7 at Calypso —xoxo.* I had been hoping for more; I wasn't sure what. Helen was mysterious and, I thought, somewhat devious like Mother. The idea of the two keeping company intrigued me. I folded the note delicately and ran upstairs to slide it under Mother's door.

Grandma Grodzki sat upright and suffered a fit of coughing; she asked me if I wouldn't mind making dinner. There was soup left over from last night and bread in the cupboard, which I sliced into inch-thick pieces and covered with cheese before placing it in the oven. I brought Grandma Grodzki chamomile and sat next to her for a moment, leaning my head against her shoulder.

"I love you," I told her.

"You are the only reason I'm still here, little goddess. Can you salt the house before your mother comes home?"

I nodded, sifting circles of salt and lighting candles to erase the energy of Helen, to pause my grandmother's illness. I opened all the windows to allow Mother Nature to enter our home, as Grandma taught me, and when she seemed at ease again, I set the table.

I was eager for Kat to come home, and it was a strange feeling. Usually, I dreaded seeing Mother because I knew that the night would be filled with more of the same; stories about the girls at the office, and Mother's plans always included some sort of equation. I suppose that's why she implored me to study mathematics more than anything else because, she said, most girls didn't know how to manage money. She just wanted me to be her accountant.

Tonight, however, I would find a story of my own. Maybe I'd learn more about Helen. When Kat arrived home, it was already nearing 6 p.m., and though I couldn't reveal I'd read the note, I had to get Mother to read it soon or else she'd miss her invitation.

"Mother, a woman stopped by today."

She set down her purse, bent over Grandma Grodzki, and straightened the blanket around her so that it covered her feet. "Mother, a woman stopped by—"

"I heard you the first time. Where's this note?"

"I slid it under your bedroom door. The woman, Helen, said it was important that you read it immediately."

Kat removed her heels and eyed her daughter suspiciously. "That doesn't sound like Helen. She's never in a hurry to do anything. You should see the way that woman works. She pecks like a chicken at those keys. It takes her all day to complete a task I can finish in a few hours. Ha! Helen in a hurry!"

"Oh, well, maybe it's an emergency," I said. "Maybe she was anxious to have you read it."

Kat sighed then made her way slowly up to her room. She was upstairs a long time, and as I set the table, I hoped she would tell me more. Gently nudging Grandma Grodzki, I whispered, "Are you up for some dinner?"

Grandma Grodzki moaned a little. "Can you bring me a glass of water instead? I'm going to rest a while longer." She hoisted herself up to a sitting position and began coughing again. The coughing seemed to hurt her stomach, and as she bent over, she gasped for air. It was then that I first felt the chill when I touched her arm. I rushed to the kitchen to get water and a washcloth for Grandma Grodzki's forehead. "It's not just my head anymore, Amelia. The doctor will be coming out to see me soon."

"I wish I could make you feel better," I said. I brought a small saucer of soup, in case Grandma Grodzki changed her mind and wanted something salty to settle her stomach.

To my surprise, Mother stayed home that night and, much to my dismay, spent the evening discussing the dates of her paychecks and the amounts. The two of us sat on the floor at the foot of Grandma Grodzki's couch. We sat there with papers in front of us, which Mother kept in a shoebox. She asked me to add the numbers then multiply them by percentages, then different percentages. She had a million scenarios, which only confused me. I was sure I wasn't getting the right answers, but unlike my schoolbooks, there weren't correct answers in the back to prove us wrong. Mother had only an elementary school education, and she was far more tolerable when happy, so I figured it'd be best to always round up. Mother seemed to accept any answer I came up with as correct.

"I will need you to teach me. We'll do this every single night until I understand," she said. "We are soon going to have a lot of money, but I need your help."

When I looked at Mother, I saw a frightening determination. She wore the same expression before taking my brother to California those years ago. I worried what Mother would think if she knew I got low marks in my last arithmetic course. "Mother, I'm not that good. I'm trying, but I'm not sure this is right." I showed Grandma Grodzki the calculations.

"It seems right to me. According to this, after four months of working, I'll have enough money to buy shares of General Electric. This is a blue-chip stock, one that will pay us more back than we invest. We'll figure this out together." She smiled.

"I hope you don't mind my asking, but what did Helen want that was so important?"

She cringed, shaking her head back and forth before looking down at the numbers again. "Yes, this makes a lot of sense to me. I think it's quite right."

"She's a smart girl," Grandma Grodzki muttered. "Is Helen that woman who was cackling in the kitchen earlier?"

"Oh, did she wake you?"

"Briefly. I didn't feel the energy to meet her, or I would have introduced myself. She's an interesting one."

"I'm curious about her," I admitted.

Mother collected the papers and held them to her chest. "Helen is a woman you won't see in our home again. I'll make sure of that." She kissed Grandma Grodzki and instructed me to go to bed.

Chapter Fifteen: Emerson

I tried to begin at the beginning, the way Amelia had, but as I sat there, I didn't have the grace to retell Amelia's stories in any meaningful way. I didn't think Lori would understand, so I didn't string my words together with relish. I just offered glimpses and scattershot details, mentioning the drive, the indifference of Kat, the art, and the magic embedded deep in our family line. I skipped around and didn't do any of it justice.

"Sounds witchy." My sister laughed.

"Not exactly."

A balding man in the waiting room snorted. "You all go to Hogwarts?"

"Yes. Yes, we do," my sister said seriously, sitting straight.

I tuned in and could see, or imagined I could see, the man's ulcer. I wanted him to know what I felt, what real pain and loss was, but thanks to my sister's glare, he quickly turned around. It was the first time I wasn't trying to absorb someone's pain but rather willing it, and I watched as his eyes widened and his lips pursed together. Entertaining the idea that it was me causing it, I was honestly unsure. He hobbled to another chair, and I closed my eyes trying to summon my mother's presence.

"Generations back," I continued, louder. "Practices hidden to avoid persecution by the ignorant. She told me about goddesses, too, the study of women intellectuals from around the world. She may not have gone to college, but she self-educated. Women who were and still are enslaved but have a knowledge that runs fathoms deep. Do you remember those stories from when we were kids?"

"I do. I hated them. But I guess it's good Amelia has the company and an outlet. I know she has stories, and I feel bad about not seeing her more, but … it's weird around her. I know it's not contagious, but it feels like it is. It's scary, Em. I honestly agree with Dad on this. Maybe you should stay away from her."

"Because we don't understand."

"You understand," Mom whispered. I sat up straight, hugging my knees to my chest as I sat in the waiting room chair. I used to sit like this as a child. I lost my breath.

"Shit, shit, shit, shit…" I leaned over, resting my palms against my lower stomach, as my sister rubbed my back and told me we'd be called back soon, and I just needed to hang in. We were number 223, according to a small ticket we'd been given, and it felt like at least that many people had been seen before us. I breathed into my lower belly, trying to ease the grip of pain, but it was insistent.

"We need some kind of magic right now," Lori said. I looked to her, searching for signs that she was being ironic or mean. When the pain surged again, I closed my eyes and asked for strength. I wondered why I couldn't heal myself or know, for sure, what was going on.

When we were finally ushered back to a small room, there were blood tests and checklists. It all blurred together as a tired man asked me questions printed on a clipboard. I answered, one after another, and most of the questions felt accusatory and rude. Had I recently had unprotected sex? Was I pregnant? Was I sure I didn't have an STD? I took a pregnancy test and waited. They listened to my heart and lungs, and I was told everything was normal. My pulse was slow, even though there was energy thrashing behind my ribs.

A short nurse with boxy hips examined me and without fanfare said plainly, "Not pregnant. The doctor will be in soon, but we see a lot of this type of thing. It's probably just a panic attack. Maybe you had a little heartburn or period pain attached to it." He widened his stance.

"I know panic, and this feels different. It's like my body is ripping in half. I feel a tear from my hip to my heart, like someone is trying to break me open," I said firmly, wanting to knock the guy on the side of his head. He looked unimpressed by my self-diagnosis.

"Something is seriously wrong," Lori said, backing me up. "You all need to do more tests." She wasn't acknowledged.

"So you've had panic before? Tell me about that."

There was a knock on the door, and Rita cracked it open, explaining she was my mother-in-law; my father was on his way. The label mother-in-law didn't jar me as much as I thought it would, but I briefly imagined my mother coming through the door instead, sitting the doctors down with a series of questions and charming them so much that they'd give me everything I needed. She'd always been meticulous with her questioning and note taking, a fact I didn't want to correlate to the way she died.

I gripped the bed. I could see Amelia in that moment, navigating her world each day around being told what she needed to suppress. My sensation was not imagined; it was information. It was telling me I wasn't on the right path. When Rita reached for my hand, I took hers and squeezed. She wasn't my mother, she'd never be my mother, but that day, I needed her the way I needed my mother. When she squeezed my hand back, I could tell she understood.

Mustering all my strength, I asked, calmly, "Why would panic make my limbs feel numb? Why would that make my heart hurt? I feel like I'm going to die. Again, can I see another doctor?" No one was listening. I remembered screaming at my father to listen to Amelia, and now I knew intimately what it felt like.

"The doctor may suggest an anti-anxiety medication, which would help with these things by boosting your serotonin levels. The rest of your bloodwork will take a few days."

After a few minutes, the doctor, a tall woman with narrow features and long, straight hair, came in with her iPad and looked over her glasses as I tried to breathe into my pelvis to release the pressure. I waited with my hand over my navel and my other hand squeezing Rita's intensely.

She held up a notebook. "So far, everything's looking good. I want you to go here," she said, handing me directions to a psychiatrist a few blocks away. "As we wait for your blood results, I recommend you take the medication at the very least and try to remain calm. Panic disorders and the like can actually lead to real symptoms if we don't treat them."

"Are you sure it's not cancer?" my sister asked.

"Not likely."

"It could be hormones. Birth control has helped me quite a bit," Rita whispered. "I had a few emotional periods. Nothing like this, but I've had friends ...." Her vanilla scent was making me want to puke. She added, "It did make me bitchy though." She was trying to lighten the mood, knowing I couldn't imagine her saccharine sweet self anywhere near bitchy.

I glared at the doctor, then insisted I go home. Maybe it wasn't entirely fair, but in that instant, I thought about Kat, her seemingly irrational anger at the world and desire to conquer it at any cost, and I wondered if events like this had shaped her.

The idea that they wanted to give me medications to numb me, too, probably the same pills that killed my mother, caused my body to grow hot enough to almost be medicinal. The heart could burn away anything, I imagined. I just needed to tune in. I lined the outer edge of my hands up along my pelvic bones and focused on my belly. I closed my eyes, trying to summon the magic, but in that moment, I was all too human. I should've felt relief. I wasn't pregnant.

When my father came in, he asked for a rundown. "Your parking situation is less than optimal," he told the doctor.

"You must be Emerson's father. I see the resemblance," the doctor said. "We validate. Here are a few resources I recommend." She repeated, to the word, what she'd just told me after handing my father a list including the numbers to a psychologist and psychiatrist, along with an OBGYN in case I had severe PMDD. When she discussed different antianxiety medications and a mood stabilizer, he nodded as though he'd seen this all coming.

"What else can we do, right?" I said in mock resignation. "All the women in this family are insane, remember?" I imagined myself checking into The Lavender House, being ignored for the rest of my life.

The next day, I called and texted Courtney with the same fortitude that Ian called and texted me. I didn't tell her how horrible the night had been because I was tired of talking about it, but I thought I'd have the chance to reveal all that later. We usually texted daily. I just needed to hear her voice or see her message, but she didn't answer her phone.

I texted a final time, a plea: "I need you to write an expose on healthcare. This is bullshit. See you tomorrow?"

"You okay?" came in at last. When I didn't answer, she followed up with, "Yes. Tomorrow. Catch me up with you."

"Good. I need to talk to you about something. Yesterday, before I got all those texts...," I wrote. I didn't hit send, but I knew I had to come clean even if she hadn't seen the texts from Ian. Instead, I sent her the address for my sister's race, then I sat at my computer and waited for my mother. I needed her guidance. I watched the screen, waiting for a sign or presence, until the light blurred my eyes. She didn't arrive, so I wrote. The letter was short and awkward, explaining how I could relate to her pain now. I understood. I told her Amelia was helping me understand everything else, but I still felt lost. I ended with a simple plea: *Tell me what I need to do.*

Then I wrote the same note, this one to Grandma Grodzki. *Tell me what I need to do.* I printed and folded the letters and placed them under my pillow. Keeping my window cracked and the blinds up, I lay there glancing out and up at the stars, waiting for an answer. What arrived was stillness. Realization. I was *not* pregnant. Of course not. I was insane.

"Not pregnant," I texted Ian.

He texted me a paragraph-long inquiry about how I was doing and what I was going to do this weekend and whether we should talk.

"I'm in love with Courtney," I wrote. Again, I didn't send. Instead, I said, "I think I need space. I was in a bad place that day."

My breath was deep in that moment. It pushed down on my diaphragm, moving beyond my lungs. I'd once read advanced meditators could breathe through their eyes, their pores, and I imagined doing just

that. I felt the subtle ripple of hope surf my forearms and shins. The
tension in my shoulders relaxed, and I realized what Amelia had meant
by honing my vision. I began to see not only what would happen but
what I wanted to happen, and I made an agreement with the future that
we'd meet somewhere in the middle.

After a coma-like sleep, I woke with the sun. Dad suggested
that I stay home and rest, and after I refused, we left together in uncomfortable silence, headed to Canton with soft jazz playing to augment
the melancholy we both felt. Every now and then, Dad glanced over
kindly and asked if I was okay. His tone was one I hadn't heard since he
used to stay up late with Mom. I simply nodded or offered a soft yes as
I kept my head against the window. It was strange to be driven to The
Lavender House. It took only an hour by car, without all the bus stops.
We arrived just before breakfast was served, so the halls smelled of eggs
and coffee. Dad was funneled into conversations with staff, as I was left
to "entertain" Amelia. *If they only knew.*

I knocked lightly on the door.

"Come in, doll." Amelia was seated on the floor with a blanket
bunched underneath her and a mug in her hands.

"Do you want to tell me what happened?" I asked.

"Do you?" she asked, glancing down at my hand, which I hadn't
noticed was settled on my lower belly, even though I no longer felt pain.
"Your womb. The creator."

"Let's talk about something else. *Your* story. It's medicinal,
Amelia."

"Ha! Where's our friend?" She yawned, stretching her arms as
though she just woke up.

"She's busy today. Got a B on a test, and I think her parents are
cracking down."

She stared at me again. "I only have one cup. They took my
coffee maker as punishment. They consider coffee a luxury for those on
'good behavior,' Amelia said, placing the mug down in front of me and
straining to reach under her bed and retrieve a small ceramic jewelry box.

"Thank you, but no, you drink the coffee."

"This is my victory! This is how I'll get the energy to make my trip." She handed me the jewelry box, and I lifted the lid. A week's worth of pills shifted around, and I emptied them into my palm. I watched my grandmother, waiting, then returned them to the container and snuck it inside my backpack when I heard rustling in the hallway. The door was open a crack, and we watched as someone shuffled by.

"Why do you still have these? Where exactly do you want to go?"

"So I can keep track. My voice stops shaking after a week. I'll tell you about my trip. First, you tell me what happened, Emerson."

"Maybe keep a tally instead?"

"If I can study these pills, sit with them and observe, I might be able to make myself immune. There's no ritual for that, but nature always has a counter move to what's destructive." She examined the pills. "They're not that powerful. Now spill!"

"I might need to learn that trick myself. Everyone thinks I'm crazy, Amelia." I sat up straight, easing into reality as I told her what had happened with my trip to the urgent care. Amelia, nodded, not surprised, as though she had been there, too, or had a vision. Her long fingers reached out, lightly grazing my lower belly, and she closed her eyes.

"A shooting star—you will birth other things," she said. "I promise. You are carrying the pain and potential of many women."

"What? I don't want to be pregnant. I just want to feel normal." I rested my head in my hand and asked, "Will I ever stop being afraid?"

Amelia smiled—her face a profusion of color and grace. She tore a page from her notebook and handed it to me. It was a recipe for tea and a practice of bowing in the woods to appease nature and reconnect. "Bow to the earth. Bow to your inner truth," it said. "This is not a cure. Your journey is your own, but this is a practice like everything good and bad. You will never be alone in your pain if you give it to the earth. Fear like yours ... such things show up when you're not living your truth. That's the secret. Are you insane, or is the world that's trying to mold you?"

She cracked her neck. "You can read more about that later. For now, I'll tell you what happens next in *my* story. I have to get this thing out of me, and you'll have to fill our friend in. She needs to hear the whole thing. It's important that she hears. I need a writer. I need it all captured, and I need it to end with love."

Chapter Sixteen: Amelia

I stood in front of a mirror with my brother's shaving blade and imagined the moon. The idea I'd brought up to Helen circled around my head. If I slashed my own cheek, I'd be a warrior. No man who wasn't truly kind would want to marry me, and I'd be free.

In the mirror, I saw Jake then. He was an old man in the image, so incredibly kind, and he offered me his hand. I would have to decide whether to take it. Even if I slashed my face, he'd offer me his hand. Especially if I did. Knowing that, I could taste a different future, but as I stared in the mirror a little too long, I heard footsteps. Grandma Grodzki knocked on the door, and I put away the blade.

She sat me down when I finally came out, insisting on tea, which I dutifully made with two sugar cubes. I poured Grandma Grodzki's cream, until she lifted two fingers signaling me to stop.

"Amelia, please listen closely. Lean in." She lowered her chin and waited until I scooted in closer. I could smell the spices and cream on her breath as she said, "In order to own our power, we have to accept that we all have a side of us that is not pristine, not good. You understand that, right?"

I shook my head no. "Are you talking about Mother?"

Without answering, she told me the story of the night goddess Selene, the embodiment of the moon, who controlled time and sleep. There was always a dark side to these goddess stories, as there were of any allegorical stories. Selene kept the love of her life in a state of permanent, peaceful sleep to maintain control, my grandmother explained.

"She is the goddess of the moon because the night was to bring peace and equilibrium, but there was always energy that could not be contained during the late hours. We all have a side to us that we'd like to keep hidden."

I felt like I should be taking notes. When I was around Grandma Grodzki, I could be myself. I was connected to another world that didn't exist outside, around my mother or at school. I stayed up that night and tried to will a better vision for myself, a vision of that might enable me to escape.

My visions allowed me to see everything for everyone then, but I couldn't see what lay ahead for me. I fell asleep that night in our small home in Cleveland beneath a full moon at the mercy of time. I woke up realizing that I didn't control anything. I was a girl who was late for school.

Betty and I didn't realize so many boys even attended the school until we saw them all congregated on the stands that surrounded the blue mats at the center of the gym. It was rumored that many of these boys would soon be drafted, and this thought kept me standing in the doorway a moment too long. I scanned the crowd, trying not to think about my brother as some of the faces I both knew and didn't know seemed already faded, destined for loss no newspaper could predict.

Betty smacked me on the back. "Let's move. There are people behind us. With this many desperate boys, we might be married before we walk out of this room."

"I wonder if we're even allowed in here," I said.

There was a small cluster of girls in the stands across the room. Each wore a school coat with their boyfriends' initials on the chest. "I wonder if one of those girls is dating Jake," I said.

"He's in love with you, and you're in love with him. I can tell," Betty said and made a kissing sound.

"Oh hush."

She grabbed my forearm and tugged. "Let's just sit and watch. We'll see who he stares at when he comes out." We found seats near the cluster of girls and exchanged smiles. One girl was in my English class, and she waved us over.

"Which one is yours?" the girl, Janice, asked.

"What?"

"My boyfriend is competing in the wrestling match today after last bell. His name is Oswald. Don't tell anyone, but he always loses. See, the one with the blond hair."

"He's handsome," Betty said. "Amelia here likes Jake, but she doesn't know if he's courting anyone. Do you know him?"

I was suddenly so embarrassed I wanted to run out of the room and, as if on cue, Jake appeared in red spandex and a head piece. His body was muscular and dark in the low light. Just the sight of him caused my eyes to lock. Maybe I *was* in love.

"Oh no, he's not taken at all," the girl said. "He's a strange one. Kind of bad. I hear he might get kicked out of school for grades."

"Really? He seemed so smart when I talked to him." Smart to a fault, I thought. I was still watching him as he stretched, and when he caught my gaze, I summoned the moon.

"My brother is one of his friends. Maybe we can get a Coke sometime, like a double date and I can vet him for you. If you can promise to fill me in about that story."

"Oh, she'll fill you in," Betty said. "That's a neat idea."

"Um, yes," I said. "That sounds fine."

I allowed my mind to wander during the various wrestling matches, until Jake's name was announced by the burly coach. I sat up straight and examined the competition. The boy Jake was facing appeared to be at least twenty pounds heavier. It didn't seem fair, even for a person without premonitions. I wanted to save him from the pang that came with defeat—I had to somehow stop the match. Maybe if I were to make some sort of distraction, to faint or scream, I could stop it, but before I had a chance to do any such thing, a hand was waved and the boys began to take wide steps around the mat, trying to intimidate each other with angry stares.

It all seemed so barbaric. The heavier boy rushed toward Jake and grabbed at his bony legs, but Jake was quick enough to pull out of his grip just in time. Jake hobbled around in a circle and plunged head-first into the boy's fluffy stomach, propelling him backward; then, in a matter of seconds, Jake had positioned his long legs around the other boy's so he couldn't move. His arm was against the boy's chest—which was heaving now, and the same man who had waved his hand moments earlier, tapped the mat. Jake won round one, but I knew his victory was short-lived.

"That's enough of that," I said. I stood and made my way back down the bleachers, desperate not to see another minute of this ridiculous fighting. I walked past all the freshman boys, who were closer to the match, and received a few cat calls on my way out. Then I heard a voice lift above all the others.

"Thanks for coming." It was him. Watching me. He gave me a salute, then shook out his legs, readying himself for another round. As Jake jogged in place, I rushed into the hall. I couldn't go back in there, but I didn't want to go home.

The cat calls came again as Betty ran toward me. "Why did you just run off like that?"

"I still like him, but I don't think I want to date a boy who fights like this for no reason." As we stood in the hall, a roar from the crowd, replete with gasps, funneled into our ears. We glanced it to see Jake rocking in pain.

"Amelia, it's what boys do. I hope he's OK."

"Well, I don't want to watch such a thing. It's stupid, and it makes me worry about Gene, out there fighting, out there risking his life." I thought about Selene, the temptation to place something you love in a pristine condition, a perpetual sleep so he'd never be hurt.

Betty put her arm around me as people gathered around Jake. He was alive. He would be fine, but he was clutching his leg. If only I could heal, like the goddess Panacea. I pulled Betty along, unable to watch. We walked past the empty lockers and took a seat on the steps which, we realized after sitting down, were freshly mopped. I felt the seat of my skirt dampening and laughed. Betty stood up and had a wet round on the back of her skirt.

"I might have a sweater in my locker. Come on." Giggling like actual children at the fact we both looked like we'd just peed ourselves, we ran down the hall when, out of nowhere, the door to the boy's bathroom opened and Jake came out. "Oh no," Betty said, laughing harder now. "Amelia, this just isn't your day."

He was limping, and his face fell, as though this was a personal attack on him.

"I sat in water," I explained, turning around. I shocked myself by my lack of embarrassment.

Jake's eyes narrowed as though he were trying to conceal a smile. "Hold on. Just stay right here. I can help."

"We should help you," I said pointing to his bruised shin. He ignored my comment and limped back into the gym.

"If he's going to tell his friends so he can make fun of us," Betty began, curling her fists, but before she could get it all out, he appeared again, holding his lettered jacket.

"Here. Wrap this around your waist." He shoved the jacket my way, somewhat clumsily. He appeared fatigued. "I'll find something for you," he told Betty.

"Thank you," I said. "I'll need to leave, though, so you might as well hang on to it. I have to get home."

"No, keep it. Can I walk you home? I mean, I have to change, but I can do that in a jiffy."

"No. I really have to get going. Here," I said, handing him his jacket.

"You don't have to leave," Betty said. "Listen, I'm the one who needs to get going. Amelia here was just being nice because she knows I don't like to walk by myself. But I'll be fine. I'm going, Amelia." Betty widened her eyes at me, as though to say I better not argue. "Congratulations, Jake. I'm assuming you won, right?"

He hung his head. "I wish. I might be done wrestling for the year," he said. As Betty walked away, Jake looked to me. "Really, wait here. You'll see. I'll be right back."

The school felt so peaceful, only quiet murmurs escaped from the gym. I looked around to make sure no one was watching and held the jacket to my nose. It smelled a little musty, and with the hint of something cool, maybe a cologne. I couldn't help smiling in my solitude, thinking maybe the fate I feared could be avoided. I tied the jacket around my waist and began walking along the lockers, catching the metal vents on my fingertips as I went. If I could connect with the elemental energy and see futures I had no interest in seeing, why couldn't I see what was in store for me? Why couldn't I see a future with Jake?

I walked toward the cafeteria and stopped in front of my artwork. The paper was pristine behind the glass, and I wondered if my painting would be there long enough to turn yellow the way the pages in books sometimes do. I wondered if it would stay there until after I graduated, and if students many years from now would look at it and wonder about the artist. Probably not, but it was fun to imagine. I hadn't created art since this piece, and I worried nothing I would ever create from here on in would ever be as good.

I was still staring at the work when I felt a tap on her shoulder. "It really is remarkable," Jake said. "I wanted to tell you the day your award was announced, but you never showed up at the cafeteria. You were too busy scrapping." He laughed.

"I feel bad about that day," I said, realizing he wasn't the only one who engaged in barbaric activities.

"Some people deserve to be put in their place. JoAnne was bound to get kicked out for one thing or another."

"You sound like my brother. You know her? JoAnne?"

"Kind of."

We began to walk, silently but not uncomfortably. Once outside, in the crisp fall air, Jake stretched his arms out, as though he wanted to hug the breeze. "Do you want to tell me why you ran out of the gym?"

"I didn't like watching you fight."

"Most girls love it."

"Girls just put up with watching that stuff because it makes boys happy. I don't want to see anyone fight. I don't want to fight myself. I don't want my brother to fight this stupid war."

"If anyone hears you call this war stupid, you might have to fight all of America."

"I know. But I hate the thought of him over there. He had just come back home after a long trip with my mother when he left. And he was the only person in my house who seemed to care anything for me." She thought about this and added, "My grandmother cares, but she's sick."

"Your father?"

"He's not around."

"Did he leave your family, or is he a soldier?"

"Why so many questions?"

"Listen, my father died, so I guess I just like to know about other people's fathers. Sorry if I offended you."

"You didn't offend me. My father is dead, too. I think," I said.

"Oh, gee, sorry." He looked down solemnly.

"I don't know anything about him. He died while Mother was pregnant with me."

Jake put his arm around me and gave me a soft squeeze. I felt his body weight lean in some, and I wondered if it was to offset the injury. "I'm sorry if I'm out of line, but I'll tell you this. Your father is still with you. He lives in you. You might have gotten your talent for art from him."

To let someone into my life like this felt wrong, even Jake. Suddenly, all I wanted was to be left to my imagination so I could be at peace. We were only two blocks from home now, and we continued in that comfortable silence.

When we got to my door, he smiled, but I could see his pain. He'd wrapped his leg, but I could tell it was throbbing. "You hang on to the jacket, Amelia. And hey, I know what it's like."

Jake began showing up at the corner of Cuba and 4th at the end of my street each morning so he could walk me to school. He carried my books, and we walked silently together until Betty, with her bubbly morning chatter, met us halfway.

He became a person to count on and soon people began referring to him as my fella, and much like the first time we met, Jake would often go into long silences in which it seemed he wasn't present at all. I wondered if it had anything to do with his father's death.

We would sometimes chat about everyday things: the weather and homework, how a girl who had dropped out of school had been rumored to have gotten herself *in a way* or how the boy who had dropped out early must've been drafted. We didn't talk much about ourselves those days, but there was something nice about keeping some mystery, at least to me, and I grew to enjoy his silent company, to expect it. It was a great comfort because home life was teetering.

I brought Grandma Grodzki fresh washcloths for her headaches and changed out the small wastebasket that was kept by her station. I filled it daily with tissues that contained traces of blood among clumps of mucus by the end of the day. Grandmother's cough was relentless. Meanwhile, instead of helping, Kat was away more than ever. She said she was working extra hours to pay for the hospital. Betty would sneak over meals from church dinners, to help us out, but from what I could tell the bills were all paid.

Kat often returned at the wee hours of the morning, sometimes waking me by standing over my bed with another person, always a man smelling of gin and Shalimar, smoke and a trace of sweat. I would never move. I would keep my eyes closed, kept still as a board and imagined light around my body, until Mother and her friend left, and the door to my room was closed with a clumsy slam.

Each nightly visit felt enough like a dream I figured they may well have been, but sometimes I'd wake up and still smell the cologne. When Mother was around, she would worry over Grandma Grodzki with artificial sweetness, often trying to feed her desserts she had picked up from a downtown baker.

"I brought you some of the best cinnamon rolls in all of Cleveland. I had them made with extra love," she'd say, forcing the sweet thing on Grandma Grodzki, who would politely take a bite or two and leave the rest of it there to harden, the butter and sugar to congeal and grow shiny. Mother would then look quite satisfied with herself and saunter off to her mysterious places.

I sat with Grandma, relishing the silent moments, and I tried to recount the stories of goddesses. On one of her calmer evenings, I held much of Grandma Grodzki's weight as we walked outside. It was the fresh air, that brief gasp, that brought her to life for the last time. Druantia—the goddess of birth, death, insanity and creativity—I told her, trying to get it right, offers inspiration with the rustling of leaves and reminds us we are connected to the stars.

"Very good, girl." We had to go back inside before getting anywhere near a tree, but as I sat at Grandmother's feet, there was an entire evening of peace. "I'm not really going anywhere," she told me. I couldn't fully accept that yet. I wasn't ready, but it was true.

When Mother made the arrangements to have Grandma Grodzki moved permanently to hospice to spend her last days, I felt more alone than she could believe. I couldn't imagine living with only Mother. I tried to picture it as Mother sat across the table picking at the potatoes I'd boiled after school, but I couldn't.

Mother rarely spoke to me the last days of Grandma Grodzki's life, and when she did, it was only to revamp her plans, to complain about how Grandma Grodzki's illness had put a burden on their finances, to comment on my hair or dress that day. The only times I could be in her presence without feeling a deep-stomach sickness was mornings, when I knew I'd see Jake or before the few times we were able to visit Grandma Grodzki at the facility as she began to lighten and soften toward the earth.

It was the last time I saw her in the nursing home. The women in our family must listen for final words. She told me, quite plainly, "There is a bit of cash stashed away behind the stairs. My cards. There are publications there, too. Publications your mother used to read."

I took this information in, holding her weak hand. She was only a trace of her former plump self by this time, and she had a yellow tone to her skin, as though something was staining it from the inside out. I was sitting bedside, trying to emit warmth. I closed my eyes and saw the space beneath the stairs, women's writing, magic and money. A treasure trove waiting for me and only me. Unless…

"Have you told Mother?"

"I see no point," Grandma Grodzki said weakly. "She has plenty of money." She wore a sort of strange smile I had never seen before. She was stoic, a woman preparing herself for transition, or perhaps more accurately, patiently waiting on its arrival.

"You're old enough now," Grandma Grodzki said. "You need to get away from her."

"Grandma, I'm scared. Mother will fall apart if I leave; then I'll have no one. What am I supposed to do in the world?"

In a moment of dogmatic strength, Grandma Grodzki took on her old disciplinarian stare and propped herself up on an elbow. "Your mother won't fall apart. She's too full of herself to fall apart. That woman is as solid as concrete."

"But you love her," I said, rebelliously.

"I love her, too, but I know she's no good for you. I see it— she's going to hurt you in ways you can't imagine. Unless you leave."

Tears streamed, but I didn't feel sad exactly. What I felt was too complicated. I couldn't humor the usual theatrics that went with crying. I just had to let it flow through me.

"Your mother is finding herself, young one, and until she does, she's dangerous. I've tried to find you support. I've really tried." Grandma Grodzki worked her way up to a sitting position, which appeared to be a painful venture. She withdrew her cold hands from my grasp and placed them on my thigh. I immediately thought she was hallucinating. "Listen to me, Amelia. You're a good girl. You've taken such good care of me, but it's up to you to take care of yourself now, and that's always far harder…"

I kept a hand on Grandma Grodzki's arm and squeezed gently as a fit of coughing pushed her straight back down into the bed. She heaved and began to shake, so much so I could no longer hold her hand.

I ran down the hall to the sink to get her water. When I returned, Grandma Grodzki appeared almost transparent. "Thank you. Such a good girl," she whispered.

"Grandma, I won't tell anyone. I won't tell Mother a thing."

"Won't tell Mother what?" Mother said, appearing in the doorway.

Something took me over then. "Mother, Grandma Grodzki doesn't want you to know she might not have long." The lie was seamless and perfect.

"Oh, Mother," she said, rushing to Grandma Grodzki's side and weeping overzealously, another scene from a motion picture.

I walked out, telling them I had to go to the lady's room.

I walked down the long, pale-yellow hallway, which smelled of rubbing alcohol and mildew, and I found a door to a small courtyard where I'd never ventured. I sat on an empty bench across the way from two nurses who were smoking Chesterfields and laughing about something.

"Can I bother you ladies for a smoke?" I asked. My pain and the cold air, I was sure of it, made me look like a patient.

"You seem a little young to smoke," one of the women said, but as I looked down, nodding, the woman handed me a small white cigarette. She pulled out a fancy silver lighter, and as I gripped the cigarette between my lips too tightly, the woman lit a small flame and moved it toward me. I took a puff, expecting to cough awkwardly and gag, but instead I took the piercing smoke into my lungs with zeal. It felt right.

After a few puffs, the sensation from the smoke had worked its way up to my head, and I thanked the ladies. I was ready to rejoin my family. I knew I would have to find a way to get Mother out of the room, but there was a strange drive welling inside me. I walked back down the hall and into the room, where Mother was now pacing and recounting all the things she was worried about happening in the impending days.

It was sickening to watch; Mother's healthy body and angry mind being comforted by a kind, otherworldly woman on her deathbed, a woman who had quite given over her life's days for the sake of her daughter and two grandchildren. I only wished Gene were there with me.

I stood in the doorway, still a little dizzy from the nicotine. "Mother, one of the nurses out there, the brunette who's smoking, asked if I would get you."

She hadn't noticed me come in, and she stopped dead in her tracks. "Oh! I must have left my compact out there. I'll be right back."

As soon as her thin heels were no longer audible in the hall, I pleaded with Grandma Grodzki, "Please, don't leave me. I need you. I need you to tell me everything."

"The three thousand is saved up from the fortunes I've told. Some of your teachers were my best customers, you know. It should be more than enough to last you all until you graduate high school. After that, it's going to be up to you. You have abilities. You won't have to worry. You need to run and keep practicing. Keep my cards safe. They could get you in trouble if someone finds them."

"Run?"

"You need to run if you want to live your own life. Your mother is planning..." Grandma Grodzki took a long, hard look at the doorway. I wondered if she was considering sticking around. "You have your brother," she said. "You have yourself. And me. And those who came before me. We're with you."

"Gene hasn't written us once, Grandma. He might be away for a long, long time. The war is ... I need..."

That very night Grandma Grodzki died in the same manner her mother had, the same way a great-granddaughter she'd never meet would, ultimately, of heart failure. It was near-impossible to survive at her age, the doctors told me, and I felt a surge go through my body.

"She was a tough, tough woman," one of the nurses added. "One of the kindest patients I've had, and it was an honor to watch over her during her last days."

Mother and I stood silently in the doctor's office, listening to kind words until the nurses were called off to work, and they dispersed with heartfelt apologies. I watched them go, too numb to cry.

Over the next few days, Mother became stoic and, surprisingly, productive, which allowed me the privilege to fall completely apart. Mother made the funeral arrangements and sent for Gene, requesting he get leave so he may attend the funeral, but Gene, apparently, was unreachable, so by the time the message had been received, he couldn't attend.

Gene's absence left me to grieve alone as Mother boxed up clothes and cleaned house. It seemed she couldn't rid the place of any trace of Grandma Grodzki fast enough.

"Mother, I don't know if I can go to school yet," I said, watching her fold Grandma Grodzki's old flower print dress, the ones she wore most often around the house.

"You don't have to worry about that. I've already called, and you're excused for the entire week, my dear. Come here and help me fold. Keeping busy and cleaning house is the way to deal with death. You see, we must respect the deceased by allowing them to move on."

As I folded Grandmother's clothes, I began to hum, feeling the flower prints in the fabric of a dress as I imagined the soft cotton expanding and blanketing me, keeping her warm and safe.

We walked two boxes of clothes and hats down to the shelter, where they would be donated to other women who were in a tough spot while their husbands were away at war, but, as soon as we placed the boxes on the ground as instructed by the Volunteers of America worker, I shed my first tear since losing my grandmother. With the release of that single tear, something opened inside of me. Mother simply walked home, singing hellos to those we passed as I felt myself drowning in a new truth. I thought I had Grandma Grodzki forever. As such, when I lost her, I would lose myself.

Chapter Seventeen: Emerson

I sat with my chin heavy on my fist. Amelia relaxed as she told her story, as though she were truly releasing it from her body. "The more you understand, the less you try to control," she said, standing and moving to the window. "You metabolize. You work through it. Em, you act like you're interested in magic and our stories, but you don't live. You're boring. You're afraid."

The wind was heavy as the clouds began to bruise. It felt like everything was moving around me, and I was a stagnant thing, a fixed point of unease and fear. I tried to explain. "I keep hearing Mom's voice. I'm not a bore, I'm insane." If insanity was nothing else, it wasn't boring.

"Shhhhh ... You're boring *because* you're worried about going insane. Who isn't? *Boring*. Figure out how to trust yourself, and do it asap," she said. "That way you can build a bridge and get over your own issues ... help me out a little. I'm old. I don't have much time."

She looked down at the jewelry box in my lap. My legs were stiff, and I realized someone would be checking on Amelia soon. I tucked it away and walked down the hall to the common bathroom, more to grab a quiet moment than anything. I dialed Courtney's number. Nothing. I texted, "Hey! Still studying?" Nothing.

I stood in front of the sink, staring at my reflection for a long time. Was I boring? Jenny came into the bathroom and jumped when she noticed me. "You scared the daylights out of me, kiddo! I'll be damned. Did you sign in?"

"No. I thought Dad signed me in," I said.

"You probably only have a half hour with her, you know. Amelia needs to go to therapy. It's art therapy, not the talk kind where you're on the couch. But the therapist is there. Sometimes it helps them to open up."

She began reapplying eyeliner but really didn't need it. "You know, this is an art. Took me a year to learn this little swoosh. Want me to touch you up? I'll make it look like the sun bent right over you and you alone, just to kiss your cheeks and give you good angles."

I thanked Jenny and told her I'd consider. "She's telling me a story—I need to get back."

"Oh, I love your grandmother's stories. Here with your father today, eh?"

I shrugged, then waited a moment for her to ask me about Courtney, but she didn't. Outside Amelia's room, Dad met me in the hall. His shoes squeaked on the freshly mopped linoleum as he paced. "Amelia, we'll be in in a minute. Em, come chat." He didn't say anything for a while. The windows lining the hallway reminded me of an airport terminal. "They're not threatening to kick her out yet," Dad said at last, "but I think she's trying for it. I need you to help me out and not cheer that on, Emerson. You don't understand her history."

"I understand Amelia better than you think," I said. "Why can't she move in with us?"

"If Amelia plays by the rules for a few weeks, all will be forgiven. They suspect she's been the sole reason at least three nurses have quit over the last few months. Only the receptionist seems to like her. We're going to try a new medication and new method."

"No one likes a woman who knows too much," I said.

My father grabbed my forearm hard. "Emerson, don't let her manipulate you."

I pulled away sharply, reaching for Amelia's door, and when I cracked it open, she was pretending, not too convincingly, to stare out at the pond unaware. "She can hear you," I told him.

"We should go," Dad said. "We might even be able to make your sister's meet on-time. Let's say goodbye and discuss on the way home. Text your friend and make sure she can still come. It'd mean a lot to your sister."

He turned and headed toward the door without saying anything to Amelia. His disdain was palpable. I bent down to kiss her gently on the cheek. "We're going to heal," I whispered. I looked back, before following

my father and saying, sarcastically, "Right behind you, Sir. Yes, Sir."
Amelia called out. "Trust, girl. Trust."

On the way home, I texted Courtney again, then turned to my
father. He drove with his body leaning back, lounging, and his chin forward.
When I was a kid, I used to say he looked like a hedgehog when he drove,
which had made Mom laugh. She would sit up straight, leaning slightly
forward, alert.

"When they find out I can't have kids, that's not the worst thing,
right?" I asked.

Dad shot up straight then and stopped the car suddenly, almost
hitting the berm. "Are you afraid that's the case? No doctor said that."

"No doctor needs to say it," I said. "I already know it. And I
guess ... I guess I'm just trying to let you know." I was not being cold or
inquisitive, I was being honest. I was telling him what I knew at the time to
be true of my body, and I was telling him with all the heart I had, as though
I were presenting a new way to see, but I was suddenly overcome with
stoicism. Perhaps for the first time since I was twelve, I felt my mother with
me completely. Not just as a disembodied voice. Not as anything to fear.

"I know you're scared. But please don't talk that way. Don't say you
know things. You don't know! You can't know. Your mother used to talk
like that, and you can't feed into that stuff."

"Why? You always dismiss Amelia and Mom. They had intuition—
they could see things. Amelia warned us about Mom. How can you deny
it?"

I tuned into my father's energy, and it wasn't worry. It was pure
anger. The same anger that swelled inside him when Mom died. He took
a strong breath and said, "We'll get through it as a family. But I think you
need to see someone about this magical thinking. We need more than talk
therapy. We need medication. We can stop it before it's too late."

He was trying so hard to be nice, empathetic, but he didn't
understand. Deep down, he wanted to smash his fist into the window. I
could feel the heat radiating from him. He wasn't angry at me but at his
loss, the idea he could lose more. His daughter, too.

"Maybe it's not just magical thinking," I said.

"Em, it is. Look, I need you to take this seriously. It's okay to be dreamy, but you're treading on dangerous territory. Your mother had headaches, yes. But they were just part of it. She used to talk like this, say she could see things and know things. And then the headaches would come. It was paranoia. I hate myself for not forcing her to get help, but she said she was fine. She said they made her delusional, but she started withdrawing. I should have been there for her," he said, resting his forearms on the wheel. "I didn't want you to think you were destined to be the same way. You were always a level-headed kid. We got you evaluated when you were younger, and you were fine. Even after your mother passed, it was *you* taking care of *us* and trying to advocate for your grandmother. I was the one who couldn't keep my shit together. *You*, Em. You were the one who wasn't afraid to keep her memory alive."

I felt the urge to comfort him, to promise to live inside the box that I was supposed to live in. I stepped out of the car and looked at the long road stretching out, the pine trees lining each side of us. The world was not too small, I realized, only perceptions of it were. In that moment, I allowed the rest of my body to tear open. I felt a beam of light work through me as I looked down at my hands, and instead of panic, I felt something else.

Each line on my hands told a story. A narrative that spanned time and space, and I felt every one of the women who came before me at my side. Catching my reflection in a small, still pool of water, I waited. I watched the reflection until it changed. I changed. I eased back into the car, where my father was wiping his face.

"I understand," I said. "I need to you to trust me, Dad."

"This is tough stuff, Em."

No. It's not. I closed my eyes, and I summoned my mother with new resolve. Not only could I hear her but now but could feel her sitting in the backseat with a knowing smile. She remained with us the duration of the drive, soothing my father. Nothing was strange anymore. Everything felt more expansive and connected, but I still struggled to find the right words to get Dad to understand.

"I need Amelia in my life. I deserve to have a grandmother," I told him. Mom gave me a slow clap from behind, which almost made me laugh. "I deserve to hear her stories and know her rituals. It's nothing evil or wrong. It's an inheritance."

"She was trying to hurt herself, Emerson. She could have hurt you girls."

"She was trying to help."

He turned the crimson color he turned all those years ago, but Mom placed her hand on his shoulder and shushed him, soothed him in a way she couldn't when she was in her body. After a few miles, Dad reached over to squeeze my shoulder. I thought I saw something like compassion in his eyes, a hint of knowing. But then it dropped.

"Em, I want you to start medication. I need you to understand that it's not just about you. Your mental health impacts all of us. Me, your sister, Rita…"

PART FOUR: MADNESS

Chapter Eighteen: Amelia

Grandma Grodzki never warned me of her death or all that was to come after, but she must have known. She simply moved out of her body and into everything, leaving me with the mystery of how to communicate with her again. She returned in my dreams from time to time, but it took me longer to speak to her now. There was nothing more painful. It felt as though my skin had been ripped off, and the world could see me raw.

In grief, I didn't have visions or feel connected to nature. I felt hollow, unable to recognize those who were supporting me, and I began to hatch practical plans, listening to my mother and her myopic views of the world. I craved safety, the idea of just getting through the day seemed insurmountable that first week.

Schoolwork was piling up after I'd taken so much time off, but teachers allowed every concession. Even the kids I never spoke with brought me baked goods and cards with kind messages. I wasn't used to such treatment and hadn't seen anyone else ever get it, so I couldn't help but feel a bit suspicious. Mr. Oham said I was excused from the lessons I had missed, but I asked him to let me make up the homework on variables. He seemed shocked. "Most girls despise math. With everything you are going through, I'm quite impressed you want to attempt this. I'm sorry about your mother. Don't worry about the homework you owe me."

I wanted the homework, but something else he said stopped me from saying so. "My mother?" When the thought crossed my mind that something happened to her, I felt a wave of lightness before the worry. When he tilted his head down, peering at me over his glasses, I realized that he, and probably other teachers, thought Grandma Grodzki was my mother because she was the only person to ever show up to or sign off on anything.

"Such an interesting woman. She always sent me holiday cards with the kindest messages."

Grandma Grodzki's kindness, and likely the readings she'd delivered in secret, had earned me compassion from those who'd never so much as looked my way. Or maybe she was orchestrating it in that moment, telling these people to treat me well; it almost didn't feel fair when so many others suffered in silence at the loss of their brothers and fathers at war. I thanked him, not bothering to correct his mistake. In many ways, Grandma Grodzki had been my mother, after all. And there would always be time to learn about variables.

By the first Friday back, Jake was waiting after school with a fistful of sunflowers and a small box of chocolates. He hadn't been at school himself. I knew because, despite the cloud of my grief, I had been looking for him in the halls all week. When I saw him, it was as though we hadn't seen each other in years. He looked older somehow, and I'm sure I did, too. His eyelids heavy and smile slight, he handed me the large stocks with too much exuberance. "I missed you while you were away. I wanted to see you earlier, but I had to take care of some things."

"What things?" I placed the chocolates in my bag and felt the softness of the petals. I could barely wrap my fingers around the thick stems, but I loved this about them. Jake didn't bring roses like everyone else. He brought tough, vibrant flowers. I noticed a ladybug walking across a yellow petal, and I gently nudged my finger underneath its legs until it was crawling around my hand.

"My brother was drafted."

"Sorry."

"No, it's good. He likes the bottle too much. The Army is probably safer."

I examined his kind face. He held compassion in a way I'd never seen. "Well, thank you. These are perfect."

"Did your mother tell you that I stopped by your house?"

I stopped walking. "Really?"

"Your mother told me that you were in your room, and she started asking me about who I was, who my family was, and why I had an interest in you. She's an intimidating woman. She acts like a man."

"Right. Mother is tough," I said. "I don't like that comparison though. Kat's tougher than any man I've ever met." I watched his face soften.

"Good point. I didn't mean offense. She told me you're accustomed to a certain lifestyle and wouldn't accept anything less than a well-bred boy." He nudged me and laughed. "Sounds like your exact words, eh?" For the first time since Grandma Grodzki had died, I laughed, too. "I thought I had the wrong house, the wrong person's mother. But she warned me that I had better be 'damned successful' if I wanted to court her little Amelia, so when she said your name, I knew I was in the right place after all. Anyway, I told her I supposed I must have looked like a tramp to her. She didn't seem to think it funny."

"Hope she didn't scare you."

"It was interesting. You know, I have met a man that mean. For the record."

I was relieved he wasn't so much intimidated as he was intrigued by Kat. "Mother's obsessed with money."

"Oh, she made that clear."

"She wants us to be well off. I don't understand why—if you want to know the truth, we never have been."

I walked at a fast clip. "My mother is also a liar," I added.

"Do you want to sit and talk awhile?" Jake asked. "I'll listen. I'm fairly good at that."

"She's a dirty liar," I said with more heat in my voice. I could feel it rising in me. And without a second thought, I told Jake everything, everything Grandma Grodzki had told me, only leaving out the bits about the hidden money.

"I don't know how to be mad at her *for this* because I'm always mad at her, but I love her, too, and I respect her. She makes me respect her. When I'm old enough, I want to just leave."

Jake didn't seem to know what to say, I could tell. He shifted awkwardly, then asked if he could carry the flowers for me. My hand was beginning to get tight, so I handed them over as we walked for two blocks in silence. "Even though he doesn't want anything to do with me, I sure wish she'd been honest. I wish someone would tell me my father was still alive."

"People do a lot to avoid embarrassment, but it is odd. That's the thing about your mother. I got the impression she doesn't care what people think. But this is wild. Your father … what all did she say?"

"It's not like a story in a book; he doesn't want me. Grandma said he didn't want to be a father. I can't just tell him he wants me. I can't make him. He has a wife and a quiet life somewhere. I've been trying to get mother to love me forever, and that hasn't worked." I shook my head and sucked in hard to keep my breath. It was as though something were finally being released inside of me. "It's overwhelming."

Jake put his arm around me. "Your presence is overwhelming."

He'd said it seriously, intensely, and the comment worked its way into my stomach in a strange, unexpected but pleasing way. I was processing everything out loud, and I'd never truly done that before—not with Betty, not with anyone. Not even Grandma Grodzki. With her, I knew to listen. I couldn't give up even a word for fear I'd miss something she wanted to offer.

I leaned into Jake, and he leaned into me. The pressure of his lips on mine felt both soft and forceful. To lock into him like that was more than I could have imagined, but it also felt different. I didn't want him to ever pull away.

Within days, Kat's saccharin demeanor began to fade, revealing the intensity she usually exuded. The temporary domesticity she'd shown was gone, perhaps a side effect of grief, and now she didn't so much as empty the trash in her bedroom. Accustomed to "office" life, she had taken to leaving her wastebasket outside her closed bedroom door so I could empty it. I was expected to do everything, and even entertain the men and women Kat brought over from time to time.

For me, weeks passed in a blur. Jake was with me every day to walk me home, and every school day, we kissed. Every day, Jake asked me about myself, and I told him. I became used to sharing what went on in my mind. I even told him about the occasional visions, and how they felt more like a burden than a gift.

"I understand," he said. And he did. I couldn't have imagined a man understanding—but the way he looked at me in that moment, I knew he meant it.

"Mother doesn't get home until six most days," I told Jake. "Want to come in? I can't allow the house to fall apart, but I can invite you over to talk while I clean. Perhaps we can study together?" I was going to ask him to accompany me to the place behind the staircase. I was finally ready to see what was there.

"I wouldn't want to get caught by that mother of yours. Can you imagine?"

"She would murder us both," I agreed. There was no hint of exaggeration in my comment, and Jake seemed wise to this. "But I could make absolute sure she would be gone before I invite you. She usually goes out to meet a woman on Tuesdays, Thursdays and Fridays. They have cocktails. Maybe I can drop a hint that I'll be looking forward to spending the evening with her one of those days, and when she admits she'll be away, I'll know for sure she'll be gone. I'll invite you."

"What if she changes her mind and thinks it would be quite a nice idea to spend time with you?"

This made me laugh so hard my stomach ached.

The plan was set. I wore a checkered skirt that Tuesday and, at breakfast, asked Mother if she wouldn't mind doing my math homework with me that night. "We're going over percentages, and it might be interesting for the business," I tempted. "I'll make chicken and rice, and we can have a girls' night in."

"I'll be out tonight," Kat said, eyeing me. "Let's look at the percentages on Wednesday."

"Wednesday is okay."

"Amelia, don't you try to guilt me into staying home. I have two days of the week I go out, maybe three, and that's not much. Now that your grandmother is gone, it is difficult for me. Don't be spoiled."

I thought about how I did everything around the house as I

said, "Yes, Mother. I apologize. Wednesday is fantastic. So, you won't be eating tonight, then? I don't need to keep a plate for you?"

"I might come home after work. Go ahead and fix me a plate. Keep it in the ice box. I'll take a nibble." Kat planted a sticky kiss on my cheek and whispered into my ear, "You're a good girl, and I want you to know I appreciate it."

She pulled back and, still in a near-whisper so that I had to concentrate to hear, she added, "This is going to be excellent training for you. You'll make a remarkable wife. And we will find you a distinguished husband. You have my word."

"I don't want to think about a husband, Mother. I want to get through school first."

"We'll see. And by the by, I know about that dark-haired young man who's walking you home from school. I've checked up on him, and he's only good for a little fun. Don't get too serious. His family has nothing—this is not the kind of man your pretty self can catch. This face! No boys, unless I approve, hear? You're all I have left." She ran her palm across my cheek admiringly. "You'll thank me later. I promise you."

"Mother, please! It makes me sick to my stomach. And that boy is nothing. He likes me; I don't like him," I said as convincingly as possible.

"Mmnhm. Well, good," Kat clapped her hands. "Good, good, good. Good girl."

It was a plan. I would let Jake in through the back door when I was cleaning the kitchen, a time Kat was sure to be gone. It wasn't the most romantic way for him to enter, but it would have to do. Kat couldn't suspect later.

The thought of Jake in my home was delightful, something like knowing I was about to eat ice cream and had the night to myself to draw. I ran home from school, insisting on leaving before him so that nothing looked suspicious. Once home, I waited eagerly.

Kat was home when I got there, which was odd, but she was getting ready to go out. I worried she might suspect, but maybe it was something else. Kat looked especially fetching this night. She wore

Grandma Grodzki's pearls and an emerald-colored dress; the better
Mother looked, I had come to know, the later the night.

"I left work early today. Can you believe? All caught up. How do
I look?" Kat asked.

"Like a movie star, Mother. Would you still like me to make you
chicken?"

"Are you senile, little one? I told you I'd be out. This is an
important social event. Important people from the office will be there,
and I'll be working the room until the wee hours." Kat always called her
nights out important social events, but I imagined Mother meeting Helen
at a bar and dancing all night long. "Give your mother a kiss," Kat said,
gesturing to her cheek and bending down. I gave her a soft peck and tried
to contain my excitement as she walked out.

The house suddenly looked so filthy and humble. I began
sweeping and ran around, cleaning every corner and dusting all the bookshelves. I took a wet rag to the couch and double-checked there were no
stray dishes, that the crystal ash trays were cleaned and sparkling.

Before I knew it, it was 6:30 p.m., and the house looked as good
as it could. I eyed the staircase as I sat there, almost out of breath from
busying myself. Looking around as though someone might appear out
of thin air, I felt a twinge in my stomach as I crawled into the space
beneath the stairs, finding exactly what I believed I would. There was a
cheap-looking magazine opened to an article on women and equality by
Crystal Eastman called "Now We Can Begin." I sat, reading it, forgetting
time and space. Even Jake. The old article was published the year before
I was born.

There were notes in the margins—not my grandmother's hand-
writing, but Kat's. I imagined her longing for freedom as I read the words,
"Now they can say what they are really after; and what they are after, in
common with all the rest of the struggling world, is freedom." When I
finally realized the time, I retrieved Grandma Grodzki's Tarot cards. I
tucked them in my waistband of my skirt and crawled back out, adjusting
the wood panel that covered the space.

The only thing left to do was to collect any trash, so I ran upstairs to check the wastebaskets in the bathroom and outside of my mother's door. I stopped at the vanity mirror to check my hair and noticed a few streaks of dirt on my shirt. Probably from the crawlspace. I tried to brush them off with my hand and smoothed my hair, setting the cards down in front of me.

Placing my palm on the cards, the way Grandma Grodzki would before readings, I felt a warmth. I slid one card to the top and glanced down. They were imperfect, made by a local printer and probably illegal. The card I selected said "judgement" and depicted a threadbare woman with arms extended upward toward the sky. An angel looked down. This would mean rebirth and absolution if the card was facing the opposite way. For me, it meant something else. The inverse.

On the vanity were a variety of powders and creams, lipsticks, and bobby pins. I sat up straight on the dainty white chair that Mother loved and I disliked for the exact same reasons.

There was a soft red lipstick that I dotted onto my lips and blended with my thumb. Instantly, I appeared ancient and, somehow, cold. I kept on, lining my eyebrows with a brown pencil and looked older still. My reflection was pale, soft, and for an uncomfortable moment, I saw more. I could see the future. Myself as a wife. No happiness. No Jake.

I added a bit of the creamy lipstick to each cheek and blended it upward, the way I'd seen Kat do so many times. My feet became ice as I stared at this possibility. The reflected me was just possibility. One of any number. This is what I told myself, that it wasn't a prediction, it was just possibility. An option. I could follow my mother's path and finally endear her to me.

But I knew better even then.

I examined my reflection one last time. "You're so beautiful. You'll find a rich husband. Blah, blah, blah." I looked myself right in my eyes and stuck out my tongue.

Placing everything back where it was, carefully, to remove any evidence of my trespassing, I ran out of the room. My feet wouldn't warm, and suddenly I heard the whispering again, followed by a scream and something breaking in the far reaches of my mind. I closed my eyes and waited for the sensation to pass. As I stopped at the doorway to pick up the wastebasket, I spied a tightly folded piece of pink-hued paper similar to the one Helen had left the day she came over. I knelt and unfolded it.

"Tonight is the night, my love. We got in. We're VIP," the note said. It was the same loopy cursive I had read before. It must have been a note from today. I tossed the note among the tissues and cigarette butts in the basket and took it outside to the trashcans that lined the street, the cards again tucked in the waistband of my skirt.

"Am I too early?" a deep voice asked from the opposite side of the screen door.

I jumped, turned, and saw Jake peeking out from behind a bush on the side of the house. He'd purposely lowered his voice.

"You couldn't get here fast enough. Come on, hurry, you goof," I said. I looked around, eyeing the windows of the neighbors' homes to make sure no one was watching. We appeared to be in the clear. Rushing back into the house, I let Jake in through the back door and released my breath as I placed a hand to his chest, feeling that his heart too was racing.

"I'm good at making a quick getaway," Jake said with a crafty grin. "May I sit?"

"How formal! May you? Yes, please," I said. I pulled out a chair and sat at the small wooden table where I usually ate silent dinners with Mother or by myself as I worked on my homework. "I thought I'd still be cleaning when you got here, but I'm done. I suppose we'll just have to chat." I reached back for the cards, which were sticking me in the back. Unsure, I allowed them to be visible in my hands. "I have to put these away."

"That's a crazy-looking game," he said, and I nodded. "You know, I was going to offer to help you with your work, but truth is, A, I really didn't want to. I have enough chores of my own. Mom doesn't let me off for being a boy."

"Ha! How sweet of you to think to offer, but in case you haven't noticed, this place is pristine."

"I'm not sweet." He gave me a crafty smile and reached out his hand, eyeing the cards. "I like this. I like being in a house with just you."

We kissed delicately. And after an indefinite amount of time, which might have been a second and might have been an hour, we pulled apart, still connected, and Jake looked as though he wanted to kiss me again immediately. "I want to show you something," I said.

Jake looked down. "Sure, um, yeah."

What I wanted to say in that moment is what I'm no longer afraid to say. I wanted to show him the place behind the stairs. I wanted to unearth the treasure and tell Jake, "Let's run. Let's run far away and start anew." But fear stopped me. Instead, I reached for the paper and said, "I think my mother is up to something. I know you like mysteries, and I think this is one. Be right back."

I removed the panel, throwing the deck of cards into a dark corner. When I reentered the room, Jake was sitting properly, hands crossed on his lap, and looking serious. "Why are we always talking about your mother? She fills the space around you even when she's not here."

"I want to know what she's up to, so we can continue to meet. I want to know her schedule. She's not working at any office. Or if she is, she's not there much."

"Interesting. You think we could do this regularly? Meet like this?"

"If I know what she's up to!"

"Well, I'll help you figure it out." He grinned a moment, then went to his silent place.

"Thank you and that happens to be my favorite book. But, first, you're right. We talk about my mother and me all the time. The mystery of Kat. But what about the mystery of Jake? We never talk about you," I said. "One thing I know from my mother is a secretive person always lets the other talk, and the secretive person does this because he has something to hide. I'm not saying you must tell me anything deep and dark, but I don't know much about you. Tell me something."

He reached for my hand again, a gesture I'd never grow tired of, and held it in a loose grip, then stood to his full, towering height. "You're a smart girl, but you're wrong. I have no deep, dark secrets. I'm an open book. I just haven't been read."

"I love to read," I said. "We can read each other."

"How about we read you first."

My feet still felt like ice, but they were slowly melting. A wedding veil flashed in front of my eyes, and I saw Kat looking satisfied. I heard a whoosh of words: *She's up to something. Something bad. They're looking for him. They're recruiting him. They're going to win.*

Jake kissed me again, and I felt as though I awoke with his touch, but I was startled at the way the steady stream of words had paraded over my thoughts. Whatever the whispering was, whatever the visions were, they would pass. They had to. I had to be present. I looked Jake in the eyes and felt his sobering stare warm me.

"I'm sorry. I don't know what's wrong with me. I get stuck on a topic, and I can't stop thinking about it. It's this feeling, these … words and images that flash."

"The knowing," he said. "I get it. Let's talk about ordinary things. If your mother is really on your mind that much, we can talk about her. Go on. We'll talk about me one day."

I didn't miss a beat. "I don't know. She goes to a place called Calypso and stays out until morning. She comes home acting strange and sometimes brings people home. I hear them. Sometimes I hear them in my room. I worry she's trying to put me on display like a purse or dress to sell. But sometimes I think it's just dreams."

"You think she's bringing people into your room?"

"I know she wants to. Or will. That's where my brain gets fuzzy. The reality and the visions…"

He put his hand on my knee as my face grew hot. I was embarrassed by my inability to articulate.

"I know where Calypso is. It's just a few blocks toward the river. We can go scope it out," he said. "Find out what she's up to."

"Tonight?"

"Well, yeah. It'll be an adventure." There was a childlike excitement to Jake's face; it was contagious. "If we know what she's up to, we can come up with a plan."

Without a word, I ran to the closet and grabbed my coat. This night would prove even more adventurous than I had imagined. Yet, I eyed the staircase. "We have to be careful," I said. "You should leave first, wait for me. I'll catch up to you at the mailbox at the end of the street. I'll put on heels. I want to blend in."

Before I knew it, Jake's mouth was pushing with gentle force against my lips again, and when we kissed this time, it was all business. I had so much to tell him, but our plan was good. If I could figure out what Mother was up to, I could plan a way out. I could avoid what I'd seen in the mirror.

For Jake and me, the partnership was established and sealed. He understood me in ways I couldn't imagine then. What I did know is if we got into trouble, we'd get into trouble together.

Chapter Nineteen: Emerson

My mother remained by my side. But as Amelia had warned, this felt a little dangerous. Arriving at the school for Lori's race after a long and silent car ride, I realized for the first time how few people attended track meets. Rita couldn't come because she was teaching yoga, and though we were early, Dad and I made up about a fourth of the attendees. We were taking our seats on the shallow benches when I noticed a dark green Hyundai speeding onto the gravel lot. It parked sloppily, at a diagonal, and Courtney emerged beaming.

She was carrying two buckets of ravioli and fettuccini from The Spaghetti Shop, which she held up proudly when she saw me, and my cheeks began to feel the strain of my smile.

"What is my friend doing?" I asked no one in particular. Dad shrugged and reached for his sunglasses.

"I brought Italian," Courtney said, plopping herself down on the bench with two vats of food.

"What in the—how are we supposed to eat that? A hotdog or sandwich would make more sense." Dad scratched his head, and someone in the bleachers two rows back chuckled.

"Maybe. All I know is that I was craving Italian, and I just aced my second pre-calculus test, which brings me up from the A- Mom was giving me hell about. It's celebration time!" I wondered if all was well between us, or Courtney was just doing what Courtney could do— showing up as though all was good while she tried to pretend to be okay with everything. Writing was her release, always had been. It allowed her to put on a good face no matter what. Trying not to tune in, not to intrude, I saw her writing feverishly and balling up papers in her room.

She wore a distracted smile, as I looked around. "Are there plates in that fancy new car?" I asked.

"Um. That would've helped. Look, I'm on Cloud Nine over here."

Courtney had been gifted the five-year-old Hyundai as an early graduation present, in place of the brand new one she would have gotten with acceptance into a "real" college program, i.e. political science at an Ivy League school, rather than journalism at a state school. She said her parents called her a "late bloomer" before they offered her the keys to their old car. My father said something neutral about how parents just worry, then he looked to me, breaking our silence.

"You're going to have to buy your own car no matter how you bloom," he said with a hint of levity in his voice.

"Ten-four."

"Maybe we'll have to wait to eat this," Courtney said, evaluating the situation in front of her: napkins and forks, buckets of pasta covered in sauce.

Now my father really laughed. I tried to join in.

"Eating pasta at a track meet is a novel idea. I think you'll make a fine writer, Courtney."

"Good one, sir!"

"That's a Dad joke if I've ever heard one," I said.

Courtney examined her food. "My brain! Ugh. I had the order in when I remembered I needed to be here. Good news is that pasta only gets better. It'll be good after the race."

I nudged her. "Thanks for coming."

She nodded as we heard the rustling of runners moving toward the start line. Lori looked up from the track. She was decked out in her spandex with an orange stripe going from ankle to armpit. My big little sister, almost a foot taller than me now, who had been there for me when I needed her. "Go, Lori!" I yelled. She waved a fist in mock-anger as her face reddened. Though my sister didn't smile, I could see how much our presence meant

It was one of the first sunny days in a while, but the air was crisp. My sister was serious business, resembling the Olympians we'd watch jump and stretch at the start line with kinesiology tape on their legs and shoulders. As she stretched in a circle of fit men and women who looked just as intense as she did, I felt my mother's presence with me. She sat somewhere in the bleachers a row ahead, clapping and screaming just as I had.

"Look at her," Dad said, elbowing me gently. "This is nice. It feels like a true family event. I'm glad we could all do this." Mom looked back at him as he smiled whimsically, and a gust of warm air arrived.

We cheered as the runners perched their fingers, lifting tailbones to the sky. There were so many of them they had to be released in heats, and with each new group to approach the start line, we cheered. As boring as I thought it would be, it was rather exhilarating to watch their legs move so rhythmically, hypnotically. It was when my sister's heat, the third to go, took off when I felt Courtney's hand on my back then waist. She tugged me gently as my sister fell into line in the first lane. With each loop, her stride seemed to extend, and when she crossed the finish line with arms up in a victory 'V,' I hopped up and down like a child. Mom did as well, screaming about how proud she was. When the small crowd settled down, Mom faded from sight.

"I'm going to get something to drink," I said. Courtney followed. We rushed down the bleachers, passing portable bathroom stations and arriving near a row of food trucks.

I felt heat near my ear. "Sorry I've been MIA. It's just crazy at home, and I had some feelings to work out ... and now, well, I feel good. I finally have a plan of my own. I didn't want to say this in front of your father, but my parents and I really threw down. It was epic. I told them I wasn't going to be a fucking lawyer no matter what and they'd have to deal. I really stood my ground. They blamed you. Said you were a bad influence."

"Me? Well, I'll take it."

"I know it's bullshit, but ... I don't know how to say this. I mean, I've been falling behind and stuck in this fantasy land. And I've been thinking," Courtney said. "About our future."

"Fantasy land?" Something compelled me toward her then. It wasn't coming from a place of anger or defense. Before she had the chance to say anything else, I placed my hand on her forearm and leaned in, kissing her awkwardly and feeling my face go hot. "I need you around," I said.

When her phone rang, we both startled. Her shoulders sagged. "Mom doesn't want me to hang out with you till at least graduation. She thinks you're the reason my grades are dropping. I love you. I love ... I love that kiss, but maybe it's not time. I mean, you and Ian..." She stepped away from me, and I threw up my hands as Amelia might, trying to control what, in that moment, I couldn't.

"I made a mistake, but I was just trying to feel something. The stakes were low with Ian. With you, they're everything. With you, it's my life. I tried to tell you."

"Emerson ... It's all getting a little weird for me," she said. "It's not Amelia, it's you. You seem overwhelmed and not on this fucking planet, to be honest." She lifted her phone but didn't answer. I tuned in, wanting to know what she meant. I could see how confused she was. My entire body swelled in that moment, and recalled our drawings of the future, seeing them come to life.

"Overwhelmed?" I asked, looking away and seeing my mother. She looked concerned as I gazed toward the distance.

"Yes, and distracted. And..."

"Crazy? Insane? Well, you're fucking boring. This existence is boring."

"No." Courtney knitted her eyebrows and gave my arm a squeeze as I realized she was asking for space not just to accommodate her own, living mother but because it's what *she* wanted. "Maybe we should take a little break, just until the end of the term," she said, stepping away as the phone stopped ringing. "And maybe. I don't know, Em, maybe I can't help you after all."

I nodded. "Yeah okay."

"I better call her back."

I wanted to stop her, yell at her, explain how much I needed her right now, but the way she was looking at me is the way one looks at a feral animal. She was terrified.

There was no one to talk to but Amelia, and I needed her, but the words wouldn't come.

Courtney dialed, adjusted her voice in pitch and tone while she walked, explaining to her mother where she was. I heard her say, "It's a few hours! I'm telling her about my priorities. We discussed this!" as she walked beyond the food trucks, the school. When it seemed she'd be on the phone for a while, I journeyed into a neighborhood with low fences and ranch-style homes that all looked the same in different colors, unsure what had just happened, unsure what I was going to say. Mom walked alongside, and I reached out my hand.

"Is it wrong I brought you back?" I asked.

"It's not right or wrong," she said. "It was time. Now that you know there's more, you can let me go."

I could no longer feel her hand. Realizing I was alone, I began to walk faster, across a bridge and into a different neighborhood. Examining the duplexes with their Victorian sharpness and gothic presence, I stared up at the attics, wondering whose memories were buried above the living and how they influenced the present. Everything and everyone held a story that became a portal to the past and future. I'd read that time is not linear but a spiral, a series of events along a causal chain that circles back. I remember drawing the spiral and thinking it wasn't quite right either.

When my feet began to tingle, I circled back. The sky was full of billowy clouds, and the air was just crisp enough to bite. There were no trees to shade this street, only wisteria and flowerpots. It was all pavement and repetition. I felt both more linked to my family and more alone in the world than I ever had.

I took my time to walk back and settled in at one of the tents with a sign out front which read, "Waters + Bananas" with rows of empty folding chairs and a small stage. I was the first one to the tent, and I took a seat up front. When Dad and Courtney arrived, each holding a large plastic bucket of cold pasta, we all sat in a cluster of awkward silence.

"You okay?" Dad asked, and I nodded. He and Courtney looked like they'd been talking about me.

My sister got first place among the women in her age group, twelfth among all the women who'd run the race in heats. Courtney and I sat on either side of my father, and we both cheered louder than anyone else in the tent as my sister received her award. Lori was happy enough to not notice the heaviness between us. We ordered heavy mochas with whipped cream and chocolate shavings from a food truck, and my sister drank a protein shake and ate two bran muffins to "warm up" for our dinner. She insisted on riding home with Courtney and me.

Donning her medal on the ride, my sister clutched the backseat handle as Courtney made sharp turns and sped home. The cold ravioli shifted from one side of the car to the next as we left Dad in the dust behind us. Lori was exhausted and proud, and she told us about the race, how one woman she sees at all the races and who always wins twisted her ankle around the fourth mile and dropped out. She said it was going to be the race she would finally beat her, and she figured the woman was faking; my sister talked about each mile, she talked and talked, and I was glad we came.

"Thanks for coming. Please don't kill me with your NASCAR driving, Courtney," Lori said from the back seat.

"I think I should drop you all and head out. You keep the food," Courtney said as she parked in front of our house. She opened the door to the car and hugged my sister weakly, congratulating her once more.

"There's a half-marathon coming up. Don't forget," Lori said. She grabbed the fettuccini bucket and made her way inside. I followed, looking back at Courtney, who didn't return my gaze. I knew better than to tune into her thoughts, but I did it anyway. I sensed her confusion, the desire she felt to stay, but I heard her parents' voices louder, almost choir-like, and she was listening to them now because she felt abandoned. I didn't sense anger about what I'd done, but she was hurt because I'd been self-absorbed and hadn't trusted her enough to talk to her. I wanted to beg for her forgiveness, to tell her I would do better, but it was too late.

When Dad arrived, my sister was sitting intently behind two small mountains of pasta while simultaneously devouring a piece of garlic bread with her free hand. She always managed to eat twice as much as any of us would before we even had food on our plates. "I'm carb loading," Lori said. "Have to replenish."

"What is it like to be a superstar? Is that thing heavy?" I asked.

"You have a math trophy from—what was it? Second grade?" she reminded me.

Rita, who had adorned the house with streamers and balloons, arrived with a small cake. "Gluten free, but there is dairy."

Dad showed Rita pictures of Lori's slim, tall body leaning in as she crossed the finish line. The night was about my sister, but it moved by in a blur. While everything ordinary was happening, I felt my mother's energy flickering, like I was truly losing her.

I texted Courtney later. "I'm sorry. I know how I sounded, and I'm sorry. Will you come to TLH one last time? Say goodbye. This will be it, and I'll be ready to move on. I know I've been scaring everyone."

"I'd love to, but I'm committed. Maybe invite Ian?" she texted back.

And there it was.

"I need you, not him," I wrote Courtney, then I scanned the texts from Ian. He was a kind person, and I'd been completely ignoring him. "I'm sorry I haven't been reaching out. I just need to move on. It was my mistake."

"No shit," he wrote back.

"I'm sorry," I texted again.

"I'm sorry," I texted Courtney.

I sat there for a long time, tapping my fingernail on the screen of my phone before powering it down. I made a cup of ginger tea, lit a candle, and wrote my final letter before venturing up to the attic to pack Mom's clothes away for donation. As I sifted through her paintings, I thought about my date with Ian, imagining her work on the walls of the theater. I cried in the attic until my face was raw. I cried curled up in a ball, forehead to the ground. I realized that I never let myself say goodbye. In the last five years, I hadn't shed a single tear because I hadn't let her go. But now I had her story. I no longer needed her things. The decision presented to me at twelve was in front of me once again. Only this time I knew what was at stake. I had to choose for myself or let the world choose for me. Neither way would be easy.

Chapter Twenty: Amelia

I wanted more. Though we can change things in this world, we can't manipulate it, at least not for long. Freedom of thought is liberation, but it's more than that. When I found this out, I realized why my mother was so tortured. Trying to manipulate leads to disappointment. We endure as we grow, and this means we need patience. She didn't have that.

She was trying to win a game of power, and it's a losing game. Grandma Grodzki knew the deeper truth—we are only as strong as we can be apart from what and who holds supposed power. What we have is connection, to the earth, to the internal pulse that reminds us who we are. We have our own mind, and it will scream at us if we're on the wrong track.

Truth is, at the time, I was trying to distract myself from the screaming by chasing my mother around like a detective. A small part of me still had hope for her because she was part of a counterculture that seemed empowered to me, a wave of post-flapper women who were tough. I was stalling on my dreams, what truly called me, because I was too afraid to do what I genuinely wanted—to run away.

Meanwhile, Jake and I felt like we were on a movie set. The worldly excitement of the moment pulsed through us. The club was dark. Long black cars were lined up out front, and a man in a small knit cap handed out valet tickets in exchange for keys. Men in long coats and fedoras exited the cars alone or in pairs. There seemed to be no women arriving with them like at restaurants. Jake whispered if he could just find a coat and hat, he'd probably be able to go in without raising any suspicion. I looked at him in the low light, and he appeared older than he was.

"Mother met you, and if she's really in that place, she'll spot you right away. She's a hawk." Looking around, I noticed a side entrance where a cluster of people were smoking and laughing. "Let's see if we can peek in."

We walked around to the back of the club where there was yet another entrance, but it was closed off. From the back, we stood tall, holding hands, and when a man walked past us in an all-black uniform, I mustered the courage to stop him. "Sir, excuse me, I think my sister is in that club, but I'm not sure. Will they let me in?"

The man, who was balding and round, bit his lip playfully and looked me up and down like a predator. "My dear, I think any room would welcome you."

"Yes, yes she could," Jake said, putting his arm around me protectively. "You wouldn't have a smoke on you?" He was trying to sound like a man. A tad annoying, a tad endearing.

"Sure thing. Would you like one, too, my lovely?"

I wanted to laugh at the man's speech. Instead, I said, "I'd love a cigarette. Thank you."

The man revealed a neat metal case and gave it a good tap. Three cigarettes slid halfway out, like magic. He offered one to me first, but Jake reached over and grabbed two. He handed me one, eying the man, and stuck his behind his ear. He refused to acknowledge Jake's stare. He exposed a flame to Jake without taking his eyes off me, which made me remember something Grandma Grodzki had suggested.

"Imagine pink light all around you for protection."

I was uncomfortable, but also oddly flattered. I leaned into Jake, pressing my cheek to his chest as he guided me away. The round man waved, then offered me the light. "Have a good time, kids. Maybe I'll see you inside after my shift."

We started walking toward the side where, much like at the front, there were only men.

"Hello there," a tall man said from under the awning. He was giving me the same look, and I was beginning to feel as though I was on display. I stopped walking, which caused Jake to stumble a bit. His arm was still wrapped around me.

"I don't know about this place. Are you sure there isn't another Calypso?"

"Ha! Are you sure you're not the new act?" the man asked. As he got closer, I could see that he was older than I'd thought, probably in his fifties. He spoke out of the side of his mouth. "You're the spitting image of Hedy Lamarr. In fact, you might be too beautiful to work these rooms. The men are rich, but they can be vulgar. Only a few of them are as refined as we look." He turned to Jake and asked, "What's her name?"

"Why are you asking me? She has a mouth."

"And a brain," I added. "What do you mean, act? Is this a burlesque or something?"

"We host all kinds of talent," the man said. "We're not hiring. But this young lady is a real catch. You sing?"

"She's not here for that. She was looking for someone. But never mind. We'll leave."

"Ha! I know exactly who she's looking for," the man said. He got close, and as Jake put his hand up toward the man's chest, the man simply brushed it away. "I'm not going to hurt the girl. I'm just looking at her." He stared at me hard, but not in an invasive way, as the man in all black had; rather, in a genuinely appreciative way. He seemed amused, and, suddenly, he snapped his fingers in the air and pointed at the sky. "God, please! Grant me the serenity to accept the things I cannot change."

"This man is insane. Let's go before I have to knock him down," Jake said, barely moving his lips. I could see how upset he was and wanted to tell him I wasn't afraid. In fact, the man intrigued me as much as I seemingly intrigued him.

"You're the daughter of a remarkably interesting woman. Am I wrong?"

"Sir, please. Please don't tell her."

"You're not supposed to be out this way, eh? I won't say anything. Secrets are always safe with me. Bob Rand." He extended his hand, first to Jake, then to me. "You come back when you're older. This isn't a burlesque club, it's a whole other world. A world of art. You, from

what I hear, can appreciate such a world." He grinned, tipped his hat.
"See you in a year or two, Amelia. You better get going. Your mother
could come out here for a smoke any minute. The other women smoke
inside."

He smiled at me in a knowing way before turning back to the
other men, who were now toasting snifter glasses to something and
laughing voraciously. I felt I knew Bob Rand in that moment, as though
he'd reached inside my body and taken up space.

"I don't think your mother works an office job," Jake said.

"Huh." It was all I could manage.

"That guy in black was lucky I didn't knock him out cold. You
know? But the Bob fella was different. I guess your mother does have
some serious secrets," Jake said after a long, silent walk. "Maybe he's a
gangster."

My head was swimming with the possibilities. I couldn't see
Mother as a performer. Not even with using all my imagination and
intuition combined. I closed my eyes and tried to infiltrate the club, tried
to see what I could not. Could Mother be dating Bob Rand?

"He could be a gangster, I guess." I stopped walking and lifted
my foot. "These heels are horribly painful to walk in. I've never worn
them this long."

"I'll bet. I wouldn't want to be a girl … You know, I don't
hold anything against those burlesque dancers. They shake a little tail in
exchange for rent. I don't blame them. No, sir."

"You're not a normal boy," I told him. Had I been any other
girl in the world I would have been offended by half of the things he
said; instead, I could see that he was genuinely trying to figure things
out, holding up his mirror to the world. Jake spoke to me with the same
candor my brother used to. "My mother has simply confused me more,
and I didn't think it possible."

"I'm only saying if she's a dancer, that's not so bad. You'll have
to be smart about this now. You can't go around telling all those pious
girls you hang around. They'll burn you alive, and their mothers will
clean up the evidence. If I were you, I wouldn't think badly of her."

"If I think anything bad about Mother, it won't be for hanging out at clubs. It'd be for everything else." In this case, I was wrong. I was too distracted to pay attention, to connect the dots. What was to come would be so much worse than I could see at the time, but I knew my mother was connected to these people in a different way.

We reached the mailbox and shared a long hug that worked to combat the chill of the night. It's truly magical how something as simple as a hug can feel life-changing, but it did.

"I won't say anything," Jake whispered. "But I do want to be with you. Next week? We try this again, what do you say? I bet if we go later, we can sneak a look in the side door."

"Or we could visit here. I'll let you know." I walked off, purposely exaggerating my hips to be funny, but he didn't notice, which made me love him even more. I hurried home.

Once inside, I rushed up to Mother's room. This time, I wasn't careful at all. I rummaged through the closet. There was nothing suggesting Mother was a performer: no tassels, no scanty underthings, nothing. There were only suits and reasonable undergarments, except for a silk robe which, though racy on Kat's generous chest, I couldn't imagine as a costume. I checked the room for notes. I was driven to find something, some other clue before Kat came home that night. I had to brace myself for what might happen if Bob broke his word. An internal nagging told me to stop, to smoke a cigarette and calm down. It was my craving—a self-serving purpose, and it felt necessary to indulge.

After straightening Kat's clothes, I stood by the icebox, pushing my tongue to the roof of my mouth. The stale taste made me sick. The nicotine coated my cheeks. I worked the events around in my head and decided I would return to the club at another time and talk with Bob Rand. I'd have to convince Jake to hang back. If I spoke to Bob alone, he might tell me about Kat, where she got that money she wanted me to do numbers on. Was it gambling?

When I heard my mother wail from the other room, I knew not to investigate. The next day, I felt like myself again. No more stale taste in my mouth or sense of curiosity. I just wanted to feel like a kid. I made

Mother dinner and wore Grandma Grodzki's apron, which wrapped around me twice.

Kat was at the table reading the news as I set the placemats and plates down. She didn't so much as move her paper aside or look up for a long time, then, out of nowhere, as I sat down to eat, Kat smiled brightly and folded the paper. "Darling daughter, I think we should buy you a dress this weekend. I think you deserve it the way you've been working so hard around here."

"Mother, really? Thanks." I immediately imagined Jake's reaction to me in a new dress. He might laugh at first, but I knew he'd secretly like it. "That's swell. Can Betty come with us, to help pick it out?"

Kat twirled her fork. "She's a mouthy girl. But I suppose."

"Thank you." I rarely got new clothes.

"We might get you a sweater, too. I got quite a big bonus from work. Boss said I was the absolute fastest worker he'd seen. He said things were running smoother than ever, so he gave me a bump in pay, too. I even have a new title: Office Manager."

"That's great." I was relieved the meal was going so smoothly—there was no awkward talk of Bob Rand and no evidence of her having noticed I had been in her room. I kissed Mom on the cheek gently before clearing the plates.

"Oh, and Amelia, Sunday, I'm going to take you on a trip. We have a car on loan from a friend, and I think I'm going to introduce you, officially, to my friend Helen. She lives out a ways, up north where all the farmland begins."

The second after Kat left for the club that next week, Jake showed up at the backdoor. He rushed in, apologetic for his appearance. The apology was warranted, I thought.

"You look like a ragamuffin."

"I had to come quickly, after practice, and it was a tough practice. Something just told me to come."

"Well, you do look quite manly." I laughed. "Are you up for this again? Nancy Drew and The Hardy Boys?"

"I don't think I would feel right if I saw your mother performing. Well, that and I'm far from fancy-looking right now. We have a few hours though, right? Maybe I can clean up."

"I don't want to leave until dark. And Kat is no dancer. We agreed on that."

"Probably not, but there's a chance. And Amelia, if you don't mind, I'd like to keep all my focus on you." He got close to me then, close in a new way—face to face—and this gave me a sharp, almost painful tingle. It was exhilarating being so close to him without kissing, then I took a whiff of him.

"You smell horrible." I laughed, pushing him away.

"I'm sorry. I just couldn't wait to see you. I ran all the way here as tired as I was. In fact, you're lucky I didn't collapse to the ground when you pushed me just now. I'm exhausted. Mind getting me a glass of ice water?"

"I suppose. But in exchange for this water, will you promise to try on one of my brother's suits?"

"Now we're talking." He reached for the decorative glass. He drank the entire thing down in three gulps and handed it back for a refill. "You're a lifesaver. How tall is Gene?"

"A little under six feet."

He shook his head. "The suit won't work."

"You have to try. Kat says she's come into money from a promotion. She says she got a raise and that she's going to buy me a dress. It worries me."

"Because of her secret life?"

"She isn't like that. She never bought me a dress from an actual retail store. All my clothes are handed down. She spends money on only two things: herself and her investments. This is strange."

"One way or another, tonight we'll expose whatever it is she's doing." He sat in the same chair, by the window he'd chosen the last time he was over. He stretched out, comfortable enough to relax. I imagined us creating a home here, raising children and keeping a garden. "Amelia, do you remember what we talked about the last time I was here?"

"Secrets," I said without hesitation. "Cheese toast?" He nodded. I was placing pieces of buttered bread onto the oven rack, each with a thick slice of cheddar on the top.

"That's right, secrets. Like I said before, I've never met a girl who's as honest as you are, so I'll tell you all about me. I don't know that my life is nearly as exciting as yours, but we all have our quirks."

"Oh boy! I'll sit down for this." I rushed over to the table and sat at the edge of my chair. His light brown eyes were gleaming, and he had a subtle crease above his brow. Although somewhat hesitant, he started speaking.

"I'm telling you this, about my family that is, because I'd like you to meet them one day." He paused, reached for a wallet that held a few small photographs. "This is my mother. She was a housewife; now I suppose she's a house mother. She's lax with me, but she rides my sister hard. My sister's much older, already married. The thing I want to tell you, though, the thing I should have told you the day you told me about your father, is my dad wasn't so great either."

"Well, he left a lovely family."

"Mother is duller than yours. She's not a bad woman, but she has her problems, too. She cries a lot when she thinks no one can hear. She runs a tight household, everything in its place, and she spoils me to death. I sometimes worry when this war ends, when all her friends' husbands and sons are coming home; she'll be lonely. See, she has a lot of friends, but she's the only widow."

I watched his face as he spoke, and I could hear his pain whisper to me. I closed my eyes.

"When we used to travel with Dad, Mom was different. She didn't have friends at all. He had a horrible temper, and when I was growing up, he'd just lose it for no reason. He'd yell at her, slap her around, and then yell at her again for being sad about being slapped around."

"That's terrible."

"When those two were together, things weren't good. He hit me a few times too, but I could handle it. If he were alive and tried to do it today, I'd wrestle him to the ground. Do you remember when we first met?" he asked.

"How you said you'd hit your mother back?"

"I didn't mean it. When I turned thirteen, I decided no one would hit me or my mother ever again. If anyone dared it, even if my father came back, I'd wrestle them to the ground. But that same year, my father shipped out. He died from friendly fire. And as harsh as he was. Well, it's hard to explain, but I still miss him. I miss him, but I don't want to turn into him. I tell you because, well, I might. I mean, I just said that that day."

"And," I interjected, "I might turn into my mother."

He chuckled a bit. "That's impossible, but if we both did, I guess it'd be a good fight. You know, my sister would sure like you. She'd probably start following you around like a little puppy. She loves anything beautiful."

My cheeks flushing, I looked down at the table, examined the wood. "I suppose I'm too scared of my mother to hit her back. Maybe one day I'll fight back, too."

"I'll fight for you," Jake said. He kissed me, but this time it wasn't innocent in the least. His tongue was in my mouth, barely. He held my hair in his hand and made a fist around my curls in a gentle way. He tilted his forehead to rest on mine a moment, kissed my temple, my cheek, then began kissing my neck.

"Oh! The toast." I broke away and rushed to the oven. With a thick rag, I pulled out the crispy sourdough slices. The cheese had a hard, glossy look and was black on the edges. "It's burnt."

"It's fine," he said with a smile. "I came to see you; the cheese toast was just a bonus."

As the doorknob to the front door turned, my desires fled the room. Romance and hope crashed before the words even came. "You better run." When Jake refused, I knew I was doomed. I took a breath. "I'll say it again. You better run."

After dropping her keys and purse on the table and removing her shawl, Kat looked directly at us. The front room and hallway to the kitchen became the island of safety separating. It was mother and daughter, face-to-face, finally ready for a showdown.

Jake stood tall, holding on to my shoulder both in support and, I thought, for support as Kat walked slowly toward us.

"Well, well, well. Brave."

"Mother, erm, Kat, we were just making some cheese toast, and it seems to have burnt."

"I bet it did burn." She looked at Jake. "You get the hell out of my house. And, my lovely daughter, I'll deal with you later. I'm heading back to the club. Left my cigarettes." She opened the freezer door and grabbed the white pack, dropped it in her purse. "You heard me, young man." As she walked away, she added, "If I must, I'll have you removed."

"She might call the police or something," I whispered. "You should go. I'll see you at school tomorrow."

"We were being completely innocent, ma'am, just so you know," Jake said.

"I know, my dear," Kat said with a flirtatious smile. "Come here."

Jake didn't move. Instead, he stood stiff and at attention as she sauntered over to him.

"You're a nice-looking boy, but I think you should know Amelia told me all about you. She doesn't like you, and she's only spending time with you because she's lonely. That's a fact. Further, I know your mother, and you don't want a woman like that disappointed in her only son. And I'll make sure she's disappointed. Heartbroken. Hear? Do yourself a favor and find another girl."

"Mother, we're just friends," I said.

"I like your daughter as a friend," Jake said.

"Call me Kat, and let's be clear. Let's be clear, 'friends' between a fella like you and a girl like my daughter doesn't exist. Now, as the owner of this home, I'm going to ask you once more to leave. And now that you've been here; now that you've disrespected me and my daughter, I don't want you near her again. No more walking her to school."

She turned to me and added, "And no more wrestling meets.

You're no cheerleader. I have eyes all over, and if you don't respect me from here on in, I'll find out about it."

She motioned toward the table, the very chair that Jake had warmed only moments ago.

I sat, knowing better than to meet eyes with Jake as Kat walked him to the back door. This was my chance to fight, and I didn't have it in me.

After what he'd just told me, I was impressed by Jake's ability to listen to Kat and not become rattled. He merely left, quietly. He had a way of doing everything the way I wanted him to, and I imagined him finding a good hiding place, showing up later. I knew he must be seething inside.

"Amelia, Amelia, my beautiful daughter. Too beautiful for your own good, eh?"

"We're just good friends."

"I saw you two," Kat said. "If you start lying to me now, you'll lose. Best thing you can do is admit what you were doing, admit your error, and stop seeing that boy. If you lie to me again, I already know the moves you'll make next. I'll know them because I've done them. Show respect! We'll have a talk later. We'll have a real nice talk, and you'll understand why I'm strict with you, young lady."

"I like him," I started to say, but paused. "I respect you, but—"

"No but. Good. Good start. Now, when I begin to believe you, we'll be golden. I know what you need." She pulled a glass off the top shelf of the cupboard. The tall glasses Grandma Grodzki used for holidays; they were the only glasses Kat would drink from. She filled it with milk and took a long drink. "You need another boy to make you forget all about this one."

"Most of the other boys are just plain offensive to be around," I said, thinking about the cat calls Betty would get from those less respectful boys.

"Take the night to study. Keep your mind busy. I'm going back to club." Kat kissed my cheek. "And if you're thinking about running off…" She grabbed my cheeks hard, digging her sharp nails into delicate skin.

"Mother, you're hurting me."

"We have bigger goals, Daughter, so if you're thinking about running off, think better of it." In the heat of anger, Kat threw the glass, still half-filled with whole milk, at the wall, thick, white liquid briefly trailing like a tail. The glass bounced and fell to the ground, where it shattered and sprayed out. A few pieces of glass flew toward my feet. Kat smiled and pressed her lips together tightly, and her eyes all but said 'You'll clean that up.' When she actually spoke, she was calm again, almost darling. "I'll be home around midnight. Maybe. Sleep in something pretty."

After Kat left, I rushed to the small crawlspace behind the stairs. I looked everywhere, feeling the floor and backs of the stairs until, at last, I felt a small bundle of bills taped to the back of the lowest step. I pulled at the tape and released four-hundred dollars, then made my way back into the kitchen. I sat still, money tight in my grip, hoping Jake was hiding somewhere. I sat there without thinking or moving.

I wasn't in shock exactly, but my mind had slowed to a near-stop. I had no desire to move. I knew the next thing I did would determine the course of my entire life, then the thoughts began to flood in, too quick to contain. If I ran off, which Kat must've expected, I'd be on my own for good. Perhaps Jake would want me to do this, but what if he didn't? He didn't have an income; he couldn't support himself, let alone me. He might be drafted. He would be drafted. How could he not be?

If I stayed, I'd become Kat's clay; I'd have to be even more malleable. I knew her plans for me; I knew I wouldn't love the man she found and that he'd be rich. I knew my life would be one of clichés and subservience; I saw it all. I knew Kat would always be at arm's length.

If I stayed, Gene would one day return and maybe then the two of us could leave together. Or maybe he wouldn't come back at all, and I'd be completely alone. The fear of loneliness is what destroys us.

It was one time I wished the chill would come, the premonition of something different or more insightful, just so I'd know, but there was nothing. What a horrible thing, if he didn't come home like Jake's father, and what a cruel thing if he returned injured and I was gone.

He hadn't been happy in California. He wouldn't be happy here, and I wasn't sure he'd received my letters. Chances are, he didn't even know about Grandma Grodzki. I'd read about the way soldiers are easily overwhelmed when returning from war. I couldn't leave him alone.

The milk was pooling alongside the kitchen island, where the floor dipped. My sinuses throbbed, but I couldn't cry. Instead, I swallowed the tears, every salty bit; I tightened the knot on my apron and put the bills inside my pocket. I got onto my hands and knees, hoping Jake would show up at the back door and try to change my mind, hoping I'd have a reason to use the money and start over. I walked around for hours, looking for him, waiting. He never returned.

For a long time, neither did the magic. You see, it changes when we start to compromise. It turns into something else completely.

PART FIVE: THE FUTURE

Chapter Twenty-one: Emerson

I knew that my grandfather's last name was Rand. I'd heard his name from Mom, though she rarely spoke of him. There were two pictures of the two of them together, sepia framed scenes where they held hands and stared at the camera as though waiting patiently for the photographer to be done already. The thought of these images and where Amelia was in the backdrop chilled me. Why were our journeys so complex?

The week leading up to my next visit comprised doctors' appointments and school. The "normal" stuff. I wanted to text Courtney, letting her know how *normal* I was being. How I'd even started a low dose of medication that sent tiny surges through my brain. I had really expected her to text me back, so I had the opportunity to convince her there was no "fantasy land" here lately. I was okay being boring. But it wasn't entirely true.

"Mornings mean a fresh start, new plans," Amelia said, handing me a warm mug of chalky instant coffee. "How are you feeling? Nervous about graduation?"

"No," I said, pressing my palm to my navel. I truly wasn't.

We were sitting in the pale green cafeteria, drinking out of purple cups. It was Sunday. Most residents were in chapel. I examined the paintings on either side of us, magnanimous and expansive. Two owls had a quiet fire in their eyes, as though ready to fight for something noble. They were done in oil, and they looked as though they might fly out toward one another, likely to meet in battle above us. I was consumed by the paintings and content to sit in silence a while as I imagined the stories behind them.

Only two other tables were still occupied, both by staff, at the far corner of the large room. They wore hairnets and bored expressions. The Lavender House was quieter than usual, and I wondered how different life would be for Amelia if she was still living on her own. Did she really have to stay here? Amelia watched me stare at the paintings, and I noticed the odd smile on her face.

"That only works if they're not trying to kill you. Where's the journalist today?" she asked. "Standing us up again?"

"What does that mean?"

"Never mind. So, Courtney. Spill."

"It's complicated. She's mad at me."

"She's in love with you too. But you should be patient," Amelia said. I spit out some of my coffee. "You don't need magic for that. There's nothing wrong with love. There's only pain when we fight it."

I dabbed at the coffee, feeling the eyes of staff on me and refusing to look back and put my hands up. I considered telling her what happened, how crazy I'd felt, how Mom seems to have left me for good, and what I did with—or to—Ian. I wanted to share it all fleetingly, but it was too strange a conversation. Instead, I asked, "Are things better around here?"

Amelia glanced toward the staff. "I'm like enemy number one around here," she said loudly. "They insist we all go to church, but when I try to go to the woods to pray in my way, they act like I'm breaking the law."

"Because you're probably breaking their law, and they said you had a posse."

"There are others who are interested, quiet ones. They just don't know it yet."

"The congregations probably feel that way too." I smiled, imaging my grandmother recruiting women to march off the premises. I wondered how she lured them, and whether they could sense her power or were just incredibly bored.

"The air is so dry in here. My body aches from being inside and in that damn courtyard all the time." She lowered her voice to me again and added, "It's time, Em. An hour drive is all I need. I don't want you to worry, but I need to find a way to detox from this place and make my goodbyes. The new nurse holds me down each morning, holds my mouth open and shoves the pills in until I gag. She pours water into my mouth, so the pills begin to dissolve. I almost drown. The bitterness of it! Each time I think I can resist, but each time I swallow. They've doubled my prescription."

I leaned in and covered Amelia's hand with my own. The two tables of staff were taking their trays to the trash cans, laughing as they collected the empty trays, and walked back toward the kitchen. They weren't listening at all, and for the first time since I was a kid, I worried my grandmother might be legitimately ill. Her eyes darted around the way they had that day, so long ago, when she repeated my mother's name.

"What if the pills aren't so bad? What if there's just an adjustment?" I asked.

Amelia turned my palm up, and I felt how rough her hands truly were. She gave my hand a gentle squeeze to examine the map of my future. She stared at my palm for a long time, as though she couldn't quite make out what she knew was there. She reached for my other hand and did the same.

"It's the dead, the ancestors. The way you now spoke with your mother. They all go away when I take them."

"Mom left me."

"I know. It's dangerous to speak to your mother, Emerson. But you can't always be safe. You can communicate with the living this way, too, but don't get trapped by trying to force things. I try not to do it, but sometimes I tell Jake things that I can't tell anyone else. Not even you. He thinks it's all a dream. I've always known I'd never connect with anyone like him again, but I need to see him in the flesh to say goodbye."

"Why do you keep saying goodbye? Everyone can't leave me at once."

She grabbed a sugar packet and ripped it open, poured its contents into the coffee slowly, then grabbed another. Soon, there was a pile of sugar packet paper, which made me laugh. She took a drink of the coffee without mixing it, smiled sleepily and said, "You need to say goodbye too, you know that?"

"Where are you going?"

"Saying goodbye to your mother was hard but necessary. You were both stuck. I know it's hard. I didn't want to let her go either."

The coffee was as cold as the room. When Amelia stood and gestured for me to follow, I did. I laced my arm underneath hers, and we walked to the window. In the light, I could see her wrist appeared to be darkened, perhaps by paint.

"Can you tell me about that night?" I asked.

"Your father was right. I'd been a danger to myself that night. Never to him or you girls—I want you to know that. But I was ready to leave this world. I wanted to take her place. I would have done anything to take her place, and there is a spell I'd been studying."

I didn't know what to say. I remembered the gleam of the knife, the smoke. I could only imagine what she would have done if we'd left with my father that night. "It can't work like that," I said.

"It can and has. And does."

A pigeon bobbed along on the sidewalk we could see from the window. A few more joined him, finding tiny bits of bread overlooked by the squirrels and geese. "I heard you were doing art lessons in here."

"Look at that pigeon. Look at him. He looks so puffed up and full of himself, so content to be what he is." She gestured as I looked closer at her wrists in the light and realized that they were the eggplant purple of day-old bruises. "Amelia, did you do that?"

"I need to see Jake while I'm lucid. You know, Jake and I had been like Nancy Drew or the Hardy Boys. We went after Mother, to find her out, and it was quite the adventure. I don't know what I wanted to find. Like you, I just wanted answers. Something that would give me a way out. I just wish I'd had a little more heart back then. You come to these times where you just decide what you're willing to risk. I wish I'd known how to trust myself then. Things would be different." She examined the room. "I didn't know how to listen. I looked everywhere else."

With the staff now gone, the silence in the room felt like a wall. The only thing cutting through was the rhythmic ticking of a clock. "It's time for my bus, Amelia. Come with me if you'd like. If I take you home, Dad will deal with it. I mean, you are family, and no one can keep you here like a prisoner."

Her eyes lit up. "Let's plan for something like that. Next week. We need Courtney."

"Deal," I said, unsure I could fulfill what I was committing to.

When we walked, I saw the wobble. She was weak. "It's our stories, Emerson, where we find strength. It's our stories that cut through anything the world does to numb us." She was moving slowly, leaning her bodyweight into me. I could tell how tired she was. She eased to a seated position on her bed, and when I sat down beside her and felt a spring digging into my thigh, Amelia let out a long sigh. "Did you ever read about the Bona Dea?"

"No."

"She was an oracle, but only some people knew. Only women. Only a few people truly know me," she said. She began to wring her wrists, and I could see her skin reddening around the bruises.

"Please stop, Amelia. Take a nap."

She leaned in to leave a waxy kiss mark on my cheek before I left. Before I was out of the room, I felt the weakness in my body, a shot, and I knew I was on the clock. I was no longer afraid. I looked back at Amelia and imagined all our relatives there with her. My mother on the side of the bed holding her hand.

Red kiss mark still in place, I checked the time, marched up to Jenny and took a long breath. I had to be calm if I wanted information. "You look lovely today," I said with a plastic smile. She was wearing a plaid shirt with two buttons undone over a see-through white tank and a gray mini skirt with black stockings. Her bangs were teased to impressive heights.

"Why, thank you, Amelia's granddaughter. I'm having one of those days, you know, where you just feel like putting in the extra effort."

"Yeah, I wish I had those more," I said. "I've never been here on the weekend. It's quiet. I'm curious who Amelia's new nurse is?"

"You mean Beverly? She's our bad cop around here—the one nurse who gets some of the stubborn ones to take their pills."

"Must be her technique," I said. "My grandmother's wrists are bruised."

"Your grandmother rubs her wrists. We've found her doing a lot of questionable things lately."

"Yeah. Well, maybe the medication is wrong. She seems worse, not better. Why can't she have a say as to whether she takes the medication?"

"That's up to your father and her, ultimately, sweetie. They probably adjusted the dose. She signed the papers to be here herself. But really, Emerson, I can't even have conversations like this." She gestured to a sign-in sheet as a woman entered and rudely talked over us. "Here for Betty Walldorf."

Jenny winked at me. "You have a good trip home, Emerson. I'll look out for your grandmother. I promise." The first time I called from the bus, Courtney's mother told me that my friend wasn't home, so I called every hour until her mother got frustrated enough to say, "Tell her yourself," and handed the phone off. I worried Courtney would hang up on me, so I spoke quickly, loudly.

"You can hate me, but I need your help. I love you, and I'm sorry. I need your help researching."

Dial tone. She wasn't answering her cell, and the rings were so short, I was sure she'd blocked me. I texted: "Please. Life or death."

I called and asked her mother if I could stop by and apologize, but she was getting annoyed by my persistence and suggested I leave her a voicemail.

"Courtney, I know you're busy and everything about me and my family is strange. I know I'm an idiot for not telling you how much I love you. I'm not sure how to—I'm not sure I'm ready for anything. But this isn't about me. I need you to help me with A. It's not about me."

I stared out at the flatlands, the cows and corn, and I smiled as the bus barreled forward. When I saw her number I answered and, without missing a beat, launched into my plan. I told Courtney about the bruises and how worried I was about Amelia, and just as I thought she would, she hung up on me. "I also need you to forgive me right now. I'm not asking," I texted. "I know what I need to do, and I need your help."

The next morning, the green Hyundai was out front honking incessantly. Courtney stuck her head out the window and yelled, "Let's do what we need to do. Starting with driving up there right now and kicking some nurse ass." I saw neighbors' faces peering out of windows, and I waved.

As I sat in the passenger's seat, I couldn't help but smile at the cinnamon broom that Courtney had dangling from the rear-view mirror. "I know you think I'm insane. Like everyone, but it's hard to explain. I've felt so compelled to see Amelia because I'm terrified of ending up like her, in some small room in the middle of the woods with only memories."

"You said life or death."

"I did."

"Where are we going?"

"The library."

"Of course." She started the car.

As we sat in traffic, I tried to explain that somehow I knew it was a time of transition. My grandmother deserved her love story, and we could give it to her. I couldn't explain how I knew, but I knew she was fading. "She deserves to find Jake, to take her trip. She deserves to live before she dies. She's never had advocates, and we're it." The two of us sat there with news radio low as Courtney waited for specifics. "I want to break her out just long enough to visit Jake, and I think we can find him," I explained.

Courtney gulped her iced coffee. I took note of her eyeliner. I'd never seen her wear makeup. "Why did you disappear on me?" I asked.

"You're selfish as shit! You crushed Ian, and you could have come talk to me about any of it, all of it, but instead I had to find out by reading your texts. I love your grandmother, but you are self-obsessed, witchy or not, and it's not all about you," Courtney said. I noticed she was wearing lip gloss, too. It didn't look overdone or forced. I'd been

in my own head, so much so that I'd forgotten the rest of the world.
I closed my eyes.

"It's not about me." I repeated, nodding.

Courtney lightened her tone. "How about we bake or buy Jenny
brownies as a sort of ice breaker? You can buy mascara, so her guard is
down. You have, like, no eyelashes. We'll find a way to sneak her out. Or
ask for Jenny's help."

"That might work." Jenny was a wild card, and I needed to
think about how to position our ask. "Nice makeup yourself, by the way.
Bully."

"Remember how we met?" she asked, offering me the comfort
I needed to breathe. But before I had a chance to think about breath, I
leaned in, kissing her on the cheek. At a stoplight, bookended by trucks,
she tilted her forehead toward me. I felt her eyelashes graze my brow,
and just before she whispered, "Let's get to work," our lips met, a soft
pulse, and everything inside of me illuminated.

We sat in the 80s style research room at the library with its
bold-print carpet and red chairs as I printed the information, which
included the address of a house sold to a Jacob Gutowski in 1966. He
lived on Pennsylvania Ave. near a park an hour away. I took a picture of
his military record that showed retired captain status, a Soldier's Medal
and Army of Occupation Medal on his record. He retired military, it
seemed, and he married military. Her name was Gretchen, and she died
the spring of 2004, a few months before my mother died.

Courtney came toward me with no less than a dozen paperbacks
tucked under her arms. She was beaming. "It's time to play out this love
story."

Every thought I had left my mind as I walked to Jake's front
door. I began to deny my intuition and tell myself this was a mistake. My
mind raced—we had to make sure it was him. And even if it was, would
he remember her? Would he want to see her? No stakes seemed higher.
My grandmother was fading, and she deserved her love story.

There was a small welcome mat made of a material that looked like grass, which my feet sunk into as I knocked. Courtney rang the doorbell two times. "Stop. He'll think we're bill collectors or the police or something."

The curtains parted, revealing only darkness, and a moment later I heard a series of chain locks being released. Courtney blew out a stream of air and gave my arm a squeeze. I tried to shift on the AstroTurf mat but couldn't.

"Can I help you?" a slender man with a round belly said, looking past us as though to make sure we were alone. He was in house slippers and a white t-shirt that hung loose everywhere except for his midsection. When he realized that there was no entourage, he opened the door fully. Everything was familiar about this man; he was a story brought to life.

"My name is Emerson," I said.

"I'm Courtney."

"Are you selling cookies? I like the coconut ones." He gave me an extended glance.

"I wish," Courtney said. He stepped back, taking the whole of us in. His light brown eyes settled on me for a long time.

"I know you," he said to me.

"You know my grandmother. That's why I'm here."

Leaving the door open, he turned to lead us into a small living room with a pathetic arrangement of neutral colored, worn furniture. He was nodding as he walked. Courtney took a seat on a small brown chair and sat up as straight as she could.

"Can I get you something to drink?" I could see Jake was tall, taller than most people I knew, but he hunched over like he'd used a cane longer than not. I didn't want to bother him, though my mouth felt dry.

"Water would be nice," Courtney said.

When he returned, he handed us each a cloth coaster and a clouded glass, then looked at me again as though it was the first time. "Tell me more," he said. A soft smile crossed his face.

"Sir, I know this is strange, but I looked you up. I looked you up because I wanted to talk with you about my grandmother."

"Call me Jake."

"Jake, it's about Amelia," Courtney blurted out.

"Amelia is my grandmother," I repeated. "She's okay, but not great. She's an amazing woman. She's got, um, the idea that you're going to visit her, or she can come visit you. She's at The Lavender House. Well, right now she is anyway." I struggled to find my breath—it was thin, as though I were breathing through a straw. "My grandmother is deeply lonely."

Jake put his hand up, stopping me before I was able to say anything else. "Nancy Drew. She's been hiding from me." His smile was broad and full, and for a moment, I saw the younger version of him clearly in a flash. I saw them together. "We didn't think we had a choice then. There was war and there was marriage and there was loss. There was no room for love."

I reached for a glass of water, suddenly at a loss for words. The glasses were clouded, but not so clouded as to hide the fact that food remnants were floating there. I almost took a sip, then set the glass down.

"There's room for love now," Courtney said.

"I don't leave the house too much."

"Maybe there's room for love now," I repeated, louder. It sounded corny, but he smiled wistfully, glancing at the corner of the room as though he had a glimpse of the past.

"Guess it's time for an adventure." The time that Amelia promises us is an illusion became just that. We thanked Jake, and before leaving I asked him if I could put the glasses away. In the kitchen, which had a small window overlooking a hummingbird feeder and four pots of dying tomato plants, I washed and rinsed the glasses thoroughly.

There were pictures of those I assumed were grandchildren on the walls. There was a clock the shape of a cat with moving eyes and a small, framed letter I couldn't read.

Before we left, we agreed on a time to pick him up. We figured it'd be safer to bring him to Amelia than Amelia here. Jake agreed. "Don't tell her," he urged us. "She'll know, but still…"

Chapter Twenty-two: Amelia

This is the blurry part of the story, but I tell it plainly. My marriage was an imposed disaster, and its aftershock took my daughter. I should have run away sooner, but I couldn't see a place to go, not even in the farthest corner of my imagination. I should have listened to who I was and not been concerned with who the world wanted me to be. It wanted me to be nothing. Less than nothing.

But I was terrified. I'd made the decision to stay with Kat, as opposed to listening to everything inside me that told me to run, because Kat was sure. She didn't waver, and what I didn't realize at the time was that she too had embraced her gifts, just the wrong way. In an unknowing way. We must listen to ourselves even when there are no clear answers.

I didn't listen. This is when things unraveled, my magic—as it is wont to do—became madness. I'd chosen the life every other woman had chosen because I was afraid. I went to classes, but my grades fell. Jake made no attempt to contact me, or even talk to me during this time, thanks to threats from Kat. Though I did see him in the hall from time to time, we averted our eyes, as instructed. We were puppets.

Kat's habits didn't change. She was still going out every Tuesday and Thursday, still coming home late and expecting me to take care of the household. The gentlemen whispering over my sleeping body, negotiating with my mother, were no longer dreams. The only reprieve I found from my solitude was in art books and the occasional time I spent with Betty.

Over breaks and on weekends, I read everything Grandma Grodzki had given me and everything I could get my hands on about famous painters and artists, goddess mythology and the history of Slavic rituals that used fire and water to tune in to the world; there were some similarities to what I'd been taught, but the old traditions were not easy to find. I read about anything that showed women as medicine keepers, as seers. I made deals with the school librarian so I could check out upwards of five books each week.

This time, as I filled my head with all I could, was manic. And I'd soon find out why. I knew what was coming. I wrote Gene longer and longer letters, filling him in on everything. When folded, the pages were so thick they couldn't fit in a regular envelope. I wrote Jake and Grandma Grodzki letters, too, though I would burn them beneath the willow oak, asking Mother Nature to deliver. Everything about my existence was an illusion, theater.

At school, I was still dedicated to my studies, staying up late, reading works by Buck, Eliot, Fitzgerald, Hemingway and Steinbeck, along with the bootlegged papers on the transformative movements women had catalyzed all around the world. I read all the short stories in my literature books and even checked out books from other, more advanced classes. None of this would soon matter, however, because before the academic year ended, Kat showed up at school and excused me from class. "There's an emergency," she told the professor loudly, in front of a sea of nosy students.

"Gee, your mother is a real looker," said a girl with short hair and cat-eye glasses, a girl who I often saw looking over at other students' papers. I ignored her and, quietly, gathered my books, worried something had happened to Gene, even though I didn't feel that in my bones. Once we were in the hallway, I looked up at Kat, expecting the worst.

"Please don't say we got a letter from the military. Please."

"No, darling. Gene is fine, I'm sure. We haven't heard, and no news is good news," Kat said, beaming. "No, today is about us girls. We are going on a special trip, my dear."

Outside, waiting for us, was a massive Packard Clipper, an impressively large car which seemed to take up more space than the road allowed it. "Looking ahead?" a popular radio commercial voice would ask. "Well, skipper to the Clipper!" a man's deep voice answered. The commercial repeated in my mind, the jingle playing in my head as Kat led the way. The jingle replaced thought. It worked for a while, until the backs of my legs froze. My calves became ice. I was walking into my future.

"That's right, dear. We're traveling in style today."

A man exited the driver's side and came around speedily. The man was tall and dark, wearing a deep blue suit and a cap. He made a gesture like a magician revealing a dove from an empty hat. He opened the door to the backseat.

"Are you going to give me a clue?"

"Just get in," Kat chided. "You're a queen today."

The seats were as soft as silk. I sat during the quiet ride, watching the winter-parched trees ease by as she ran her palm along the seats. "This is comfortable," I said.

"Get used to it," Kat said with a soft laugh. The driver lit a cigarette, and the car filled with gray smoke. It was like traveling in a cloud, and I breathed in deeply, trying to feel that light-headed sensation that would carry me farther from my fear. "I told you, young one, just stick with me and I'll take you places."

The car ride was over too soon. The Clipper stopped in the circular driveway of a hulking white house Kat rushed me toward. She straightened my dress at the door and led me into a foyer the size of Grandma Grodzki's entire house. I held on to Kat's slender hand.

"Don't be intimidated, little one. This is where you belong. You deserve nice things, as do I, and we will have them here. Breathe it in. Have a seat on that couch in there. I'll be back."

Kat had opened the door without a key or a knock or anything, which meant she must've been to this house before. She rushed up a curved set of marble steps and called out a name that I didn't quite make out. I heard mumbling and began walking around carefully, quietly. Worried I'd break anything I touched; I kept my hands clasped behind my back.

"Did you explore?" Kat asked.

"A little. I just saw these divine bookshelves. So many books."

"My little egghead. Now come here, I'm going to fix up your

face. Robert should be down soon. He's just finishing up a little business on the telephone." She revealed a compact and a bottle of foundation. "Pull up your skirt," she ordered. Kat took a makeup sponge out and began to apply large quantities of shiny liquid to my legs. "Stockings in a bottle," she said, chuckling. "Our little secret."

I imagined planting my feet into the ground then and there. Waiting this scene out, I would stop Jake in the hall next time I saw him. I'd tell him we needed to stand up to Kat. We needed to run away.

Kat continued: "Robert is an investor. He writes screenplays in his spare time, and his family is quite instrumental in the running of the papers around here. For his part, he runs nightclubs and fine restaurants. He's very well-off, as you can see, and this is your interview. Make a good impression, hear?"

"What should I talk about? What if I don't like him?"

"Unacceptable. Don't be nervous. You read; he's a writer. Talk about books. In fact, go back in there and find a few you've read. I know you had to have read a few of them. Then bring up those books as though you're studying them in school right now. And you are confident, no matter what. Say it."

"I'm confident."

"You're a beautiful, confident young lady. You remember that. We'll never have to work another day in our life, no worries about the small-town gossip." She clapped her gloved hands. "I'll call you when I hear him coming."

The twisted marble stairs would make any man look important, if only he walked down them with enough care. But the man who arrived in my view had already left an impression. His angular body gave him away before I could see his face. Finally in front of me, extending his hand to take mine, in a suit with a skinny, teal tie that matched his eyes so precisely I wondered if he'd had it been custom dyed, was the man I'd seen that day at the club.

Kat clapped her hands together again and held them there in a prayer position. Without his hat, Bob had a thick, wavy head of silver hair that worked in his favor, making him almost handsome for an older man. I wondered what he looked like when he was younger.

"A stunning young woman indeed," he said, kissing my hand.

"Very nice to see you, Robert. Your home is phenomenal."

"Phenomenal! Oh! What a word." He lifted his eyebrows toward Kat but continued to speak to me. "I have the sneaking suspicion you have not one clue why you're here today."

"Correct."

"I'll leave you two to chat a while," Kat said. "You don't mind if I raid your icebox, do you, Robert?"

"Not at all. I know you like those sweet things. Ask Mary to make you cinnamon rolls. I make sure they are prepped and on hand most days, so that she can just bake them up and serve them warm in a few minutes. Tell her I said to make us all a batch. Drink anything you'd like; there's a full bar."

"You're too kind." Kat disappeared and was immediately heard barking orders at Mary, which made Bob Rand laugh. I never spoke much to Mary, an older Scottish woman with an accent who offered the comfort of a warm meal, but I smiled at her that day and trusted her immediately. Some years later, she would be a fleeting but important woman in my life.

"I knew I would see you again; I made sure of it, and there was no need to get you in trouble with your mother. I'm surprised your curiosity didn't get the best of you, you know."

"I figured it was best to not find out."

Bob laughed raucously at the concession and said, "My dear, you are honest despite yourself. I love it. Well, sit here on the couch and I'll satisfy your curiosity."

I didn't rebel. In fact, it was only that fall when I married Bob Rand. It was almost like being alone, so it wasn't all bad. I adapted to a life of privilege and was able to invite Betty and her husband over from time to time. I ignored Kat when she told me it was my destiny to wear designer dresses and accompany my husband to elaborate parties that she sometimes hosted at the mansion. To me, it was still all theater, unreal and to be acted out between delicious hours alone during which I'd read or write letters.

Kat found a renter for Grandma Grodzki's old home and stayed in Bob's guest room across the hall from the library, though she was often out with Helen and "the girls." I wondered what or who she was selling now. I wondered if the renters had found the cash tucked under that step. I hoped they had, and I hoped they needed it. More than anything, I hoped that I'd get an opportunity to go back.

I never did, and it didn't take long for my intuition, my ability to see what was coming, to become nightmarish and wake me up in the middle of the night. There were screams beginning so deeply inside my body I would hear them as though they were miles away. It was always a woman's voice, or a cacophony of voices, telling me to leave. I tried to ignore them because I knew they were right. I began to write letters to Grandma Grodzki then, asking her for advice. One night, as I wrote the letter, my ink pen began to take over. She began to answer me, to explain that I must find a way to leave and I must create boundaries around myself until I did. I began to grow herbs in the backyard that would make calming teas, and I'd serve them to my husband to calm his energy. I'd create a ring of candles and set a prayer inside that I would find freedom.

Though Bob Rand had well-meaning moments, as far as men like him could, he was also well-off enough and irritated enough to try to "fix my head" a few times before giving up. When he walked into my bedroom as I prayed, he screamed. "That's not Christian behavior." This was such irony that I laughed. He insisted I go to every doctor in town, and they were so professional and insistent I began to believe there was something wrong with me.

In the end, my madness made for a short union with Bob Rand, one during which we created a lifetime of damage. Maybe generations of damage. One during which we created a miracle—your mother.

I continued to set intentions and study the patterns around me to create safety, Bob began to lose interest in trying to fix me. As he began to court other women, I was sent to harsher and harsher doctors.

I was labeled hysterical, then "cold and disturbed." I was told this so often for so many months I began to worry Kat and Bob Rand's versions of life were more near reality than what I knew to be true. As I spoke to these bespectacled men who asked me question after question, I told them the truth. I told them I heard a woman's voice from deep inside and she tortured me.

At that time, electro-shock therapy was the rage for wealthier people. It was for the elite and connected, those of us women who caused their husbands to suffer in any way. Nightmares, visions and voices were all reasons. Peculiar behavior, but what's more, an inability to arouse or please a husband. It was with those rounds of treatments I lost a piece of my life—it took years to reclaim who I once was.

The first time I received treatment, I was in a room the size of a closet and color of green peas. It was supposed to be a calming color. There were flowers on my gown and cap. Kat had been the one to take me to treatment, and even she seemed to hesitate at the door of the center. Everything about it was wrong. I heard what sounded like a whimper in another room before they retrieved me.

Men in white coats strapped me into a chair, explaining the body would writhe a bit, but I'd be fine. They'd start out slow. "Just a bit of electricity," one of them said with a smile. His face was like rubber. His gloved hands squeezed my knee. There were metal plates strapped to my head and a jolt which came with so many promises. The therapy had been advertised in the paper. It was supposed to be safe, and maybe it was, but the way my body seized is something I'll never forget. I was not the same for a long time.

Grandma Grodzki arrived before my dreams to counter the treatments, but I screamed at her then, too. Due to my screaming, I was also given injections. I began to hear the woman's voice—the one I didn't recognize who lived deep inside me. She was persistent, warning me to reconnect to my truth. But I called her a witch, I writhed and tried to tear myself apart when she spoke, whispering truths in my ear. She whispered them so many times, softly, gently, that I slowly began to remember. Cloudy as I was, numb as I was.

Then the day came when I was released. Tired, wan. I recovered in the mansion with a stack of books on my nightstand. Yet, I could no longer read. I learned to whisper to the voices, rather than scream back at them, and they gave me the strength to tell my husband only a year after we'd been married, that I had to leave. I told him I was better, but I would never be able to be enough for him. I made my case that it was about what was best for him—not me.

I remember how Bob clinked his spoon to his mug, stirring a sugar cube into his coffee, the way he did every morning. He took a sip and licked his lips, then pursed them. "That seems about right, Amelia. How about an apartment, then? I will pay for everything, and we will keep this hush hush for a time."

"No more treatments," I said. "I will live quietly."

I didn't know at the time I was pregnant with Celine. I asked Bob not to tell my mother I was leaving until we had to, and he agreed. My mother had been grating his nerves, trying to over-manage his staff and carve out a place for herself at his club he hadn't offered. "That woman needs to relax, too," he said.

I moved out quietly on a Sunday afternoon with Mary and Betty helping me to settle into a small, womb-like apartment with pink walls and tiny appliances. It was perfect.

Though Betty was conflicted about my choice, she helped me to settle in, and we'd often play cards. Tortured by the fact that she wasn't yet pregnant after the first year of marriage, she often cried on my shoulder, asked me what was wrong with her.

I said what I could, explaining that things weren't always so simple. But to her, to her family, she was defective. Mrs. Jamison, she'd told me, had outright asked her what sin she committed to receive such punishment, and she was genuinely trying to figure it out. "After two years, he's sure to leave me, then what? I'll be on my own?" The way her shoulders retracted, I could see that she understood what she said as soon as she said it, but I didn't take offense.

It was around this time that I realized how free I was. This is when I began to tell my friend the stories Grandma Grodzki told me. She didn't listen at first, but after a while she couldn't get enough. I began going to the library and reading about myths and magic and wondered if Kat had found Grandma Grodzki's stash of readings.

Despite my growing belly, I was getting used to being on my own in downtown Cleveland, from riches to rags, and I was beginning to think I could make it work. I took the train to Grandma Grodzki's home one last time, asking a kind couple who were renting from Kat, to let me check under the stairs. There, I ducked into the space, which seemed so much smaller and dustier than I remembered and found what I had left: the essays and notebooks my grandmother kept. Notes from my old Latin books that correlated to tales of women who could shift the earth on its axis. Hugging my knees in this space, I felt Grandma Grodzki place her arms around me. Strong as Mother Earth herself, she kept me steady.

I would have stayed there the rest of my life if the young couple hadn't have knocked out of concern. They were cordial about me taking the notebooks and offered me a sturdy canvas bag and a ride home. In the letters and stories, I found—or remembered—my freedom, but my diagnosis and my solitude followed me everywhere. As did this new voice, which I worried the therapy had brought on.

Kat would never visit me, not even when news of my pregnancy would reach her, but she still hung around the same crowd, which included Bob. He refused to divorce so soon and instead played the victim by telling people I had gone insane. To the world then, he was sticking by my side. The hero.

When Celine was born, I hollered out in joy. I sat in the hospital bed and felt the entirety of my being filled. A doctor whispered to me that she was the most beautiful baby he'd seen all year. I asked a nurse to call Bob, but I didn't have any expectations. What I didn't realize was that he had already rushed there. He had staff paid at every hospital in the city to alert him if I arrived, so when a worker I barely knew, a host named John, walked me into the hospital and gave my name, Bob got an alert.

He'd been sequestered to the lobby when he arrived because my contractions were so close together. He puffed on his cigar as I made the final push, and our child was born. When he was able to see her, I noticed the quick assessment and approval. Offering a tender smile, he said, "She's healthy. Her eyes are bright." He held her for a while that day and arranged a car to take me home. He stayed with us until he got a call from one of his clubs.

Celine would continue to charm her father. Her magic didn't elude him as mine did. He would send Mary to watch her while I worked long shifts at the restaurant and would take her on extravagant trips while I worked doubles. After her first birthday, he hired a nanny to accompany him and whisked her off to Disneyland. After that, each year he'd take her somewhere new and special, places I couldn't afford, such as the zoo or the carnival. Then, he got tied up with business at the club. At first it was every weekend, which turned into every other week, which turned into monthly visits.

When he stopped coming around, Mary was sent weekends to help. Celine would cry when she left, screaming in my arms as I rocked her and tried to convince her it would all work out.

"She'll be back tomorrow," I cooed.

After a while, Bob began helping with the bills, but just enough that I still had to work part-time. Being a single mother in the forties was a story in and of itself, but I became steady. Strong. Stronger than anyone could have known. This is when I finally began to revisit magic by reading.

I began to worship at the altar of women who had done more with less and tried to convince Betty, over long phone conversations, that she too was strong. And though people thought me eccentric as a single mother who would often write long letters in the cafeteria at break time, rather than gossiping about shoes, I learned to listen deeply to the voices that came. And I realized they weren't ancestors. It wasn't Grandma Grodzki. Nothing had been haunting me. The voices were me. The me within me.

The shocks reverberated and kept me unable to speak very quickly. This too made people somewhat wary of me. Little rattles in the brain that arrived sporadically kept me from the hostess station days at the diner. Ultimately, Management told me to work in the kitchen, where I'd wash dishes or unpack boxes. I preferred this work. It kept me strong physically. Mentally, I found strength in hope. I began to think about trying to find Jake, but the grind of each day wore away my resolve.

I wouldn't see Kat again until my brother's funeral. It was news that arrived to me via a short letter with no signature and an informal invite to a church ten miles away. I had to ask Bob for a ride, but my mother refused to travel with me, so he had to send a friend, and I arrived late.

Gene had been career military, a pilot. He never met my daughter. Celine was not yet two when a small fire started in the engine of the plane Gene was flying. I stood with Grandma Grodzki and all the women I imagined before her. I stood tall, as military officers saluted and Kat, once my mother, sauntered past me in black lace.

A flag was folded, and I cried over a coffin. I hadn't seen my brother since I was in high school. We rarely spoke, and I thought him dead so many times I couldn't count. Now that he was no longer of this world, he too stood at my side. I didn't acknowledge Kat.

When Celine and I walked away, hand-in-tiny-hand, I heard her call after me. "You've become cold. Like ice. Like me."

I continued to walk.

When she was older, Celine would try to stay with her father, by this time, my ex-husband (hush, hush), and she wouldn't want to come home. She'd smell like Kat's perfume and come home accusing me of being disgusting, a thing only Kat would say. He would always be the normal one to Celine. I tried to teach her what I knew, but she didn't believe me. She followed a suitable path for a nice young woman, laid out by her father. The only thing she kept close to her heart was painting, but from her perspective, I was the one to be taken care of. She was the adult.

I tried. I did everything I could with what I had to teach her what I knew, but it only made things worse. She knew I'd had electro-shock therapy and believed I was fried. What I could not do at that time was pretend to be normal. Instead, I worked hard and taught her about the divine feminine, implored her to read Gloria Steinem and others who were coming out with brilliant and freeing work. I went from working at a café to working at a small shop that sold fortune telling cards, like my grandmother's, and crystals. I didn't know the poison Kat was feeding her until it was too late.

Until Kat broke her heart too, by disappearing from Celine's life without a word. Abandonment can be the greatest source of control. She died when she was eighty-nine, in California, with over a million dollars in her bank account from real estate and other investments. Out of daughters, she married herself multiple times, only to soon divorce and collect settlements. She left all her money to her two cocker spaniels, listing me as the residuary beneficiary.

For the first time in my life, I was able to travel. No longer reliant on Bob's allowances. I took Celine where I could, across the country. Overseas. This is a whole other story. Each summer we'd go somewhere new, and I would allow the ancestors to guide our way. They were joined by others, a band of magical women. The problem was Kat. She would cut through. When you let in others, they present both the light and dark.

Grandma Grodzki kept me safe. She reminded me to look deep into nature wherever I was to study the truths that glimmered within each narrative. When the dead visit, we must not follow them if we plan to return to our world.

When Celine began dating and finding her place in private schools, she also began to rebel by mimicking the mendacity, the normalcy, the perfect as possible bullshit of the world, saying she didn't like the same kooky things I did and just wanted to have friends, an ordinary life, a life that allowed community. She became overly serious.

I didn't know what that meant, but it scared me even then. She was beautiful when she laughed. Striving for normality in a dysfunctional world steals joy. I tried to give her space. I tried to be a good mother and let her learn, even though I had no model for that. I saw the sensitivity of my daughter. I saw her ability to see, but I also saw the desire to fit in that kept Kat so tortured. It was at this time, my middle age, with all the diagnoses and stigma to surround my identity that I began to realize the greatest freedom was to be in the world, not of it.

Chapter Twenty-three: Emerson

It felt like a reintroduction to the world. Amelia had laid claim to her own death at last, and she refused to allow what she knew to die with her. She held my hand tightly, and I could feel the surge. The transfer.

"Keep what resonates. Create something better of your life," Amelia said, motioning to a shoebox full of small decorative journals with tiny, almost unreadable text. Her words held all I remembered from the rituals I had seen as a child. The way to burn herbs and honor the dead, to communicate with animals, to hold reverence for the earth, to live unapologetically. None of it was crazy.

There were short retellings of myths with question marks or notes in the margins. Amelia had made study of the world in ways I imagined most scholars couldn't touch. As I flipped through, I found lists of books and papers, illustrations of various meditations and quotes attributed to no one. Recipes for teas and tinctures. Astrological formulas. Prayers for connecting with the earth and ways to tune in or tune out. There were notes on contemplation that enabled a different way of seeing, but nothing was underlined or starred. There were only question marks.

"Thank you," I said.

"Don't rush." She was careful to remind me that without focus and intention, without integrity, all of it would be worse than useless. I held her hand, which was frail but warm.

"I can't really tell you anything more," she told me and smiled wanly before closing her eyes.

I read and reread the contents of a silver notebook with a dragon insignia and landed on a page with the sacrifice spell Amelia had tried those years ago. "When someone is tasting death, you can take their bite." An older woman was roughly sketched in the middle of a ring of flowers beneath my grandmother's writing. The only other writing I could decipher was "Too many versions."

The handwritten notes were more legible as I went on. Those I could decipher contained question marks and instructions to ignite and extinguish a million small flames. I remembered my grandmother those years ago pacing, creating this very circle of sacrifice, lighting match after match. My father was right. She had been a threat to herself the night Mom died. She was trying to make a trade.

I quickly closed the book, taking a long breath. "You, er, sure you don't want to stay up and pull a few cards?" I asked.

"You don't need me to." She tapped her cheek, and I kissed it gently. Taking note of her gestures and the way she smiled with increasing distance, I felt the slowing of time in my grandmother's body. The cool charge I felt the night my mother left me returned, but this time I refused to be afraid. I closed her door, knowing I'd have to move quickly.

Courtney and I were about to take our last trip to The Lavender House, and I was getting excited. Jake was bad about answering his phone. I worried he'd never hear it. Armed with the journals alone, I found myself feeling the chill of panic and looking to the book for answers. As I sought relief from the pages, I found instructions to allow my body to be while it swelled and pulsed.

When Rita knocked on my bedroom door and asked how I was, it took everything in me to respond.

"I'm fine, just wrapping things up," I managed to say.

"Let me know if you need anything," she said.

"Will do," I called, extending my hand. She looked dubious of the unexpected outreach, and I couldn't help but laugh as she edged toward me. When she squeezed my hand, I squeezed back. I told her I was sorry. It was a step forward.

That night, I dreamed that Amelia's body began to fade as she joined her own grandmother and others whose stories had yet to be told. In a way, I knew they surrounded me as well. It wasn't magic that

I knew this, it was simple observation. A refusal to normalize or deny the enchantment.

When he finally answered, Jake agreed to meet us earlier than planned. I rushed over to Courtney's house to strategize. Her mother, who had always looked like she ate something sour when she heard my name, let alone saw me, forced a smile when she opened the door. Courtney lived in a trendy part of town, and her family's old Victorian home included a foyer where I stood and waited for maybe the third time since I'd met my friend. Instead of the usual, awkward silence, Mrs. Marshall offered me peppermint tea and explained that she had found a specialist for panic disorder that I might want to look up.

"Courtney told me about your pain. I can relate to what you are going through," she told me over her flat-ridged glasses. "I think a lot of people can. Something must be in the water. Or soft plastics." She handed me a card for a naturopath.

"Thank you," I said.

When Courtney rushed down the stairs in saggy jeans and a tee shirt beneath a plaid blazer, I beamed. "I've been thinking, and we need to make it a surprise," she said innocently.

"Thanks again, Mrs. Marshall. I'd love a raincheck on the tea," I said as we rushed out the door.

"Take care."

We ran toward the car. It was almost my grandmother's birthday. Just before graduation, before Rita married my father in traditional Polish dress with a beautiful ceremony at a park near our home, before Courtney got an internship at a well-respected online newspaper, before we found a small apartment near my father's home, before Lori began coaching high school track, and long before I would find out that I would be the one to tell this story.

Jake answered the door in an all-brown suit. His hair was combed with a sharp side part, and as we drove, he continuously checked for lint, brushing off his thighs and straightening his back. When we arrived at The Lavender House, Jenny signed us in immediately. I didn't want to upset anything about this plan. It couldn't backfire. When Jenny told me she had brought in the spring line of eye shadows just for me, I told her I'd buy the entire collection when I found a job.

"I'd like to sign Grandma out, just for an hour. Her friend here, Jake, hasn't seen her in decades. It's a reunion." Jenny smiled at Jake cordially, but her body went stiff. Her acrylic nails tapped on the glass counter near the clipboard.

"Wait, so your father approves? I can't get fired from this job. I'm only Level 2 in sales—not quite enough to live off yet," she said, gesturing toward her bag of makeup. "Technically you aren't eighteen yet."

Jake approached the counter and leaned in, whispering something, which made Jenny shove a clipboard toward him almost immediately. "One hour. There's a park a mile down the way." She glanced toward me, a tear forming in her eye. "Don't mess this up."

I nodded, glancing back. "Wait in the car. We'll be out soon," I told Courtney and Jake. The reunion couldn't happen in the waiting room. It all had to be orchestrated and perfect. She had to be free.

"Mind telling me a little more about yourself as we walk?" Courtney asked Jake.

"You ask an old person something like that, and you better settle in. We always have a story at the ready." Jake's laugh had a rattle to it. He looked from Courtney to Jenny to me with a smile.

Before I could rush down the hall, Jenny leaned forward with her elbows on the counter as Jake launched into a story about the perfect fire at camp, before stopping them and saying, "Jake, come here a minute. I have one more thing to discuss." My heart stopped. When I saw her pull out a dark blue bottle of lotion. "You need to make sure your hands are not like sandpaper, hear?"

"Make sure you're gone when we come out," I reminded them. I took slow steps down the hall. When I knocked, the door opened easily. Amelia was spreading cards out on the floor. Her single-serve coffee pot was brewing next to her. She was radiant, her thick gray hair freshly brushed and color in her cheeks.

"The graduate," she said, smiling.

"I'm going to make it. Barely." I laughed.

She was silent a long time, still looking down. "It's all patterns. Plants and trees upturn their leaves before a storm, opening a million tiny mouths. We flinch at the warning signs, the lighting and thunder, but the rain feeds us."

"Poetic, Amelia." I sat down on my heels to catch her gaze. "Are you up for a walk?"

She was more serene than usual, not looking at me as she spoke. All the ordinary animation and optics that usually surrounded her had been replaced by a deep calm that weighed down time. "You will be able to relate to the world in ways I never did," she said, turning a regular playing card. "And you have to remember you're in good company. You don't need to take on the burdens of others to understand. You will birth other things. You will help the world to understand. And the right people will listen."

"Thank you. I will try. Um, I was thinking…," I smiled broadly. All I could hear was my own heart drumming as I imagined leading her outside, beyond the boundaries, to meet Jake. She turned over two more cards and began to shuffle. I straightened the pillows on the bed.

"Sure, I can walk."

"Wonderful!" I grabbed her white sneakers and helped them on. "Amelia, I have something exciting to share."

"Call me Grandma." Finally, eye contact.

I didn't miss a beat. "Are you ready, Grandma?"

She nodded, and I leaned back to glance toward the hallway. Courtney had texted that Jake was "in position." They were waiting at a picnic bench at the park, near a gazebo.

"Come on, Nancy Drew. I'm breaking you out," I said.

Grandma tilted her head, then placed the cards in her sweater pocket. Her tennis shoes squeaked on the linoleum as I held her elbow. I winked at Jenny as we eased out the front door and slowly made our way toward Courtney's car.

"It's about time," Grandma said with slight surprise.

"My lady," Courtney said, opening her passenger's side door.

"They had us watching a documentary on New Mexico yesterday. I'd like to go there, please."

"That's a hell of a drive," Courtney said as I eased into the back seat, feeling my phone buzzing. My father was texting me, asking where I was. I texted back that I was working on a project, then I turned off my phone. Just as the car started and began to back out of the space, two men in white appeared at the top of the hill and began pointing at us. For a moment, it looked like they were about to charge, so Courtney eased the car forward, turning down the gravel road.

I watched from the back window as Jenny rushed out and started gesturing back to the building and nodding her head affirmatively. The two white-clad workers looked dubious but ultimately followed her.

When we arrived at a small park a mile away, Grandma was shuffling her cards. I'd never seen her nervous about anything, and I rubbed her arm. It was an odd moment, a moment when I realized we never did things normal grandmothers and granddaughters did. We never hugged or showed affection. We never took an ordinary drive together.

He was visible the moment we pulled up, and I watched as Grandma adjusted her glasses. Jake sat with a few wildflowers on the picnic bench in front of him. He hadn't heard us drive up, so by the time he raised his head, we were already parked. I wished I could see her face as she walked toward him wordlessly, but I imagined it softer than I'd ever seen, knowing. As I leaned against the car, trying not to stare, Courtney grabbed me by the chin gently, leaning in. "Don't stare at them."

"Don't tell me what to do," I said softly, holding her chin in the same way. We waited there a moment as the energy welled up.

Neither Jake nor my grandmother appeared to say anything for a long time. They continued to examine each other, until, finally, my grandmother's eyes tilted slightly downward, the way they did when she smiled. She revealed the deck and turned over a card, the queen of spades. We could barely hear her say, "I could feel you coming, Jake. You finally broke me out."

"Of course you could," Jake said, "because Amelia Grodzki knows and has always known everything. Besides, I'm pretty sure you came for me."

"True." She flicked the card in his direction playfully and added, "Well, they couldn't keep us apart forever."

"No one could," Jake said.

Like children, Amelia and Jake sat awkwardly close, all knobby limbs and stiff movements. Their knees slightly bent, leaning in and away from each other, they examined each other. Holding hands, gripping tightly, they were ready to weather anything that tried to shake them loose. The different worlds they inhabited became one in that instant. The moment swelled and contracted. Time stopped, and I felt my mother arrive and leave like the wave of a wand.

Courtney kept trying to distract me, so by the time the van arrived, and stiff bodies rushed toward us with serious faces, we'd been laughing about old times. One of the nurses led Grandma back, and my father was called. Jenny was with them in the back of the car and didn't seem to be in trouble. She'd only been able to stall them. Of course my father raged, and of course I was banned from seeing her, but none of that mattered. Everything had already changed. The story was over, and Grandma knew it. She wrote her own ending.

Less than two weeks after our visit, one of the newer residents at The Lavender House, a man named Lars, who was "doing time" for schizophrenia in the east wing where my grandmother was now living, began screaming in the cafeteria. Staff rushed in to find him looking up at the sky and talking to Amelia, asking if she'd take him with her. When staff restrained him, they saw my grandmother's body. Once Lars calmed, he said he'd been eating oatmeal across the table from Amelia, and she'd been smiling, talking about what she planned to paint in art group, when everything became quiet. She fell from her chair. This man, who had known her a matter of weeks, wept for days.

When we met him at the funeral, his eyes raw and a resident by his side, he said that she'd saved his life. She taught him how to release his anger. One day, he explained, she had walked him just beyond the gazebo to a tree that she told him was sacred. She helped him tie his rage around the branches.

"Amelia said that Mother Nature could take my pain. That *she* could handle it all and more. *She's* stronger than all of us," he told me as he shifted on his heels. I stared down at his tennis shoes and felt my cheeks get heavy.

The official account from the staff was that the stroke took her out painlessly on a day when she was displaying no paranoia. "Seems she left the world content," a nurse said. He was genuine, and as he spoke, he gave a slow, gentle nod.

There were more stories at her funeral that recounted how my grandmother touched residents' lives and got them in trouble in equal measure. My father's tears were silent as he listened, but his face was pained. There was something unresolved between them. Lori's tears were surprisingly loud. They moistened the ground as we said goodbye.

Jake stood near me, clutching the letters to his chest, looking toward infinity. Courtney gripped my arm tightly, as though trying to fend off her own tears. But my grandmother wasn't gone. It would take a lifetime of study to fully understand all that she knew. I wasn't yet sure how to dive in and what was true, but I knew she would feed my work in the world.

As we congregated around a willow oak, I felt grounded to the earth beneath my feet, and I stood tall. After Lori, Courtney and I spread her ashes at the base of the tree, I pressed my palms to the bark for a long time, feeling for a pulse. I allowed the reverberation to move through my body as I said goodbye. Jake joined me, and, to my surprise, so did Lori, though she looked slightly uncomfortable.

The everydayness of life propelled forward, shifting daily patterns, and shoving me into adulthood with force. Courtney and I moved into a small apartment and began to explore the world as inelegant but driven college students with part-time jobs and no free time. Courtney worked for the college publication, and I spent nights studying psychological theories for my courses. After homework, however, came the deeper study.

An inner knowing came alive inside me as I explored my grandmother's writing. This story lived in my womb, and it wouldn't allow me to stay small—not in a world that was itself insane. When I had trouble figuring out how to move forward or feeling like I needed to fit in, Grandma would arrive in dreams to remind me to trust. My mother would offer reassurances and story. Amelia would push me when I was afraid, and Grandma Grodzki, wrapped in a quilt that went on forever, would remind me how to use my instinct and look to nature. Their voices were a chorus—not madness but momentum.

Courtney handed me a water bottle as we hiked beyond the trees toward a creek on a mid-August day two years later. The citrus she'd added to the water stung as the sun beat down and I continued to drink. Courtney always insisted on putting lemons or limes in water, despite the damage they do to tooth enamel. It was a benign argument but one we kept having. Amassing recurring conversations like this, like a couple who had been together decades, felt good.

I gave the bottle back with a puckered face, earning a defiant smile from beneath the brim of a tattered ballcap. Courtney took a seat next to me on a fallen tree. We removed our shoes and stood. Though we hadn't practiced many of the rituals my grandmother found solace in, we spent many nights over the last years up till 4 a.m., working and writing. We read and typed until time began to move differently, like the staircases in an Escher painting. Other times, it moved with abandon.

I looked up, remembering what it was like to fly kites with my mother near this park when I was a child. Back then, we would sprint, praying for the wind to pick up. On rare occasions, the wind listened, offering us an adventure if only we'd let go. We always did then. The small red kite would drift into the neighborhood as we pointed and laughed, eager to see where it would lead us.

Mom and I would comb the streets then, glimpsing something red behind a car tire or in someone's backyard, and we'd walk toward it, only to find a flattened package or an abandoned sock. Though we replaced many kites, there were also the days we found the soft fabric resting on a windshield or a flapping against a telephone pole, and the victory felt inevitable. We never knew where we'd end up, but we always knew when we were headed in the right direction.

Courtney and I walked, our feet connecting with the electricity of the earth, and time was simply generous. Limitless. Reaching for her warm hand, I tried to imagine that lonely girl I used to be, afraid of going crazy or losing my worth. Instead, I listened for the chorus and, as I felt my way in and through a world that wouldn't always understand, I relished the moments of harmony.

ABOUT THE AUTHOR

Jen Knox earned her BA in English at Otterbein University and her MFA from Bennington College. After teaching creative writing for over a decade, Jen began to coach writers and offer idea-to-publication services through Unleash Creatives, a holistic arts organization she founded and co-owns based in Ohio. Jen's books include the short story collections *The Glass City* (Hollywood, CA: Winner, Prize Americana for Prose), *After the Gazebo* (New York City, NY: Rain Mountain Press), and *Resolutions: A Family in Stories* (Detroit, MI: AUXmedia). Her short stories have been featured in textbooks, classrooms, and both online and print publications around the world including *The Best Small Fictions* (Braddock Avenue Books), *The Bombay Review*, *The Adirondack Review*, *Chicago Tribune*, *Chicago Quarterly Review*, *Crannog*, *Cutthroat Magazine*, *Fairlight Books*, *McSweeney's Internet Tendency*, *NPR*, *Poor Claudia*, *The Saturday Evening Post*, and *The Santa Fe Writers Project Quarterly*, among over a hundred other publications. *We Arrive Uninvited* is her first novel.

JEN KNOX

TITLES FROM STEEL TOE BOOKS

CPSIA information can be obtained
at www.ICGtesting.com
Printed in the USA
JSHW081452020423
39771JS00001B/11